Challenge of the Court

The Other Realm Series, Book 5

Heather G Harris

Cover Design by Christian Bentulan

For my awesome supporters on Patreon, with special mention to Melissa and Kassandra. I am so grateful and humbled by your belief in me.

Chapter 1

Someone screamed as the man leapt. It was like all of the air had been sucked out of the room as we held our breaths. Tension radiated through us, our eyes wide as we watched, helpless to do anything but pray.

A moment later, cheers erupted as he caught the trapeze safely. He hung suspended eighteen feet high in the air, making it look easy. At some point in the performance he'd ripped off his shirt, and his muscles rippled as he swung his body effortlessly and hooked a leg over the wooden swing. Then he flung himself backwards, sending the ropes into a spiral. It was breathtaking to watch a true acrobat at work.

The man whirled downwards and was met mid-air by a young woman in a costume covered in peacock feathers. She careened towards him, their arms entwined and together they spun to the ground. The crowd roared their appreciation as the two artistes unhooked their limbs and extricated themselves from each other and their equipment.

They took a bow. I cheered as loudly as everyone else, despite this being the fifth time I'd seen the performance this week. Sometimes surveillance didn't totally suck.

I loved the next bit of the show. Salsa music started and the circus performers started to dance. The peacock lady's costume looked almost bland now against the riot of colour around her. She moved her hips to the beat, her feather headdress flashing as she danced. The laser light show began in earnest, flashing colours and beams in a dizzying display as the troupe danced on.

The show had been wonderful but, despite the accusations, there hadn't been a hint of magic. None of the performers bore the triangles of the Other realm. The strong man appeared to be exactly that; the trapeze artist didn't *seem* to be a griffin or a dragon, and he didn't use wings. The whole display had been the result of nothing more than hard work and human skill.

The circus had come to the Connection's attention simply because of its name, The Other Circus. Whether it was an in-joke or inferred something else, nothing I had seen indicated anything magical – anything Other – about it. And that is exactly what my report to the Connection would say.

It was a lie, of course; the fortune teller was a real seer, despite her lack of purple skin, and the strong man was an ogre. I could tell simply because of what I am, a truth seeker, but I was going to keep their secrets like I was keeping my own. The Connection was getting too heavy handed.

So what if a bunch of their citizens chose to stay permanently in the Common realm? I'd been there for nearly a week and not a single member of the circus had gone to a portal to recharge. They seemed determined to stay in the Common realm, which is the opposite of what most of us strive to do. We cling to the magical realm with all our might, grudgingly recharging when the itching gets too bad. But you can stay as long as you want in the Common realm like my parents did. It's the only way to stay hidden from the Connection.

The circus had been careful and I'd seen zero evidence of any magical powers. If I'd been an ordinary PI, that's all that I would have known and all I'd have said in my report. Inspector Elvira Garcia could kiss my ass.

As I filed out with the rest of the audience, I handed my empty popcorn carton to the young guy on the door. He touched my elbow. 'I'm sorry, miss, can you wait a moment? The circus master wants to see you.'

That touch was all I needed. I let my magic reach out to him, seeking to identify his species. Huh, he was a selkie – I would never have guessed. Weren't they supposed to die if they were away from water for too long? As well as identifying his species, I sensed his emotions: he was positively sick with worry and anxiety.

I contemplated refusing his request but his abject misery won me over. I was a total sucker. It was getting late and I wanted to report to Elvira then go home to see Emory for our date night. I also didn't want the circus boss to say anything incriminating.

I sighed but nodded to the kid and stepped aside. I let him do his job, which he did without showing a hint of his apprehension, and waited patiently until the big top was eerily empty.

'This way please,' the selkie murmured.

'What's your name?' I asked.

'Stu.'

He wasn't giving me much. I guessed he wasn't in a chatty place and I couldn't blame him; it was the last show of three that day, and he was probably all out of small talk. I got that. I'm allergic to small talk, too.

He led me towards a fancy black caravan, strode up the steps and knocked once on the door, then stood back so I could climb up. I went inside and shut the door carefully behind me. On the metal door was a life-size poster of the circus master himself, dressed in his costume. It felt a little narcissistic.

The circus master was sitting at a small table. He was still dressed in his costume, all ruby-red like a fine military jacket. His eyes were narrowed and there was nothing friendly about him. The genial, welcoming smile that had beamed across his face during the performance had disappeared

'You've been watching us,' he started. His face was lightly lined and he had a dusting of silver in his dark hair. When he'd been smiling he had been handsome, but now his glare was menacing. He was broad and strong; as I'd watched him prowl fluidly under the big top I'd have put money on him being a werewolf. My best friend Lucy had acquired the same fluidity after she was turned.

'I'm a private investigator,' I admitted easily. 'I've been hired to ascertain if this circus is exactly as it appears.'

I spoke carefully. 'So far all I've seen is a highly trained acrobatic and dance troupe.'

He opened his mouth and I held up a hand. 'I'm an honest soul. When I'm hired, I do my best to do my best. I want you to be careful about what you say to me. I was hired because of the name of the circus. Do you understand?'

I wasn't touching him, so I couldn't work out what he was. Maybe he was human, purely of the Common realm, but I doubted it. Everyone I'd come across so far had been magical, so why would he be anything else?

I'd been working hard the last few weeks to expand my magical prowess. At first sitting in the portal hall trying to guess people's species had seemed a fun – though pointless – task. Now that practice was coming into use.

I had no idea why a big group of Other realmers were choosing to stay Common and pose as a circus, and I was dying to find out. But not today, not until my report was done and I was officially off the clock.

My boyfriend, Emory, hadn't wanted me to take this job. Working for the Connection was a huge no-no in his book, but I thought it presented us with an opportunity. Not everyone in the Connection was nefarious and I needed to find a few good apples that we could work with.

Despite my personal issues with Inspector Elvira Garcia, I suspected she might be one of the good ones.

The circus master was still frowning at me. 'You're dating Emory Elite,' he said finally.

'I am,' I agreed. Elite isn't his surname but a title he has earned. He is the king of the dragons – the Prime – and also king to a host of other magical creatures who had decided to bow to him rather than the Connection. That had earned him the title Elite.

The circus master steepled his hands. 'I would like to have a frank discussion with you.'

'Not today,' I said firmly. 'Today I'll make my report and then tomorrow we'll talk.'

'Tonight. After you've done your report.' He held up a hand to forestall my objections. 'It's urgent.'

Uh-oh. I don't like urgent. Urgent derails plans – and Emory and I had planned such a lovely evening. We'd been promising ourselves a night together before I was formally introduced to his court and everything went tits up. Bye-bye cinema date.

'I'll come back as soon as I've completed my report,' I confirmed, like the fool I am.

'Bring your dog.' The request bordered on an order and he seemed to realise it. 'Please.' Now his tone was imploring and his eyes were desperate. Urgent, indeed.

I nodded. 'I'll be back. What's your name?' I asked out of politeness, like I hadn't already learnt everything I could about the man in front of me. According to his online profile, Cain Stilwell was fifty-eight, a movie buff and he was single. Watch out ladies, this silver wolf was on the prowl.

'Cain.'

'I'll come back as soon as I can, Cain. Two hours, tops.'

His shoulders relaxed a little. 'Okay, thank you.'

I climbed back down the steps and crossed the field. The March weather had been warm and dry, saving the field from becoming a quagmire. We had an hour or so to go until darkness crept in and the lilac sky was still bright. I still missed the brilliant blue skies of the Common realm. Lilac used to be a relaxing colour to me but now it felt like a warning.

Lilac always told me that I was in the Other realm … and here there be monsters.

Chapter 2

Elvira studied me with her dark eyes, eyeliner still in place even though it was the end of the day. If I were wearing eyeliner, it would be half way across my face by now. 'Nothing?' she asked flatly.

'Nothing out of the ordinary,' I repeated. 'It's a wonderful circus. The trapeze artists are phenomenal. I've been watching the whole crew for nearly a week and no one went near the portal at Tococo's coffee house. No one has had a triangle on their forehead, not for a single moment that I've been there. The circus name appears to be a coincidence.'

'The man running it, Stilwell. What did you make of him?'

'I wouldn't kick him out of bed.' I grinned and waggled my eyebrows.

Elvira rolled her eyes. 'I'll never know what Stone saw in you.'

'It was mostly my quick wit and adorable nature.' And the fact that I'd treated him like he was a normal guy, rather than the Connection's hired executioner. They'd sent in Inspector Zachary Stone when the shit had hit the fan and heads needed to roll. Literally. Stone was good at separating heads from shoulders; he'd had a unique skillset.

Elvira had been in love with him, or so she'd claimed. I sometimes wondered if his wealth had entered into the love equation, but perhaps I was being unfair. Stone had died without an heir and left most of his estate to a charitable trust, though a small portion had come to me. It was all tied up in escrow, but I still felt awkward about it. Stone and I had spent a handful of days together but he'd left something to me – quite a lot of somethings. A cool million to be precise. When his lawyer had told me the news, he'd passed me a handwritten note that was with the will. It said: *So you don't need the dragon's money – Zach.*

My PI business was doing well; hell, I even had an employee these days, even if it was just Hes. I didn't need Stone's money any more than I needed Emory's.

I had decided to worry about it when the estate was actually tied up; for now, I'd do my ostrich impression and bury my head in the awkward sand. From my brief dealings with estates, I knew that settling them took at least six months so I had at least half a year's worth of breathing room, possibly more.

'Cain Stilwell looks an awful lot like Clark Farrier,' Elvira said, leaning forward to gauge my reaction.

I didn't react. Who the heck was Clark Farrier? 'Is that name supposed to mean anything to me?' I asked with a shrug.

'You don't know anything,' she bitched. 'Clark Farrier, the werewolf rights' activist? The one that nearly took over the werewolf council in the eighties before he was assassinated? That Farrier?'

'Nope. That's not ringing any bells for me. You think Stilwell is Farrier? What about the assassination?'

'*Supposed* assassination. His body was never recovered.'

'Do you have a picture of this Farrier?'

'No, his file was deleted from the system and his paper file was destroyed in a fire.' Elvira sighed.

'That makes it tricky,' I pointed out.

'No shit.'

'It might have been helpful if you'd shared your suspicions *before* I spent a week staking out the circus,' I grumbled. 'Even so, I can confirm that I've not seen one instance of someone being too strong, too fast or healing too quickly. No one has been to the portal. Everything I have seen points to them just being a regular circus.' *True.* I wasn't lying but I was omitting. I'd learned a lot from hanging out in the Other realm, including the ability to choose my words carefully.

Elvira slumped back in her chair. 'Dammit.' She scrubbed a hand through her long dark hair, making it look untidy. That was unusual for her.

Curiosity got the better of me. 'Why did you hope Stilwell was Farrier?' I asked.

'Jimmy Rain.' She spoke his name like a curse. Jimmy Rain is an alpha werewolf and the symposium member for all werewolves. He is also batshit crazy and believes in the domination of the werewolves over other species. He had started a series of events that ended with the death of my friend, Wilfred Samuel. Wilf's death lay solely at Jimmy Rain's door, despite Wilf's blood being on my best friend Lucy's hands. Or rather, her werewolf Esme's claws.

'Rain is a prick,' I said.

'He's more than that, he's unstable. He's making the human side look bad.'

The Other realm is unofficially divided into two: the humans and the creatures. The human side consists of the witches, wizards, seers, elementals, vampyrs and werewolves. The creature side has the dragons, ogres, trolls, selkies, dryads and the like. The divide is as solid as the Great Wall of China.

Not long ago, Sky and Stone, the witch and wizard symposium members, had tried to introduce a bill to tag the creatures as if they were cattle to be monitored and controlled. Needless to say it hadn't gone down well. Emory had kicked the legislation into the long grass, but the fact that it had even been suggested had strained creature and human relations further. The whole situation was a powder keg ready to blow, and the last thing we needed was Jimmy Rain.

'The human side makes itself look bad,' I disagreed.

'You would think that – you're dating the Prime Elite.' Elvira sighed. 'Never mind. Checking out the circus was a long shot. Send your invoice to accounts.' She tapped something on her computer. 'I've authorised the amount we discussed. Any expenses, you'll need to send in receipts.

I'll let you know when there's another job we can use you for.'

'Thanks.' She was being surprisingly congenial. Maybe Stone's death had finally settled the beef that had hung unspoken between us since we'd first met.

There was a knock and someone popped their head around the door. His smile faltered when he saw me. 'Oh, sorry, El, I didn't know you had someone with you.'

'Remember the time we spent two hours corralling a herd of unicorns because an idiot released them?' Elvira asked the new arrival.

'Yes.'

'This is that idiot.'

'Allegedly,' I asserted hastily. 'Hi, I'm Jinx.'

The handsome redhead moved into the room. 'So *you're* Jinx. I've heard all about you.' He slid an amused glance at Elvira. I had no doubt that the way she had spoken about me had made me sound like I was eight feet tall with horns. And a hunched back.

'This is Inspector Gordon Bland.' Elvira introduced her partner begrudgingly.

'Bland by name, tasty by nature.' He winked.

She groaned. 'You have *got* to stop introducing yourself like that.'

'What? It's my thing. Has been my whole life.'

'It may have been cool when you were ten years old but, trust me, it doesn't work for a grown man.'

'I've had great success with it!' he protested. 'The ladies love it.' *Lie.*

I chuckled. 'I doubt its efficacy, but you must do you.'

'Don't encourage him,' Elvira sighed.

'If you're all done, are you coming to Hard Day's with the rest of us?' Gordon asked her. Hard Day's Night hotel doubled as the Connection's hub, complete with bedrooms, a bar, and training rooms.

She shook her head. 'No. I'm fine.' *Lie.*

'You should go,' I said. 'Alone is a shitty place.' I should know; I'd lived there for nearly seven years with only my dog and my best friend Lucy intruding on my solitary existence. It hadn't been bad – but it had been lonely.

She glared at me. 'I'm *fine.*' *Lie.*

I turned to Inspector Bland. 'She's not fine.'

'I know,' he agreed cheerfully. 'She's been moping. Stone didn't deserve her. I'll drag her out – do you want to join us?'

'She's not our friend, she's a private investigator,' Elvira interjected.

'The two don't have to be mutually exclusive,' I pointed out gently. 'But I have places to be tonight. I'll catch you later.' I hesitated. 'Stone wouldn't want you to mope.'

'Stone wouldn't want me, full stop.' *True.* Ouch.

'Even more reason not to mope,' I advised her. 'Ring me if you get any juicy cases you can't justify an inspector's salary on.' I gave them both a friendly smile and left the office. I needed to pick up Gato and get my ass in gear. I was late for a date with a rebel werewolf circus master.

Chapter 3

When I got back to the field, the big top tent was packed up and ready to move on. In its place, a group of people were standing around a small fire in a metal bin, holding marshmallows on skewers. The kids were smiling but the adults were on edge; they had their eyes fixed on the children and weren't letting them out of sight for a moment.

I hoped I wasn't here to talk to Cain about a kidnapping but that's what my gut was telling me loud and clear. I *hated* kidnapping cases. The last one had turned out okay; I'd rescued Hes in the end, although she'd been hurt and made into something Other without her consent. I'd killed her kidnapper too, which had sucked because it had been my neighbour, Mrs H. That still haunted me. Mrs H had stabbed Hes with Glimmer, my semi-sentient magical dagger. Now Hes is a vampyr that doesn't need blood; she has the speed and the healing spit, but none of the desire for haemoglobin. On paper, it's a win-win situation but in reality she's an outsider.

Hes hasn't been welcomed into one of the vampyr clans. She might have been had she not betrayed her lover, Nate, son of the head of the Volderiss clan. I'd messaged Nate asking him for help but she had deleted the message and not told him about it. It was tricky because we were bonded and he was oathbound to come to my aid.

Nate felt like Hes had made him foresworn – somewhat of a big deal in the Other community. Nate had promised to always come to my aid, and Hes had made it so that he hadn't. Nate hadn't spoken to Hes since. She'd taken his choice away from him, something I had once inadvertently done too, but at least I'd done it by accident. She'd done it on purpose. Besides, I had saved Nate's life and accidentally bound him to me in a master-slave bond that I was always careful not to tug on. He was sensitive now about his free will and I couldn't blame him for that.

The case had given me nightmares. I'd killed my first person because of it. Yeah, I didn't feel warm and fuzzy about kidnapping cases.

Stu was watching for my arrival from the top of one of the caravans. He scrambled down when he spotted me and came through the crowd to my side. 'You're back.' Relief coloured his tone.

'I am. Where's Farrier?'

'In his office. This way.' He strode three steps before he froze and spun back to me, eyes wide with panic. 'You know his name?'

Not before you confirmed it, kid. 'Yeah, I know it.'

'Are you going to tell everyone about us now?' He was wringing his fingers.

'No. Your secret is safe with me.'

Stu nodded but his tongue darted out to lick his parched lips. 'Okay. That's okay.' *Lie.*

My internal lie detector is far from infallible because it only tells me the truth as the speaker sees it. I've been caught out a time or two by clever use of the English language. I'm learning to rely a little less on my radar – fool me once, and all that.

Gato trotted happily at my heels. He was in incognito mode, posing for all the world as if he were a big black

Great Dane, tongue lolling, not a care in the world. Truthfully, I was glad of an excuse to drag him out of the house.

Like Elvira, Gato had been grieving. My mum was dead – truly dead this time – and my dad was lost without her. I couldn't blame him; I had the drop on him in the grieving department because I'd thought both he and mum were dead for the last seven years. It turned out they'd destroyed their human bodies and transferred their consciousness into their hellhound, Isaac, and thus Gato was born. Like a three-headed Cerberus, three souls had lived within my hellhound until they'd decided to sacrifice themselves to close the portal to a daemon dimension. My mum's sacrifice had been accepted and her soul was ripped away. Three became two.

I'd let my father and Gato wallow in their grief, but now I wasn't sure if I was doing the right thing. Inactivity lets the mind remember and the heart ache. Keeping busy had been the key to my survival, and maybe I could at least give Gato that. Trotting by my side, he looked more alert than he'd done in weeks.

Stu led us to the black caravan; it seemed that the circus master's office was also his home. He gestured at the stairs again but this time he followed us inside.

'She knows you're Farrier,' Stu blurted. His anxiety was so off the charts that I could feel it without even touching him. Normally my empathy skills required some physical contact to really be optimised but it felt like Stu was shouting at me. I concentrated, just like my mother had taught me, focusing on my ocean meditation. I concentrated mentally on the sounds of the ocean to drown out his emotions, restoring my own mental peace.

'No need to worry, Stu,' Farrier said gently. 'You can go now.'

'Shall I send Bella up?'

'No, we'll go to her in a moment. Thank you.' Farrier jerked his head towards the door, and Stu left without another word, carefully shutting it behind him. Despite my increased mental shields, it was a relief when he walked out and took his ball of anxiety with him. Stu was really worried about something, poor kid.

Farrier studied me over steepled fingers. 'Have you made your report?'

'Yes. I've told the Connection that I saw zero evidence that any of you were using magic.'

'And do you believe that?'

'Technically it's true. I *didn't* see any evidence of it. But Stu is a selkie and Madam Dubois really is a seer. And you're a werewolf.'

'Former werewolf,' Farrier said regretfully.

'Being kept apart from your wolf must be hard for you. How long have you been in the Common realm?'

'Too long,' he answered shortly.

'Why a circus?' I asked the question that had been bugging me for a while.

'Why not? We get to travel up and down the country, which means all of us get to visit with our family and friends covertly at some point. And it gives us an income and a family that travels with us. The circus was set up long ago.'

'Was it always a circus for runaways?'

'From the very beginning. It's like protective custody for anyone who has fallen foul of powerful creatures or the Connection. Life is never the same once you've joined The Other Circus, but at least it *is* life. And you get to spend your days with other creatures that know exactly what you're going through.'

'How did you find out about it?'

'When I was at death's door. A witch helped to heal me and she guided me here. The witches keep us safe.'

I frowned. 'I didn't see any evidence of runes.'

'Good. That means we're doing our job.' He grimaced, presumably thinking of the trouble that had summoned me back here. 'Well, mostly.' Now we were getting to the heart of the matter.

'Who's been kidnapped?' I hazarded, thinking back to the parents I'd seen outside watching their children so intently.

He raised an eyebrow, impressed that I had correctly guessed the issue at hand. 'A young centaur, Alfie Brown. Well, that's the name he goes by now. Back in the day he was ... Arthur Bronx.' He paused dramatically for emphasis.

Clearly, I was supposed to know the significance of the boy's name, but as usual I was at a loss. 'I'm pretty new to the Other,' I confessed grudgingly. 'Am I supposed to recognise the name?'

'Most would. His father, Bentley Bronx, is a bully and a brute. He worked his way up the centaur ladder of power until he was second only to the herd master himself. He was chief forelock to the herd.'

'What does a forelock do?'

'They're the enforcers, the brawn to the herd master's brains. Bronx was called in if somebody stepped out of line, and he built a reputation for being brutal. If you stepped a hoof out of line, he'd smash one of your legs. One day he applied that philosophy to his son, Arthur. His wife, Arabella, was furious when she came home and found her son beaten to within an inch of his life by his own father. Bronx hadn't stopped by the time she came home and she tore into him in return. The fury of a mother whose child is injured knows no bounds, and it gave her greater strength than she normally had. She knocked Bentley unconscious, but she couldn't bear to kill the man that she had once loved, so she took Arthur to a witch for him to be healed and then decided to run away.'

'But instead the witch directed her to the circus,' I guessed. Farrier nodded. 'How long has she been with you?'

'Bella and Alfie have been here about a year now.' I noted the emphasis on their amended names.

'What do they do in the circus?'

'Alfie is a runner, like Stu. They show people to their seats and occasionally help serve food. They fetch anything that the performers need during the show. They work backstage.'

'And Bella?'

'She's one of the dancers in the chorus.' He hesitated.

'What? What aren't you telling me?'

'She's just started to date our strongman, Ike.'

'The ogre?' I queried.

Farrier looked surprised at my knowledge of the species but then nodded. 'Here at the circus we don't segregate the species like they do in the rest of the realm. We're too few and too lonely.'

'Do you suspect Ike is involved in the kidnapping?'

'What? No, of course not!'

'Then why did Ike come into your thoughts?'

'Because not everyone here is okay with cross-species relationships.' Farrier sighed. 'That's their choice, of course, but it leads to friction.'

'What makes you think that Alfie has been kidnapped? Maybe he's just being young and impetuous and gone for an unsupervised stroll?'

'His caravan. It was tossed like someone was looking for something. Alfie's protective rune must have been destroyed or circumvented. He didn't just walk out of here – he was taken.' *True.* Farrier's tone was emphatic; he absolutely believed that Alfie had been snatched.

'The caravan – was it his, or did he share it with his mum?' I asked.

'He's just turned eighteen and circus policy is that's when you get your own caravan. I was working on a new acquisition for him. He was still bunking with his mum, though he wasn't happy about the delay, but Bella spends most of her time in Ike's caravan so most of the time Alfie has the place to himself. To be honest, the budget this year is tight. The cost of living is skyrocketing and people have less money to spare to go to the circus. I was hoping that Bella and Ike would move in together and save me the expense of buying another caravan.'

'When did Alfie get taken?'

'We're not quite sure. He helped wrap up last night's show but he didn't show up this morning. It must have been some time during the night.'

'Any CCTV footage?' I queried hopefully.

'We only cover the big top entrance and exit,' Farrier responded, dashing my hopes of an easy solve.

'You said his rune was presumably destroyed. Where was it?' I asked.

'Each caravan or lorry has a protective rune painted on the inside of the door.' Farrier stepped towards his door and carefully untacked the poster that hung there; behind it were several runes. He replaced the poster over the witchy marks. You'd never have known they were there.

'Each night the caravans and lorries park up around the big top in a specific formation. As long as the runes are close enough together, they form a protective barrier for all of us. They're designed to keep away anyone in the Other realm. By day, we shift a couple of the caravans out of place so that anyone Other that comes to see the circus can walk in like anyone else.'

'But if anyone comes at night...' I mused. Not being able to enter the circus would be a big red flag that something Other was going on.

'It's a risk we have to take. Anyone prowling around the circus after the show has something nefarious in mind. We'd rather be protected and discovered than vulnerable.'

'And do you think that's what happened? Do you think you were discovered?'

Farrier nodded. 'I think there's every chance that Bentley Bronx found his wife and son.'

'Then why didn't he take the wife?' From everything Farrier had told me about Bentley, the centaur didn't seem the type to let infidelity slide – and I had no doubt he'd see Bella hooking up with Ike as infidelity.

'Maybe he couldn't find her quickly enough or she wasn't in the caravan like he expected. She was with Ike.'

'You think it's an outsider who's taken Alfie rather than someone from the circus?'

'As I said, there's tensions here, but most of us are family. We've been through thick and thin together. Yes,' Farrier declared. 'I think the most likely culprit is Bentley Bronx.'

'Have you seen him sniffing around? Has he come to any of your shows?'

'No, the only one sniffing around here has been you.'

A thought occurred to me. 'Why aren't I a suspect?'

He gave me a look that said *get real*. 'Everyone knows you're dating the Prime Elite and the centaurs are under his protection. You're not going to kidnap centaur children. Besides, you're a PI and you have a good reputation. When you first came here I had you checked out. My witchy friend said you were on the up and up, and that I could trust you. Anyway, I've got no choice – I can't go to the Connection with this and I can't hire a regular PI. I need someone like you who's got one foot in the Common realm and one foot in the Other realm.'

Farrier's tone became almost pleading. 'You've got to find Alfie. He disappeared on my watch. He's under my protection and I've let him down, him and Bella.'

'You didn't always run this gig?'

'No. When I joined there was another circus master who taught me the ropes before he retired. He did his time protecting outcasts, then I stepped up to the plate.' He paused then said suddenly, 'You look like your mother.'

That caught me off-guard. 'What?'

'Your parents came here once.'

'As inspectors with the Connection?' I guessed.

'No, as potential new recruits.' He grimaced. 'They died before anything could be finalised. I'm sorry. I did offer them sanctuary.' *True.* I didn't need to use my empathy to feel the guilt that he carried about that.

I turned to Gato and he gave a bark and a wag in affirmation.

There wasn't much need to conceal the truth about my parents any more. Ajay, who had been hunting them down, was dead; Stone had killed him in a battle that still gave me nightmares. That was the night I lost my mum. 'Don't worry about it,' I said. 'They faked their own deaths.'

Farrier's head shot up and his eyes met mine. 'Really?'

'Really.'

He blew out a breath. 'I'm glad. I've felt bad about them for a long time.'

'Sorry. They went in another direction.'

'Are they well?'

'Mum died not that long ago, but Dad's still kicking about.' I confirmed.

'I'm sorry about your mum. She seemed nice.' *True.*

I managed a smile but my throat was suddenly raw. She was gone. My heart ached. My eyes burned and I blinked away tears. For my own sanity, I turned the conversation back to the job. 'Can I have your phone number and email address? Would you rather daily or weekly updates?'

'Just update me as and when anything significant happens.'

That might be tricky to define but I knew what he meant. He didn't want an update if Bella sneezed. 'Fine. There's a problem, though. If I start questioning Bentley Bronx and he's not the one behind it, he'll know that Alfie and Bella are still alive.'

'Bella was too frazzled to lay any false trails, so Bentley has always known that she left him willingly. He might not know if Alfie is alive after the beating he gave him, but he knows that Bella is. When we accept a new circus member, we do our best to help them cover their trail, but in Bella and Alfie's case we didn't need to. Bentley didn't make any attempts to find her.'

'So why are you so convinced that he is behind this?'

'If not him, then who?'

Who indeed?

Chapter 4

Night had drawn in while I was talking with Farrier and the circus was ready to move.

'Where are you going to next?' I asked.

'We're supposed to be going to Wales, to Anglesey.'

'You're not planning on staying in case Alfie comes back here?'

'He hasn't wandered off.' Farrier glared. 'He's been taken. Staying in one place won't help.'

'What if he manages to escape?'

'Then he knows roughly where we'll be. Besides, he can find our current location on social media sites.' He waved my question away as unimportant. 'Will you take the case?'

I hesitated. Accepting it presented me with some difficulties. I was due at the court with Emory to meet his close circle of dragons. Obstacle after obstacle had been put in our way and we'd kept putting it off, but we'd finally set this date in stone. We'd both promised that nothing would derail it. Emory had formally announced the meeting and I was going to be presented tomorrow.

Emory's court both lived in and operated out of Caernarfon Castle in Wales. I couldn't cancel that engagement, but neither could I leave the circus hanging. Despite Farrier's certainty that Bronx was behind Alfie's kidnapping, I couldn't rule out someone else being involved. A circus member must have destroyed the rune to enable a third party to come in – assuming that the protective circle that Farrier had described had been put in place properly. I needed to be close to the circus to continue my investigations.

'Instead of Anglesey, is there any chance you can come to Caernarfon Castle?' I asked.

'We're due there in three weeks. I can try and shift things around, I suppose,' Farrier said reluctantly.

'You do that, and I'll ask Emory to help from his side. Move to Caernarfon instead of Anglesey, and I'll see you there tomorrow.'

Farrier grimaced. His Anglesey audience wouldn't be impressed; the circus posters must have already been displayed all over town. But it couldn't be helped and changes in billing happened all the time.

'Why did you ask me to bring Gato?' I asked.

'A couple of reasons. Maybe he'll be able to sniff out something in the caravan.'

'And the other reason?'

'He can send me to the Other realm if I need to recharge. If someone's coming to attack us – to bring down the circus – then I need to be ready. Having a hellhound on hand would be extremely useful.'

I turned to Gato. 'What do you think? Are you up for being a circus dog for a while?'

He barked and wagged his tail. He was up for protection detail. Somehow he seemed to stand taller and I saw purpose in his eyes for the first time in weeks.

'I need to see Alfie's caravan,' I said.

'Of course. We left it pretty much untouched.'

'Pretty much untouched?'

'Bella grabbed a few clothes from there, that's all. I'll get Stu to take you.'

'Are Stu and Alfie friends?'

'Best mates. Stu blames himself.'

'Why?'

'Because he didn't notice that Alfie was missing sooner. The poor boy is in knots.' He wasn't wrong. I'd felt the little fella's anxiety and he was beside himself with worry.

Farrier went to the door and called for to Stu to come in. 'Take her to Bella's caravan,' he instructed.

Stu blanched. 'The caravan is locked up and closed, ready to move.'

'Then unlock it,' Farrier said patiently. He turned to me. 'We're not ready to move yet. I've summoned my friendly witch and asked her to check all the runes. She's due any moment. I don't want to set up somewhere new until I know that the runes are sorted. The witch is local, so it makes sense to do it here before we move to Wales. I'll send her to the caravan when she arrives.'

'No problem. Gato and I will have a sniff around first.'

We followed Stu out into the darkness. He led us to a white caravan that was hitched up to an old Land Rover, unlocked the door and nodded for us to go in. He stood uncertainly outside the door, wringing his hands.

I stepped into the small caravan with Gato at my heels. At first blush, the caravan did look trashed but a second glance told me that nothing was really damaged. It was set up in travel mode and the second bed had been put away.

On the double bed, the mattress had been lifted and tossed to the side slightly, but it hadn't been torn or slashed. The same was true of the sitting area: the cushions were all on the floor but nothing was damaged.

The overhead cupboards were open as if they'd been rifled through. The bathroom cabinet was open and shampoo and conditioner bottles were scattered on the floor but they were still sealed.

I had explored a similar scene once before when Nate and Hes had been kidnapped. Unlike at that scene, however, here there was no residual energy hanging in the air. When I'd gone to Nate's caravan, the fury had been palpable; there had been blood present and everything had been torn apart. In contrast, this scene was calm – eerily so.

I concentrated, focusing on the image of the ocean in my mind. I listened to the roar of the waves then gradually let the sounds recede. When I opened my eyes, I swept my magic around me. All I could feel was nervousness and anxiety. With a sigh of disappointment I restored my mental barriers; I suspected I was feeling nothing more than Stu hanging outside the door.

I turned my attention to the door. There was a poster hanging on it, like in Farrier's caravan, but it had been ripped off and was only hanging by a tack at the bottom.

The door itself was covered in something red and sticky – and I mean covered. It was the wrong colour for blood and it smelled sweet. 'Here, smell this,' I instructed Gato.

He moved his large body around the small space and faced the door, then sniffed the red smear before giving it a lick. He wagged his tail; nothing nefarious there.

I reached out, touched the substance and brought my finger to my mouth. Tomato ketchup. Why on earth would someone chuck ketchup on a door? Only an idiot would think it was blood, and Farrier wasn't an idiot. He was a werewolf; he knew what blood smelled like and he wouldn't be fooled by ketchup for a moment.

I assumed that the sauce had been used to mask or destroy the rune. I still don't know very much about the magical world – maybe tomato ketchup had some sort of special properties. I had read once that feeding your dog tomato sauce would help make its pee less acidic and help keep your lawn pristine. It was nonsense, of course, but the point is that people use ketchup for strange purposes so maybe it was being used here for something other than a clumsy attempt at making the kidnapping look bloody.

'Have a good sniff around the caravan,' I told Gato, 'then tell me how many scents you can differentiate.'

I stood back while my massive Great Dane snuffled his way through the bedroom, the bathroom and the sitting-room area. The caravan wasn't small, but it certainly felt that way with me and Gato crammed inside it. Small spaces like this aren't designed for gargantuan dogs. He couldn't turn around in the area beside the double bed and had to reverse slowly. I resisted the urge to make a beeping noise like he was a reversing lorry.

After he'd had a good snuffle, I asked him how many scents there were. He tapped the floor four times. Alfie and Bella were certainly two of them, Ike was probably another, and Stu as well. But that was pure supposition on my part.

We needed to work out a way to convey which scents he recognised. Gato pointedly rooted in one of the cupboards that contained Alfie's clothes before rifling in another that held women's clothes, Bella's. Alfie didn't seem to have too many clothes. Maybe he wasn't a fashionista – or maybe he'd packed a bag and left willingly.

Gato tapped for four scents. 'Alfie, Bella, and who else?' I mused aloud.

My dog went to the door and looked pointedly towards where Stu was waiting for us. 'Stu?' I asked. Gato gave a distinct nod.

'Okay, so we have one scent left to identify. My money is on Ike, the ogre that's dating Bella.'

Gato nodded again; he agreed that the smell was an ogre's. Either Alfie had been abducted by an unknown ogre or his kidnapper hadn't left their scent here. There was bound to be a potion that you could use to disguise your smell. The Other was full of nefarious potions and those who used them with dark intentions.

Chapter 5

There was a knock at the door before it promptly swung open. Amber DeLea stood on the other side as if I had summoned her with my thoughts of potions. I gave her a finger wave. 'Hi, Amber. How's things?'

I looked at her forehead. She had the three triangles of the Other there, but the circle that would have showed her status as a symposium member for the witches was still missing. 'Still not the symposium member, huh?'

Her glare intensified. 'No, not yet. It's a long process.'

I pointed out the obvious. 'You don't want to wait too long or the witches will remain unrepresented.'

Her quick, flat look told me that I was teaching her to suck eggs. 'Believe me, I know. The covens move slower than a sloth. It's frustrating.'

'So you're the witch who helps keep the caravans safe. Won't that be an issue if you become the symposium member? At least half of these people are hiding from the Connection. Doesn't that present you with a pretty significant conflict of interest?'

'If I become the member, another witch will step in here just as I once did. I won't be in charge or know the latest information, so I can truthfully say the circus has nothing to do with me.' The Other, home to the half-truth and the total omission.

'Who do you trust enough to take over from you?' I was curious; Amber didn't strike me as a person who had a cabal of close friends.

'No one, but I'll find someone if I have to. Now, enough small talk. Move back so I can get in the caravan and look at this rune.' She climbed into the caravan and shut the door behind us, leaving Stu outside in the dark once more.

She pulled out the last tack and put the poster aside in the kitchen. 'Hey! This is a crime scene,' I objected. 'You should leave it as you find it.'

'Crime scene or not, no one is calling the Connection. Preserving the scene of the crime is a waste of time and energy.'

She had a point. 'Someone has chucked tomato ketchup over the rune.' I gestured to the sticky mess.

She flashed me a smile, a moment of humour that was there and gone in an instant. 'It's one of the pieces of misinformation that seers spread about witches. I've heard people suggest that household items like vinegar or ketchup can get rid of runes. It's nonsense, of course. Once the rune is painted, it needs a cancelling rune to counteract its efficacy.'

'Has a cancelling rune been painted there?'

'Not that I can see. Either someone really does believe that nonsense, or they're using the tomato sauce to hide the cancelling charm.' Amber grabbed a scrubbing brush from the tiny kitchen and gave the inside of the door a quick clean. She merely removed the tomato ketchup from the rune itself and left the drips in place. The perfectionist in me wanted to finish the job but a quick wipe had achieved its objective and revealed the rune in all its glory. When Amber touched it, it shone brightly and activated instantly. Not cancelled, then.

'You can have invisible runes, right?' I frowned. Obviously the troupe members were all in the Common realm so they couldn't see the runes, and the posters hid the runes from stray members of the Other realm who might stumble around the caravans. Rudimentary, but effective.

'Right, but they're expensive. Farrier opted for the cheaper option and they just hide the runes under posters. No one in the Common realm can see them anyway, so there's not much need for secrecy.'

Everyone here stayed in the Common realm in order to fly under the radar and avoid detection by the Connection. Going regularly to a portal would instantly put you in touch with the Other realm, making hiding away virtually impossible. I guessed that was what my parents must have decided so many years ago when they went into hiding. After I was born, they'd posed as normal people. I wonder if they had missed the magic, if they had regretted living the last years of their human lives in hiding.

Sometimes, I wished I had some of Lucy's ability to speak to animals then I could pipe Gato and talk to Dad properly instead of using a system of nods and paws tapping on the floor. Still, it was better than nothing. And

Dad was still here, alive, and I was still so grateful every day for that.

I ignored the sudden sharp stab in my heart at the thought that Mum wasn't here. When I looked at Gato, she no longer looked back at me. Some days losing her made my chest so tight that it was difficult to breathe. Foolishly I had thought I was done with grief, but it's a shadow that stalks your footsteps. It never quite leaves you alone, even in the blazing sun.

I didn't have the corner on grief; the witch beside me had it in spades, too. Her lover, Jake, had been killed not long ago. My mind reared back at the thought of losing Emory. We'd barely started our journey together and I couldn't cope with the idea of it ending so quickly. But I couldn't help feeling sympathy for Amber. She wouldn't accept my pity but maybe she would accept my empathy. She probably needed some support.

'How are you doing?' I asked abruptly.

'I'm fine.' *Lie.* 'Fine' often covers a wealth of sins.

'Since Jake I mean,' I prodded more firmly.

She shot me an annoyed glance. 'I miss him, obviously. What good does talking about it do?'

'People find death hard. They don't know what to say or they spout empty platitudes that, frankly, I find annoying.

Maybe it's different for you. Everyone's grief is different, I guess.'

She grimaced. '"It'll get better with time,"' she quoted.

'Yeah, or my favourite, "Be grateful for the time you had."'

She sneered. 'That one sucks. How are we supposed to be grateful when they're dead and gone?'

'I hear you. And because people are awkward about death, they don't want to admit that it happens. No one wants to be faced with their own mortality so they try not to talk about the dead. Besides, they don't want to upset you.'

'But you don't care about upsetting me?' she quipped.

'Jake's death cuts, and you're already in pain. Mentioning his name doesn't make it worse.'

'No, I don't suppose it does.'

'So how are you?'

Amber blew out a breath. 'I'm conflicted,' she admitted finally. *True.* 'Jake and I hadn't been a *real* couple for some time. We were more like best friends by the end.' *True.*

'Sex isn't what makes a relationship,' I pointed out bluntly. 'It's all those shared experiences and memories.'

'Yes, exactly, but with him being kept in seclusion we didn't have *many* shared experiences and memories. It was hard. I couldn't visit often and our relationship was mainly based on the past, on half-moments snatched here or there. I think he resented me in the end.' She licked her lips. 'Resented my freedom. It was hard,' she repeated.

'And now it's over and you're relieved,' I said astutely. I didn't even need to use my powers of empathy to tell that.

She gave me a startled look. 'Yeah, I suppose I am, and I feel just *awful* about that. He's dead and gone and I loved him and I'm relieved. What kind of a monster does that make me?'

'A human one. He was suffering, now he's not. Keeping him secret and safe must have been a huge pressure for you. You'd be odd if you didn't feel relieved it was finally over.'

'Yeah, I suppose.' She smiled, just a little, but enough for me to see her gratitude. From Amber, that was a rare thing indeed.

'If you need to talk, I'm familiar with loss and I don't feel awkward talking about grief and dead people,' I said.

She nodded sharply. 'Thanks. I don't really have anyone – apart from my driver.' She cleared her throat and turned her attention to the door. It was back-to-business time. The rune was still shining as she studied it. 'There's nothing wrong with this.'

'It's not cancelled?'

'No, nor has its intended purpose been subverted.'

'That's possible?'

'Oh yes – but it's difficult. I thought that might be what had happened, but no. Everything is okay.'

'Maybe the breach is somewhere else?' I suggested.

She stood and brushed off her long skirts. 'Indeed,' she agreed grimly. 'Time to go rune hunting.'

Amber and I went caravan by caravan, lorry by lorry, checking every rune was in place. They were, every single one of them.

'This doesn't make sense.' Amber frowned. 'All the protections are in place. Cain swears that everything was positioned correctly, so how did they get to Alfie?'

I voiced my theory aloud. 'There is nothing to suggest that he was taken in the caravan. No blood, or anything like that.'

'The caravan was wrecked.' She pointed out.

'Alfie could be a slob,' I suggested. 'Nothing was broken; nothing was ripped. I'm just saying there is no evidence that the caravan was the place he was taken from. Maybe he went out and got snatched or attacked somewhere else. I'll run his card history and see if I get any pings for last night.' I shrugged. 'It's getting late. I propose we wrap this up. I'll interview more people tomorrow.'

'The circus is moving on tomorrow.'

'I know, they're moving to Caernarfon Castle.'

Amber raised her eyebrows. 'Is Emory finally taking you to meet his court?'

'Yup.' I tried to ignore the butterflies that were starting to flutter in my stomach.

'They're a crotchety old bunch. Best of luck.' She tucked a strand of auburn hair behind her ear. 'Oh – and Jinx? Dragons like their tests.'

'What sort of tests?' I didn't want to be handed a bundle of algebra equations when I arrived. Maths isn't my strong suit.

'Not the essay type. Character tests. Be wary because nothing will be as it seems.'

I huffed. 'Just an average day in the Other realm then.'

'I don't know the ins and outs of the challenges you'll face because the consort challenges haven't been run for at least a couple of centuries. Emory won't be able to warn you or guide you either. Any outside interference and you could be ruled unsuitable to mate with the Prime.'

'That's a thing?' I asked incredulously. 'They could stop us being together?'

'Not for a normal dragon, but for the Prime? Yes, in theory. In practice, I expect Emory would abdicate to be with you.'

'I don't want him to have to abdicate!' I squawked, my heart hammering. 'He loves being Prime Elite.'

'So just ... don't screw this up, okay?'

'Jeez. No pressure, Amber.'

'I'm just warning you.'

I blew out a breath. 'Consider me warned. Thanks.'

She brushed away my thanks. 'Good luck.' Then she walked away without waiting for a response. I watched her climb into her chauffeur-driven car and motor off.

I was going to be tested and Emory hadn't even warned me. Not even a little hint. The butterflies were gone – but something else was simmering instead.

Chapter 6

By the time I got home, I'd worked myself into a right snit. I was hurt that Emory hadn't said anything about this whole 'challenge' thing, and that hurt had spiralled into annoyance. I hated being vulnerable. Plus, I'd left Gato with Farrier as an extra security measure for the circus until we got a handle on who was behind Alfie's abduction. Not having Gato by my side was like chopping off my dominant arm and it made me grumpy. I kept starting to talk to him and he wasn't there. Talking to yourself is supposed to be a no-no. Some people say it makes you look crazy.

Without Gato to give me his flat looks while I ranted, I'd ascended into full-steam mode. Emory and I were supposed to be a team and he hadn't even hinted that I'd have to face tests! I hated tests. They always left me feeling slightly dumb, which wasn't a feeling that I relished. I already felt wrong-footed in the Other realm; I didn't need a lousy test score to confirm it.

There weren't any cars on the drive but that didn't mean that Emory wasn't there. He didn't drive, so one of his team often dropped him off. If he was here, Tom would be outside somewhere lurking in the bushes, being one with nature.

'Hello?' I called as I walked in. 'Is anyone in?' 'Anyone' encompassed Hes or Emory. Hes used to come to my house a lot. After the poor judgement call on her part, I hadn't revoked her roommate status but she'd chosen to stay away. She felt bad and I let her; her misjudgement meant that people had *died*. I knew that I was probably being unfair and I was working on forgiving her. She was young, and people made mistakes.

'I'm in the lounge,' Emory called.

I could already smell the delicious waft of pizza-goodness in the air and I felt my snit waver. Maybe I was a tad hangry.

I walked into the lounge where Emory was sitting on the sofa. He usually wore a black, expensively tailored suit; I was half convinced that he slept in them, though he never looked rumpled. This evening he was in casual chic, wearing pale washed-out jeans and a burgundy-red Abercrombie and Fitch top. He looked delectable.

Although he was dressed for the date that I'd already bailed on, there wasn't a hint of annoyance in his gaze. He understood my work, and I tried to be understanding about his.

My righteous fury drained away. That the Other was a realm of secrets wasn't his fault.

He opened the pizza box on the coffee table and pushed it towards me. 'You're hangry. Eat, and then we'll talk about whatever it is that's bothering you.' We were halfway to being bonded so we could sense each other's emotions. The closer we were physically, the easier it was.

I reached out to the bond. He was tired and, despite his easy smile, he was disappointed that our date had been cancelled. Damn. I hated that. 'I'm sorry,' I started.

He waved away my apology. 'There's nothing to be sorry about. Come and sit down.' He patted the sofa next to him. I sat, pulled a slice of pizza free from the box and devoured it in short measure while he fiddled around finding some music on the TV. It was a chillout acoustic playlist; he liked classical music but he knew I wasn't in the mood for that.

Finally he looked around with a frown. 'Where's Gato?'

'I left him at the circus.'

'Is he off realising a long-held dream to become a trapeze artist?' He asked with a smirk.

'No, he's on protective detail,' I explained.

The smirk faded. 'I thought you said everything was above board at the circus?'

'No, that's what I reported to Elvira. I didn't see any evidence that the circus was linked to anything Other, and that's what I told her.' I slid him a glance. 'It's total bullshit, of course. The whole troupe is magical. But you knew that, didn't you? That's why you were so against me accepting the job.'

'I didn't want you to be put in an awkward position. I know how you feel about lying, but I also know that you're too good a person to expose innocent magical people who are just trying to get away from trouble.'

'It's like a witness protection programme,' I hazarded.

'Yes, exactly that,' he confirmed.

'My parents spoke to the circus master about joining them,' I admitted.

'How do you feel about that?' he asked evenly. It made me imagine him as a psychologist, with some sexy glasses and a chaise-lounge I could recline on while I poured out some deep seated childhood trauma about how my parents wouldn't let me play with unicorns as a child. I got it *now*; unicorns are scary bastards.

'I'm ok with it. I'd be a different person if I'd been raised by the circus.' I grinned. 'Perhaps I'd be a super bendy acrobat.' I gave him a salacious wink.

He reached for me. 'You're perfect the way you are.' *True.*

'Charmer.' I moved to straddle him and looked into his emerald eyes. How on earth had I gotten so lucky that this guy loved me? 'I'm so sorry I had to cancel our date.' I gave him a long slow kiss in apology.

'We're both busy people with important jobs. Getting our schedules to align is like arranging an eclipse. But it doesn't matter. We have the here and now.'

'Seize the day.'

'Or the 11pm,' he quipped. 'So why did the circus master want to see you?' I could almost see the wheels turning in his head; he was worrying about why I'd been summoned.

'A kidnapping. A young man has been kidnapped – a centaur.'

'How was he taken?' Emory asked, sitting upright with a frown.

'We don't know. But he wasn't in his caravan in the morning.'

'No CCTV, I suppose?'

'Nothing so useful,' I sighed.

'Were the runes working?'

'You know about the runes?'

'I paid for the runes – on the down low, of course.'

'Why?'

'It's always a good idea to plan an escape route.'

I snorted with laughter. 'One of your back-up plans is to run away to the circus?'

'One of many.'

'Well, that's handy, I suppose. Luckily for me, the circus will be at Caernarfon Castle from tomorrow if I need to escape from your court.'

'The people in my court are not so bad. Their hearts are in the right place.'

'But there will be tests.'

'We call them challenges.'

'What sort of challenges?' I demanded. 'We're not talking Anneka here.'

He laughed. 'You're too young to have watched *Challenge Anneka*.'

'There were repeats on TV. And you're dodging the question. What sort of thing will they chuck at me?'

'Honestly? I don't know and they won't tell me. There will be nothing that will harm you physically, but that's the only guarantee I've managed to wrangle out of them. The last consort challenges were administered before I was part of the court.' He was looking at me like he was giving me a hint.

'They challenged Audrey and Cuthbert?' I asked suddenly. 'They're not part of the court any more, are they?'

'No.'

'So they could tell me a little about what to expect?'

'Perhaps.'

It was too late to call them, but I would phone Audrey and Cuth in the morning before we headed to the castle. I felt better for having a plan of action, and I was grateful that Emory had given me the idea. 'How are we getting to the castle tomorrow?' I asked.

'By helicopter.'

Of course. I needn't have bothered asking; the helicopter is Emory's favourite mode of transport apart from flying when he is in his dragon form. I shuddered to think how much money it took to have a helicopter and pilot on permanent standby. Thinking of money...

'The circus could do with a little more cash,' I said. 'The cost of living is going up and audiences are down.'

He pressed a kiss on the back of my hand. 'I'll arrange a donation. The luxuries are the first thing to go in a recession.'

'I loved going to the circus. I've never really understood the appeal before, mostly because I imagined clowns with red noses and pasty white faces. I was expecting a bunch of slapstick but it wasn't like that at all. It was amazing. I loved the dancing and the trapeze artists and the riot of colour – it was very uplifting. There was lots of humour and sleight of hand.'

'The circus has moved on from slapstick humour. The audience is more sophisticated. Everything is fast paced these days.' Emory sounded wistful.

'Poor Grandpa, do you miss the good old days?' I teased.

He tickled me a little in return. 'Cheeky. I'll get you back for that.'

I giggled and wriggled under his ministrations. Writhing on his lap had some very predictable consequences and it wasn't long before we got totally distracted and left the pizza cooling on the side.

Chapter 7

I felt bleary when my alarm went off at 7am. I reached out an arm next to me, but the bed was empty and cool. Emory was up and about facing the day while I drooled into my pillow. So sexy…

'Morning boy,' I called out automatically to Gato and looked at his bed on the floor. He always padded in when Emory left but this time there was no responding yap and tap. I sighed as I remembered he was at the circus without me. It didn't feel right not having him next to me.

I felt restless, so I dressed in some running clothes. As I headed out for my morning run, I spotted a croissant and a cinnamon roll on the kitchen side. Next to them was a note from Emory: *I'll be back to pick you up at 11am. I love you xx.* He was a dragon on the go and he'd undoubtedly been up since 5am. He'd probably bought two companies before I even stirred.

Emory is a millionaire, possibly even a billionaire. I haven't enquired as to his exact wealth – it wouldn't matter to me if he didn't have a single penny to his name. But Emory is a dragon and he acquires wealth like other people breathe. He loves to buy a company that isn't operating at its full potential; he swoops in, buys it low, fixes it up and watches the profits roll in. Maybe it's his age and experience, or maybe it's something innate to dragons, but the man has the Midas touch. Coming from nothing has made him want to accumulate everything.

I set off into the cool air and let my mind clear. Running is meditation for me. My run was fast, hard and rejuvenating. Normally Gato popped me to the Common realm for my run so I could see the baby-blue sky but, without the security of his presence, I would have felt too nervous to be in the Common. Still, I missed him and the blue.

When I got home, I showered and dressed quickly, anxious to get started with my day. I made a cup of tea and ate the pastries that Emory had left for me. I was eating the calories that I'd just burnt off, but that hadn't been the purpose of my run. Now my head was clear and my focus was back.

I opened my laptop to do some work; I didn't have time to go to the office. I had an email from Hes, sent at 7:31am. I felt my eyebrows rise – she wasn't usually a morning person. I guessed I wasn't the only one with forgiveness on my mind.

I scanned the report that she had compiled. It was thorough, detailed and well thought out and I responded telling her exactly that, then fired off the report to the client with only a couple of minor amendments. Another email had pinged in overnight from a regular Common client asking me to serve some papers in Liverpool that afternoon. I forwarded it to Hes and asked whether she could do it for me since I would be in Wales with Emory. She replied instantly in the affirmative. She was earning brownie points. I emailed the client and confirmed that Sharp Investigations and Other Services would handle it for the usual fee.

I dictated a report about Alfie's abduction, mostly to get all the thoughts clear in my head but also because I like to keep a proper record. I corrected the dictation errors where it said things like 'sent more' instead of 'centaur', then I drew up an action plan and assigned some tasks to Hes's diary.

Point 1: run a full digital background check on Alfie, including accessing his phone and bank records. The latter was a smidge illegal without his express consent or that of his mother, but requesting the records through the proper channels would take weeks that we didn't have. Luckily we did have some helpful software that Mo had installed for me. Mo was my Common realm tech guy. He worked for me on a 'don't ask questions' basis but I always got the vibe that he was a good guy. A good guy who sometimes did nefarious things. A bit like me.

Point 2 of my task list was to run a full background check on Bentley Bronx. I flagged both as urgent so she would know they needed to go to the top of her to-do pile. She should have time to get both searches up and running before serving the papers later in the day.

I hoped that doing some legwork in the morning meant that I could focus on meeting the court. Hes would progress the case for me in the meantime; I usually preferred to do the scut work myself because I struggle with delegation, but I was working on it. Besides, the report she'd just done was top drawer and she deserved a chance to redeem herself.

I checked the time: 9:30am. That's a totally reasonable time to ring your potential mother-in-law, right? Audrey and Cuthbert may not be Emory's biological parents but they had raised him since he was eight years old. They are his parents in everything but name; he had legally become their ward even though they had never formally adopted him. I guessed none of them felt like that was necessary; they hadn't needed a piece of paper to tell them that they were family.

I took a sip of the cold brew next to me. Yuck. It was sacrilege to let a good cup of tea get cold so I microwaved it before dialling Audrey and Cuthbert's home number. They were still old fashioned enough to have a landline.

Cuthbert answered. 'Hello?'

'Hi, Cuth, it's Jess.'

'Jessica, how wonderful to hear from you. Are you well?'

I probably considered the question more than it warranted. 'I'm okay,' I said finally. 'I'm nervous about meeting the court and I'm nervous about their secret challenges.'

'Ah yes. It's a trying time,' Cuthbert said cheerfully. 'I didn't enjoy it one bit. Some of that nonsense was downright insulting. And dragons are sneaky – they won't lie to you but they will try to deceive you.'

'Great,' I muttered sullenly.

'In truth, I miss the court. The balls, the intrigue – it was great fun. You're going to enjoy putting them in their place.'

'I have nothing to do with *their* place.'

'My dear,' his tone was sharp, 'you have *everything* to do with their place. You'll be their Prima, queen of the dragons to Emory's king. You won't inherit all of the creatures, of course – you don't get the Elite title unless each species chooses to recognise you formally. But the dragons … you get them. If anything happened to Emory, if he were indisposed, you'd be their ruler until a new dragon Prime was selected. That process has been known to take years and in the meantime you would have the brethren and the court – and indeed its wealth – at your disposal. The sooner they accept you, the better. But first, you must pass their little challenges.'

'Calling them "little" challenges makes them seem less threatening. They're not a big deal, right?'

'Oh no, they *are* a big deal. They are a series of tests that you can't study for, and they'll come with no label to tell you whether or not they're a test or a real problem. They will be challenges all right, although I understand Emory has managed to curb some of the more … feisty elements.'

'Any words of advice?'

'Disbelieve everything but act like you believe it's real in case it is,' he suggested.

'Can you tell me what kind of thing I'll face?'

'Sorry, Jessica. Each of the challenges is different. They are planned with the consort's individual skillset in mind. The point of the challenges is to test your moral mettle to see what you're made of.'

'Emory has managed to wrangle a promise from them that they won't harm me physically.'

'Good lad. I still have an impressive scar down my shin.'

There was an audible click on the phone line. 'Hello? Who's on the line keeping Cuthbert's tongue wagging for so long?'

'It's our daughter-in-law to be,' Cuthbert said. 'Which handset are you talking on?'

'I'm in the kitchen.'

'I'm in the lounge. Why don't you come through and we can both speak to her?'

'You get off the line, you old rogue. You've had quite enough time with Jessica. Now go – those carrots won't pick themselves.'

'We're having carrot and coriander soup for lunch,' Cuthbert confirmed.

'Not if you don't pick the damned carrots we're not,' Audrey snapped.

'I'm going, I'm going. Good luck, Jessica.' There was another click.

'Hello? Hello? Cuth, are you there?' Audrey waited a beat. 'He's gone so we can talk privately. How are you doing, my dear?'

I was grinning from ear to ear; their antics had cheered me up no end. My grandparents had all died before I was born but if I'd had some, I imagined they would have been like Audrey and Cuth.

'I'm fine, thanks, Audrey. A bit anxious about the challenges.'

'Emory didn't tell you about them, did he?' She sounded scandalised.

'No, not Emory. It was Amber DeLea. I wish someone had given me a heads-up,' I complained.

'Emory is duty bound not to tell you about them. You're supposed to come into them knowing nothing.'

'Well, objective achieved. Cuthbert didn't have much to say about the whole procedure either. I feel as blind as a bat.'

'Well then, that's not blind at all, is it? And it's a good analogy, Jessica. A bat senses things all around it, does it not?' Her tone was heavy with suggestion.

I thought for a moment. Spread out my senses... 'You're suggesting I use my empathy to sense what's around me?'

'I'm suggesting nothing of the sort. We're just talking about bats.' If she'd been in front of me at that moment, she'd have been winking at me.

'Right. Bats. Do you have any other useful bat facts?'

'Bats can eat up to 1200 mosquitos an hour.'

Try as I might, I couldn't see how that was supposed to apply to me. The conversation seemed to be going rather off-piste. 'Any general advice for me?'

'Trust no one,' she said. 'Apart from Emory, of course.'

'And his people like Tom, and his PA, Summer,' I added.

'Nope, not them. They'll be in on it.'

'Great,' I murmured grumpily.

'The good thing is that once the challenges are done, they're done. You'll be Prima and you'll look back fondly on all of this.'

'Like Cuth and his giant scar down his shin,' I said drily.

'Exactly.' She had missed my point entirely. 'Cheerio, dear. I must get this soup started. Best of luck.' The 'you'll need it' went unsaid.

'Thanks. Take care.'

'And you, dear. Best take Glimmer with you.' With that parting shot, she rang off before I could question her further. Marvellous.

Pleasant as it had been to chat to them, they had been about as useful as a vegan vampyr. All they'd done was make me more nervous. Well, screw that. I wasn't some sort of naïve teenager. I had life experience in spades.

I could handle whatever the court threw at me. I'd make sure of it.

Chapter 8

I packed my suitcase ready for battle. I took my bumbag, my lockpicks and some daggers. Despite Audrey's advice, I hesitated to pack Glimmer. I opened the bedside drawer where it lived in the special sheath that Emory had arranged to have made for it. I wasn't sure if it would be a social faux pas to turn up visibly armed but it would certainly make me feel better. I hooked the sheath onto my belt and slid Glimmer out of its leather cover. Happy to see me, it burst into song.

I smiled. 'I'm happy to see you too, you homicidal blade. We're going to the dragon court. No stabbing anyone and imbuing them with magical powers, you hear?'

Glimmer suddenly felt slightly sullen but its blade shone with a quick flash of a promise. It would behave.

'Good. Don't take this the wrong way but although it's nice to see you, I hope I don't have to use you.'

I felt the dagger's excitement bubbling through me. It was hoping we could make something or someone *Other.*

'No,' I said firmly. 'No making anyone in the Common realm Other. Behave. And only stab dragons that attack us.'

Or kin, I sensed it say.

'Yes, okay, brethren too. But they have to attack us first. And even then, you only disable them and do a little maiming.'

Light maiming, it agreed. I wasn't sure what constituted 'light' maiming but I had to accept it.

'Good, we're on the same page.' Sort of. 'Goodnight now. Be ready.' I slid Glimmer back into the sheath and its alien mind slid from mine. The dagger shouldn't have existed; it was far too dangerous. I'd tried a number of times to give it back to the elves, or at least to store it in one of Emory's safes, but no matter how far away it was taken it always turned up again in my bedside drawer. It liked me. I was perversely flattered.

There was a loud clatter downstairs and my heart started to race. It wasn't Gato – he was still at the circus – and Emory wasn't due for another hour at least. Besides, he always called out when he opened the door. Shit. I had an intruder.

'Good morning,' I murmured to Glimmer as I pulled it back out of the sheath. 'I need you sooner than I expected.'

I wasn't sure what I expected as I crept quietly out of the room and down the stairs. I concentrated, summoning fire to my fingertips. Lately I'd been focusing more on my empathy and truth-seeking powers so it took a few tries to get the flames started.

There was another bang from the kitchen, followed by a muttered swear word. I crept further down the stairs, my heartbeat a roar in my ears. Weapons raised – fire and dagger – I turned to the kitchen. Then I swore loudly and prolifically. 'Shirdal! You scared the life out of me!'

'So I heard. That's an impressive array of curse words for one so young,' he complimented me.

'You scared me!' I repeated. 'How the hell did you get in?'

'Not many things can keep a griffin out. That's why we're so feared.'

'But I have my house runed up to the hilt!'

'Runes-smoones.' He grinned. 'Actually your witch didn't rune against us. We serve the mighty Azhdar, so it's awkward to rune against us. That's why Tom Smith or one of his men is always lurking outside, ready to come to your rescue.' Azhdar was how the griffins referred to Emory. I had no idea if it was a term of affection or some sort of mysterious title.

I sheathed Glimmer and let the fire fizzle out. I didn't need rescuing; I could rescue myself. I frowned. 'So you just walked in?'

'Well, there was a little lock jemmying involved.' Shirdal turned back to my cupboards. 'I'm looking for rum. Where do you keep your rum?'

'I'm not really a rum girl. Besides, it's 10:30am!'

'What's your point?' He asked blithely.

'It's too early for rum.'

'My dear, it is never *too early* for rum. Sometimes it is too late ... but not often. Rum keeps the party going.' He swung his hips around like he was dancing salsa.

'Nope, no rum.' I folded my arms.

'No rum?' He reared back as if I had struck him. 'Not even Malibu?' He whispered it like it was a curse word.

I hated to be an enabler and there was no doubt that Shirdal had a problem, but part of the problem was that he was a griffin who constantly struggled with the overwhelming urge to kill everything around him. A little drink might not be a bad thing if it helped harness those deadly urges.

'I do have Malibu,' I admitted, moving to the next cupboard along. 'Here.' I took down the bottle. It was Hes's, but I doubted she'd mind. 'You want some Coke with that?'

'Bite your tongue.'

'Milk?' His glare intensified. 'It's like a pina colada,' I explained defensively. 'Just ice?'

'Obviously.' He said drolly.

I poured him a small measure in a tumbler and popped in a couple of ice cubes. 'Now that I've done the hostess thing, what the hell are you doing breaking into my house?'

He gave me an elaborate bow. 'I am your guardian, your protector, your knight in shining armour.' The bow made him sway dangerously and I grabbed his arm to steady him. He straightened and sniffed happily at the Malibu. The fumes made my stomach recoil. I'd had too many Malibu and Cokes as a rebellious teenager and now I couldn't bear the stuff.

'Self-appointed or ...?' I trailed off.

'You have sent Bastion to help your dear wolfy friend Lucy, so I am here for you.'

Lucky me. 'Did Bastion send you? I thought you were his boss.'

'I am indeed the boss, second only to your Emory. But we decided that you might need some help in the vipers' nest so here I am. Your personal mongoose at your service.' He gave another sweeping bow and staggered again. I caught him before he crashed into the cupboards.

'No more bowing!' I couldn't help but smile. 'I appreciate your assistance.' I did – though I wasn't sure if he was going to be more of a hindrance than a help. Still, I wasn't going to turn away an ally. Not at the moment.

If Audrey was right, I couldn't fully trust Tom, Summer or any of Emory's people that I already knew, not while the challenges were in play. I'd be alone, and that didn't sound like fun. Better to have a stinking-drunk griffin in my corner than to be a solitary force against the might of the dragon court. 'I'm happy to have you.'

'Of course you are, sweetheart. I'm a fine specimen of a man.' His exaggerated leer made me roll my eyes.

'Well, now I know who's broken into my house, I'm going to finish my packing. Emory will be here soon.'

'No problem. Me and Mali will chill here until you're ready.' He cuddled the bottle to his chest.

I left him and the bottle to get more closely acquainted and hurried upstairs. I'd packed my smartest clothes – nothing with holes or fashionable rips. I'd even packed a couple of dresses and my comfiest pair of heels. I still needed to be able to run down a suspect, but that didn't stop me looking nice.

I'm not a big make-up wearer but I packed a few essentials, then I checked myself in the mirror. Black jeans, black shirt, dagger on my hip. Mascara, hair in a messy bun. I could have looked better, but I could have looked worse. Plus, I didn't know what one wore to meet a court so it would have to do. I wasn't going to pretend to be something I wasn't; the court would have to accept me, warts and all. And I didn't care if they didn't. *Lie.*

Dammit.

Chapter 9

'Ah, Shirdal. What a nice surprise.' Emory greeted him with a firm nod.

'My fine Azhdar. I trust you're well?'

'Quite. And you?' Emory's question was rather pointed as he took in the Malibu bottle next to Shirdal.

'Top of the world.'

Emory grimaced. He needn't have worried, though. Despite Shirdal's posturing, the Malibu bottle looked to be at about the same level as when I'd gone upstairs, and the tumbler was still full though the ice had melted. Had he really just been sitting there sniffing it? I'd put nothing past him; I'd already learnt that his inebriation was frequently an act. He wasn't stupid.

'Shall we?' Ever the gentleman, Emory grabbed my suitcase.

'Where's the pooch?' Shirdal asked, looking around.

'With the circus.'

'He's finally given in to his longing to be a clown, has he?' Shirdal snickered.

I rolled my eyes. 'Emory beat you to the punch with that one.'

Shirdal raised an eyebrow. 'I'm not sure our Azhdar is allowed to have a sense of humour. Airplanes might fall out of the sky.'

Emory glared and I interceded before things got fractious. 'I'm on a job. Someone from the circus was kidnapped.' I told him briefly of the circumstances, leaving out the magical nature of the circus for now.

'That's inconvenient timing,' Shirdal commented.

'You're telling me,' I muttered. 'Gato's keeping an eye on things at the circus while I meet the court.'

I locked up my house and the three of us strode to the green field around the corner where Emory's helicopter was waiting. Chris was sitting in the sleek black bird. He fired up the engine as soon as he saw us, Emory stowed the bag and we all climbed in.

Emory raised an eyebrow at Shirdal. 'You're not flying yourself there?'

Shirdal sniffed in disdain. 'I wouldn't be much of a bodyguard if I flapped along by myself, would I, your kingship?' Emory levelled a hard look at him for his irreverence, which Shirdal blithely ignored. 'Don't mind me, mighty Azhdar. I'll look out of this window. You two love birds just do what you do.'

'You wanna make out?' I asked Emory with a cheeky wink.

He barked a laugh. 'We should, if only to make Shirdal feel like a third wheel.'

'Oh, I'm fully prepared to be a tricycle this weekend,' Shirdal confirmed. 'I'm used to being a unicycle, but I can adapt with the best of them.' He brightened. 'I wonder if the circus has a unicycle I can borrow.'

I ignored his unicycle blathering and turned back to Emory. 'How did it go this morning? You were up and out early.'

'I had a few things to do so I can take a few hours off this afternoon and lounge about with my beautiful fiancée.'

I grinned. 'I don't think you've ever lounged in your life. You can't sit still and relax for one minute.'

'I can!' he objected. 'I watch movies with you all the time.'

'True,' I conceded. 'But then you check your phone and your emails and save a small country.' I smiled so he would know I wasn't bothered by his multi-tasking.

He shook his head but I could see he was amused. 'Only a tiny country. This morning I was organising a tête-à-tête later with some dryads. They're having some boundary issues. I've sent for an independent arbitrator to help smooth things over but I'll deal with them after we've had lunch with everyone.'

'So we're going to have lunch with your court?'

'The inner circle, yes. My advisors and confidants.'

'The good guys.' I cheered a little inside.

'Not necessarily. They're not my friends, they're just the people most in the know.'

I deflated. 'Oh.'

Emory gave my hand a reassuring squeeze. 'It'll be fine. I have no doubt that you'll get through this.' *True.*

Maybe he was right, but it didn't mean I was looking forward to it.

Emory told me a little about the history of the castle that we were flying towards. Wales, he explained, had always been the main home of the British dragons and that was why, even in the Common realm, the red dragon was on the national flag.

There had been a Caernarfon Castle from some time in the eleventh century. In the late 1200s, King Edward I of England had started to replace the motte-and-bailey fort with stone. Emory grew animated as he told me about the skirmishes it had survived. The castle had been held by Royalists and besieged by Parliamentarian forces three times, but that was the last time it had been used in a war. Nowadays, it is open to visitors – and dragons.

Sections of the gigantic structure were runed off to Common realmers, who thought those sections were closed-off storage areas or unsafe for occupation. The truth is that the castle hosted the dragon court in areas, like the vast banqueting hall, that were accessible only to the Other realmers. Sections of the old castle had been upgraded by the dragons, including the installation of a new kitchen and plenty of radiators. The dragons couldn't have coped with a cold homestead.

Emory looked out of the window and frowned.

'What?' I asked.

'We're flying a little higher than usual,' he commented.

'Maybe Chris fancies a jaunt in the clouds.'

Emory was opening his mouth to speak when suddenly there was a loud crash. We all tensed as Chris came on the comms. 'We've had a strange noise. I'm going to land to check the helicopter.'

'It's not unusual,' Emory sought to reassure me. 'We probably hit a bird.'

'Poor Tweety. He won't be okay, will he?' I said regretfully.

Emory slung an arm around my shoulders. 'He's in birdie heaven right now.'

There was another loud crunch, and then a third. Alarms started blaring.

'Prime, we're going down.' Chris sounded incredibly calm.

'Engine failure?' Emory said, surprised. It was rare for a helicopter to have a problem bad enough that it couldn't ride it out. Chris nodded with a grimace.

The noise of the alarms continued, ratcheting up my heart rate. It didn't sound good.

I piped up, 'Erm ... isn't engine failure a bad thing?'

'Chris can auto rotate us to land safely,' Emory explained. I was reassured by the lack of panic I could feel through the bond; Emory wasn't fazed by all of this. 'He knows what he's doing, and we're not far from the castle,' he assured me.

I tried to stay calm, too; after all, we were hardly in any real danger, right? Shirdal and Emory could always shift and let us ride out of the helicopter safely. *We were fine.* Which was why my palms were starting to sweat.

'We're not too far from the castle,' Chris agreed, 'but it doesn't have a runway or a fire crew on standby. There's a private strip not far from here. I'll radio in and ask for permission to land there instead.'

The helicopter gave a bump and a shudder – turbulence, just what we needed when the alarms were screeching. I was feeling nervous and I wanted out of the helicopter. Then an idea struck me and a buzz of excitement started to take over from the nerves.

'Hey, do you have any parachutes on board?' I asked as casually as I could.

'Of course we do, but you won't need one,' Emory promised me.

'I might not *need* one but I *want* one. I've only ever had one jump from a helicopter.' I grinned at him. 'This is the perfect opportunity for another. Let's go!'

Emory stared at me for a beat before grinning back. 'Sure, why not?' He reached behind him, passed me a parachute and helped me with the leg and chest straps as we continued our unplanned descent.

'Wait, is there another 'chute for Chris?' I asked in sudden concern for our pilot.

'He won't need it but yes, there are two more. Coming, Shirdal?' Emory called.

'Obviously,' the griffin replied with another eye roll. If he wasn't careful he was going to knock something loose in there.

Emory tugged the door open and frigid air swept in. We were descending from our previous height of 15,000 feet, but we still had a good 10,000 feet left to play with. I had no altimeter so I'd have to eyeball it.

'What's the AAD set at?' I asked Emory. The Automatic Activation Device fired if the parachute was falling too fast at a set height in case the skydiver had passed out or something.

'Two thousand feet.'

Plenty of time. Butterflies were racing around my stomach. I was nervous but also excited; I couldn't wait to get my knees in the breeze.

Shirdal stood in the doorway and, without a change in expression, simply fell out of the helicopter. Even though I knew he could shift in a blink, I still dashed to the door to peer out. Glorious white wings swept out and the golden griffin screeched at me, mocking my concern. Yeah, yeah, he was okay.

'Shall we?' Emory grinned as he took hold of my arm and we leapt out, leaving poor Chris to land the helicopter.

I had expected Emory to shift into his dragon form straight away, but he surprised me by staying human. We both banged out an arch, flattening our bodies so that we could flat-fly together, then linked hands so that we were in star formation and facing each other. The wind was screaming into my ears and I regretted not wearing a helmet, but this was *fun*. It was even more special to be sharing a jump with Emory.

Emory squeezed my hands and then let go. He did the hand sign for a full turn and I obliged him. I did a full 360-degrees, enjoying the scenic Welsh landscape around me. When I turned back, he'd stabilised after a 180-degrees turn. I grabbed hold of his shins so we were in caterpillar pose. I was enjoying watching his tight butt as we fell through the sky.

After a few seconds I gave him a squeeze and let him go. He dropped his knee and turned back to face me then waved off, the signal for me to pull my parachute. As I looked around, I saw that he was right. We were at about 3500 feet and it was time to pull.

I blew him a kiss, turned and tracked away from him. I flung myself across the sky and tracked closer to the castle. When I reached behind myself and pulled my parachute it jerked a little on my shoulders – someone had packed a hard opening on this one.

I checked the canopy above me: big, rectangular and beautiful. I reached up and pulled down the toggles, pulling the left one first before letting it go and pulling the right one. Thankfully, both worked.

I contemplated my landing options. The castle was big but I had to get over the high walls to land on the green inside it. That would create quite the entrance and I was half tempted, but it was the weekend and there would be a lot of civilians wandering around. No area had been sectioned off for me to land on, so in the end safety won out over style and I aimed for a section of dried riverbed instead.

As I flew over, I saw the huge big top tent in the field across the river from the castle. The Other circus had arrived. I hoped I wouldn't stack the landing in front of all those watching eyes.

I assessed the wind conditions and flew the canopy a bit further downwind before doing a 180-degrees to face the breeze and slow my descent. My landing was slow and controlled; I flared the parachute and landed effortlessly on my feet. Textbook.

I pulled on one of the toggles and started to gather my parachute before the wind started playing havoc with it. 'That looked fun,' said a voice from behind me – a young voice I recognised.

'David! What on earth are you doing here?' I asked. I'd met the small dryad boy once before in another wood in Wales, in Bala.

'Mum's doing her thing again,' David explained.

'Mediating a dispute?'

'Yup.'

'Whose dispute?' I asked nosily.

He looked a little regretful. 'Mum said I'm not allowed to tell anyone. Sorry.' He had learned restraint; last time he'd told me everything, virtually down to his shoe size. He was a cute kid. 'I've got some lunch, though. I can share if you like,' he offered with a grin.

'I would love to share some lunch with you, but I'm due at the castle for lunch with the dragon circle.'

'Oh! You might see Mum there.' He paused. 'I shouldn't have said that. I'll get her to arrange a clearing.' I suspected his mum might be the independent mediator Emory had arranged for the dryad dispute.

'No, it's okay. No clearing necessary. I'm great at keeping secrets and I won't tell a soul.' Clearing is when you get your mind wiped, usually by a subterfuge wizard. The name makes them sound nefarious, but technically some of my skillset come from my abilities as a subterfuge wizard and, fingers crossed, I don't appear to be evil yet. Even so, I hated the idea of being cleared.

David considered carefully, his green forehead furrowed in thought. 'Well, that's probably all right then,' he said finally. 'It's not like you know about the challenges.'

'Do *you* know about the challenges?'

'Just a bit, like I knew about the helicopter being targeted. That's why I came outside to watch.'

My nostrils flared and I struggled to keep my tone even. So much for the dragons' promise not to hurt me. 'That was a challenge, was it?'

'Yes, to see how you cope under pressure.'

'The bangs?'

'A dragon in a nearby cloud spat a couple of rocks at you,' David explained happily.

'The engine failure?'

'I overheard that part. Mum said Chris was to fake it, like a girl on a third date. I don't really know what that means, though.'

I fought a grin, my humour restored. 'Did she now?' So Chris was in on it. Thinking about it, he hadn't faked particularly well; there had been no arm flailing, no panic. No wonder he'd sounded so calm.

So that was how the dragons had skirted around their promise to Emory; I was never in any real danger and I'd willingly leapt out of a perfectly safe helicopter. Of course, they had no idea that they'd just helped me fulfil a dream of mine – skydiving with Emory – so suck it, dragon circle.

If they were expecting a quivering mess to come to lunch, they'd have another thing coming. And if they could 'shoot' down my helicopter, I'd damn well keep them waiting. It was off to the circus for me.

Chapter 10

I made a conscious effort to reach out to my bond with Emory. I concentrated on the feeling of impish mischief and sent it to him along the bond in one big bundle. Almost immediately I received a text from him: *Up to trouble, Jessica? xx*

Always. I'm off to the circus for a little visit; the dragon circle will have to wait. xx

Powerplays are sexy. xx

You think everything is sexy. xx

Correction, I think everything you *do is sexy. xx*

I snickered. We were quite far apart so all I could feel was Emory's amusement. I was glad that he wasn't pissed off that I was planning to keep his court waiting.

Then suspicion curled at the edges of my mind. Had he known about the helicopter plan? I considered it for a minute as I replayed the 'crash' in my mind. Emory had seemed surprised and asked whether it was engine failure. Chris had nodded, lying silently so my radar wouldn't ping. I felt a chill. Someone in the dragon circle knew I was a truth seeker, and now Chris did too.

That knowledge was spreading dangerously and I wondered who my mole was. David's mum had been present the day I'd blurted my secret out to a roomful of trolls and mermaids, but she'd been sworn to secrecy – as had they all. I had no idea what the consequences were for breaking an oath, but they were probably hefty.

Who else? Zachary Stone had known. Was there a note in some file somewhere? He'd been fanatically loyal to the Connection, but still ... I hoped not. He'd loved me, even though I had only liked him and lusted after him for a time. Surely he wouldn't have risked my safety? After all, he was the one who'd told me not to reveal my truth-seeking abilities.

I left David and stalked down the dried riverbed towards the field which held the circus big top. 'You're going the wrong way, sweetheart,' Shirdal called. He was resting casually against a tree a few metres away.

'Nope. I'm going exactly where I need to be.' I studied him. 'Did you know that the dragon circle faked the whole helicopter-crash thing?'

He raised his eyebrows in surprise. 'No. But with me and the Prime Elite on board, you were never in real danger. Either one of us could have flown you to safety.'

'But they didn't know you'd be there, and dragons aren't supposed to let anyone but their mates fly on their back.'

'You're almost Emory's mate.'

'Almost, but not quite. If he'd let me ride on his back, I bet they'd have used that to suggest I didn't respect dragon culture.'

He grinned. 'Well, they fucked up there then, didn't they? They didn't know you're a wind-rat. You got around that one.'

'By sheer good luck,' I admitted drily.

'Better to be lucky than to be smart.' He winked.

'I don't think that's true.'

'We'll see. So where are we going?' He pushed off the tree.

'We're going to the circus.' I was trying to be good, really I was, but ultimately the dragon circle had brought this upon themselves. I had a real case, a kidnapping case where time was of the essence. I had justified not prioritising it because I'd promised my time and attention to Emory and his court. But now that they'd chucked some stones at our helicopter, all bets were off.

'Can you be discreet?' I asked Shirdal.

'I'm an assassin,' he said dryly. 'Discreet is all we know.'

'The circus is a magical one full of runaway creatures and magic users who don't want to be found by the Connection.'

Shirdal mimed zipping his lips closed.

'That's not enough,' I said. 'I need to hear you say it. I need you to promise that you won't divulge any information about this circus to another living soul.' I paused. 'Or any dead ones.' There, that should cover everything from vampyrs to dragons.

Shirdal nodded and for once his expression was serious. 'I vow that I will keep secret any information about The Other Circus and I will not divulge it to another living soul or dead one. So mote it be.' He was in human form but his eyes flashed gold as the oath took hold. *True.*

I relaxed a little. 'Thanks.'

We climbed over a wooden stile into the field where the circus big top had been erected. We weren't far from the tent when a familiar shape hurtled towards us. I was surprised at the depth of relief I felt at having Gato back.

I went on jobs without him pretty regularly, but that was different to leaving him at a scene where something nefarious was going on.

'Hey boy!' I greeted him happily. He bounded up, put his paws on my shoulders and gave me a massive lick on my face.

'Eww!' I pushed him down, laughing as I wiped the slobber from my cheek. I felt so much happier, lighter, for having seen him. 'Well, at least they're feeding you well – I can smell sausages on your breath.' He barked, chased his tail then gave me a happy wag. Yup, Farrier was taking good care of him.

'Any drama?' I asked. He shook his large head. 'Okay, good stuff. Take me to Alfie's mum, Bella.'

Gato barked once and turned tail, leading me around the big top to a cream caravan at the back. It was newer and bigger than the one that Alfie and Bella shared.

I had seen the strongman, Ike, a few times when I was shadowing the circus but not up close. When I knocked on the door and he filled the opening, I revised my estimate of his size. Even by Common realm standards he was gargantuan; he must have been knocking seven feet tall.

I gave him a brief smile, business-like but friendly. 'Hi, Ike. Can I come in and speak to Bella? Farrier has hired me to look into Alfie's disappearance.' Best not to call it a kidnapping yet; despite the rifled caravan, we didn't have any real evidence that he'd been taken forcibly and, as far as I knew, there hadn't been any ransom demands.

Ike studied me. His arms were folded and his legs were stretched akimbo. He didn't want to let me in. 'She's upset,' he finally muttered gruffly.

'That's understandable, but it would really help if I could have a few minutes of her time – and yours, too.'

I could see him wrestling with himself.

'Hmm.' He said. He clearly couldn't think of a good reason to refuse, so in the end he stepped back reluctantly and pulled the door wider. I went inside with Gato and Shirdal.

The caravan was generously proportioned but it still felt small with Ike's towering presence and five of us stuffed inside. Gato sat down, making himself as unobtrusive as possible, and Shirdal flopped on the bed. My mouth dropped open. 'Sorry about him,' I managed. 'Shirdal. Get off the bed!' I hissed.

As I used Shirdal's real name, Ike tensed visibly. 'He's not here for you,' I said hastily, 'He's my bodyguard.'

'And what a fine body it is, too.' Shirdal's voice was muffled by the pillows he was busy burying his head in. He was the most embarrassing wingman I'd ever had.

'Sorry,' I repeated with an awkward smile.

'It's fine.' Bella's voice was wobbly.

I turned and studied her carefully. Her hair was dyed black with blue undertones and it looked young and vibrant, but unfortunately it made her ashen skin appear washed out. She had bags under her eyes the size of suitcases and her hazel eyes were desperate, entreating me to give her some good news. I had none.

'Farrier has hired me to look into Alfie's disappearance,' I repeated for her benefit. 'Was there anything unusual about the way he was acting beforehand?'

'He was happy – happier than I'd seen him in a while. I've struggled with him a bit at times – he's wilful and he's strong. He's a teenager,' she said, like that explained it all. Maybe it did. 'He doesn't want to be part of the circus. He wants to leave our life here and return to the herd to face his dad.'

'And you don't think that's a good idea?'

She laughed bitterly. 'Bentley would kill us both for daring to disgrace him. Our running away like that was incredibly embarrassing for him and he'd kill us just to save face. No, returning to the herd is not an option while Bentley and his cronies still live and breathe. Besides,' she shot a shy look at Ike, 'we've found our forever home here.'

As she smiled up at him, the ogre's countenance softened. He sat next to her and she automatically slipped a skinny hand up to his bicep. His lips twitched in what passed as a smile.

'The herd would never accept my relationship with Ike,' she went on. 'I'm done running. I deserve to be happy.' She said it like she was repeating an affirmation she made every day in the mirror. Then her smile faded. 'I hope to hell that this is just another of Alfie's stunts. Any minute now he'll walk back through the door with his dopey grin, teasing me about worrying unnecessarily.' *Lie.*

I knew the answer, but for form's sake I asked the question anyway. 'Do you think that there's a chance he's gone somewhere willingly?'

She shook her head firmly. 'Absolutely not.' *True.*

In my peripheral vision I saw Ike grimace. He disagreed, though he said nothing.

'There's been no contact from kidnappers?'

'None. Is that a bad thing?' Bella said anxiously.

I smiled reassuringly and dodged the question. 'Have you got a picture of Alfie I can see?'

'Of course.' She pulled out her phone and passed it to me so I could scroll through her folder marked 'Alfy-Walfy'. Ouch. There were a lot of pictures. I picked one with a fairly neutral background and sent it to myself so I had an image to work with.

Alfie had long dark hair like his mum. I'd assumed Bella's hair was dyed but his had the same blue undertones, so unless they went to the same salon and got matchy dye jobs, the colour was natural. In the picture I'd selected, he looked surly – come to that, he looked surly in virtually every picture. Either Alfie didn't like having his photo taken or he didn't have a sunny disposition.

'What about Alfie's friends? Is there anyone he might have been hanging out with? A potential witness to what went on that night? A romantic interest?' I queried.

'No, nothing like that. He flirted with Victoria but it was harmless,' Bella replied. 'He doesn't know it, but Victoria is into other women. It's not something she's very open about.'

Victoria was a seer and the circus fortune teller, though presumably in the Common realm she was largely cut off from her powers. I'm a truth-seeker and an empath but being in the Common realm for my entire childhood hadn't stopped my lie-detector from pinging.

The strongest of us still have some access to our powers in Common, but it's a dribble compared to the deluge we experience in the Other. I had no idea how strong Victoria's powers were, in the Common realm or the Other. 'Apart from that, he hangs out with Stu a lot. He's Alfie's best friend,' Bella explained.

'I've spoken to Stu already. Is there anyone else I should question?'

'No,' Ike said firmly. Given that Farrier had told me that the circus was like a family, Alfie didn't seem to have too many friends.

Bella's eyes welled up and her bottom lip trembled. She was holding it together by a thread. 'Please find my baby,' she begged.

'I'm on it,' I promised. 'I'll do everything I can to find him.'

'The dog is yours?' Ike asked abruptly.

'Yes. He's my hellhound.'

Ike raised his eyebrows and looked at Gato with new appreciation. I didn't worry about the covetous light that appeared; Gato could more than handle himself. Once, I'd thought that he'd been piped by Ronan, a piper who could control animals. Ronan had wanted a hellhound of his own. But, as it turned out, when Ronan had piped Gato,

Gato had just trotted along willingly because he'd wanted to find out about Ronan's plans. Gato is nosy like me.

I felt a surge of anger down my bond: Emory was pissed. I reached out with curiosity and concern and felt a wave of reassurance roll back. He was angry but he was fine. I felt him get his emotions back under control and a moment later the bond went silent between us again, enabling me to focus on the situation around me.

I struggled to get back my investigative vibe. Where was I with my questions? Hobbies: I'd been about to ask about hobbies. 'What does Alfie do for fun?'

'When he can, and when it's safe, he goes for a run.'

'On two legs?'

'Yes,' Bella sighed. 'He struggled with giving up his hooves – we both have. But he still needs to run, even if it's just on two.'

'And you?'

'I can't face running on two legs. It's not the same. The freedom...' She shook her head.

'Is there anyone else Alfie is friends with, Bella? A running buddy?' I directed the question to her, ignoring Ike. He glared at me. I was making friends again.

'He looked up to Farrier. He's the father Alfie wished he'd had.'

'And his relationship with you?' I asked, looking at Ike. His lips pressed together. 'We get along fine.' *Lie.*

Bella sighed. 'They're both alpha males so they clash. But it'll get better with time. They just need to give each other a chance. Too stubborn, the pair of them. Ike and I have only been dating officially for a month or two. I just need a bit more time' she repeated. I wondered who she was trying to convince.

Chapter 11

We chatted a little longer about Alfie's likes and dislikes before I left the caravan. We discussed his hobbies. Unlike a normal teenager, we couldn't discuss his usual hangouts because the circus was constantly on the move.

Alfie had stopped full-time education at sixteen. He had intended to follow in his father's footsteps by working his way up the herd ranks. I felt sorry for him; his whole life had been ripped away from him: his hopes and dreams for the future, his centaur friends ... all because of his shitty father who probably shouldn't have procreated in the first place.

I sent Hes an email from my phone: *How much longer do you think the report will be? Can you get one running*

on Ike Sandford? He's the strongman in the circus, an ogre.
Ike was making my radar ping. He didn't seem particularly worried about Alfie. That might have been because he didn't much like the kid, but I would have expected him to care about his girlfriend's mental health and welfare. Bella was clearly struggling.

Something about the whole affair was just ... off. I itched to get my hands on those reports, but I would have to be patient.

I got an email back from Hes: *I've reached out to all of our usual sources. Roscoe says that Bentley Bronx is with the herd master today, meeting with the Connection. No sign of Alfie. Bentley has been in Liverpool for the last three days. Formal reports with you in the next hour.*

Damn: that definitely put Bentley way down the suspect pile. I didn't rule out him hiring a third party to do the snatching, but that seemed less likely given what Farrier and Bella had said about his personality. Still, I didn't discount it entirely.

I slid my phone back into my pocket. Now that we were outside, I put my hands on my hips and glared at Shirdal. 'What the hell was that? You can't go around jumping on people's beds and having a nap in the middle of an interrogation!'

For once his jovial expression was gone and he was looking at me seriously. 'People get scared by griffins. For some reason, we have a deadly reputation. People don't relax around me, but if I'm snoring in the corner they'll eventually forget that I'm there. Then they'll relax and talk to you the way that you want. Besides, I'm more of a background operator. If everyone is looking at you, I can sneak around behind the scenes.'

'Oh,' I said, nonplussed. 'Well, I guess that actually makes sense. I thought you were just goofing off.'

'People often think that. It's a reputation I encourage,' Shirdal explained with a wink.

'Like the thing with the Malibu.'

'Like the thing with the Malibu,' he confirmed.

'Tricksy.' I was impressed despite myself.

'Don't tell anyone. I'm supposed to be a wastrel,' he said cheerfully.

'Your secret is safe with me,' I promised.

'Much obliged.' He pretended to doff a hat he didn't have on his head.

I turned to Gato. 'Something is off about this whole scenario. If a kidnapper snatched Alfie and wanted some sort of ransom, they'd have been in touch by now. The other possibility is that his father is getting revenge – but then why not attack Bella?'

'Perhaps Ike was enough of a deterrent?' Shirdal suggested.

'Perhaps. But I've found out that Bentley spent the last three days in Liverpool having a tête-à-tête with the Connection, so I doubt he had time to kidnap his son.'

'The circus was only half an hour away from the Connection's headquarters before it moved to Caernarfon,' Shirdal pointed out. 'It's not beyond the realms of possibility that Bentley sneaked out of his hotel and took a quick jaunt to kidnap Alfie, then got back before anyone noticed he was missing.'

'No, it's not. But I keep coming back to the runes. They weren't damaged. How is that possible if Alfie was taken forcibly?'

'You think he walked out by himself?' Shirdal stopped mid-stride.

'It's a distinct possibility – and Ike thinks so, too. He's not worried – he's pissed off.'

'The mum doesn't think he's walked,' Shirdal pointed out.

'No,' I agreed. 'Bella is genuinely worried. I don't blame her with her history with Bentley not far distant in the rear-view mirror. It must be a constant worry, even on a good day.'

'Having your son kidnapped probably doesn't constitute a good day,' Shirdal mused.

'Not even a little bit of one. Come on, we'd better head back to the court. Hes will have a report ready for me in the next hour or so. Let's go socialise, then once we have the reports we can decide on a sensible course of action.'

'I vote for an insensible one.' Shirdal's tummy gave an audible rumble. 'Though I could definitely eat.'

'You can always eat,' I complained. I looked at Gato. 'Are you okay to stay here? I don't like being separated from you, in fact I hate it, but my gut is telling me something hinky is going on. Can you be ready to shift anyone in the circus to the Other realm if they're attacked? Hopefully I'm being paranoid ... but if I'm not, they're sitting ducks here if the runes aren't properly lined up.'

Gato barked and wagged his tail, then straightened his spine and walked back to the circus with a distinct swagger. He was enjoying being a guard dog and having a purpose. I watched him greet Stu at the edge of the caravans. The boy gave him a welcoming pat and Gato licked him enthusiastically until Stu started to giggle.

'Silly puppy.' My heart warmed as I grinned at his antics.

Shirdal and I strolled back to the riverbank. There was no sign of the young dryad, David, so I assumed he was having a nap inside a tree after his lunch.

We studied the river. There was a bridge a little way down but it would take a good fifteen minutes' walk at least, possibly more. There were also boats on the river but I didn't fancy trying my hand at petty theft. 'I'll fly us to the castle,' Shirdal offered.

'What about the Common realmers?' I worried about exposing the Common realm to flying beasts that shouldn't exist.

'The Verdict won't let them see the truth,' he explained patiently. The Verdict was a piece of magic that protected the whole of the Other realm from discovery. It was also pretty deadly – fuck with the Verdict at your peril. 'They'll see a big bird.' Shirdal continued. 'Their minds won't let them see a lady riding a griffin. That shit gets you sent straight to the funny farm.'

'We don't use terms like that anymore,' I rebuked him.

I was seriously contemplating flying on Shirdal when an amused voice behind me said, 'Breaking the rules again, Jinx Wisewords?'

I turned to face the speaker. The name he'd used for me had already given his identity away. 'Hi, Jack.' I smiled warmly.

Jack Fairglass was in the water. To the casual observer he looked like a man who'd gone for a quick dip in the river, but I knew what he was. Beneath the surface of the muddy water, a tail was swirling. Jack was a mermaid – or merman, I hadn't gotten around to checking the proper mode of address with him. He was a big deal in the water-based community, some sort of royalty, but he still knelt to Emory.

He was looking at the circus with a frown. 'What's up?' I asked.

'I thought I saw Andrea...' He shook his head. 'Impossible. She went missing years ago.' He scrubbed a hand through his long green hair. 'Sorry. I guess you never quite stop looking for the ones that have gone missing. She never returned from shore leave. Some don't.' He shook himself visibly. 'Anyway, how have you been? Up to anything nice?' he asked lightly.

'Nice?'

'You know, like saving the Other realm from certain doom,' he teased.

'Not for a week or two,' I responded drily. 'How is Catriona?' Catriona Barnes was officially a dear friend of Jack's from his childhood, but she was a friend he was utterly in love with. She had been kidnapped and her mermaid scales had been used to make a poison deadly to the Other creatures. When we found her she was desperately ill, but we'd managed to heal her and to foil the planned dirty bomb attacks before too many more people got hurt. Jack had been beside himself with worry about her. Despite all of his protests, it was evident where his heart was.

He couldn't help smiling. 'She's good. She's been seeing a therapist and it's really helping. It's been a few days since she's had a nightmare.'

'That's great,' I said honestly. I wanted to ask how he knew about what happened to her at night, but we weren't *that* good friends.

Jack looked at me pointedly. 'You know I love Catriona?'

I felt my eyes widen at his admission. 'Yes, but I thought you were still officially in denial?'

'Father won't be happy.' He shrugged. 'But he'll get over it. Though Catriona and I are not formally courting yet.'

'What is it with the Other realm always calling dating "courting"?'

'We're an old-fashioned, antiquated bunch.'

'Well, get with the times already,' I huffed.

He grinned. 'I just want you to be clear that I love Catriona. I'm devoted to her and no other.' *True.*

This was the weirdest conversation. 'O–kay.' I drawled it out, making it clear I had no idea what he was getting at.

He winked then dived back into the water, his dark-green hair flowing loosely behind him. A moment later, all evidence of him was gone. I hadn't realised that the river was so deep; I'd thought it looked kinda shallow. It felt like a timely reminder that appearances can be deceptive. 'That was weird,' I said to Shirdal.

He shrugged. 'The mer are strange. Getting water in your ears all the time makes you unbalanced. Come on. Let's fly.' He immediately shifted into his Other form.

I had seen Shirdal up close a number of times. One of those times, he'd killed a lot of men. Bad men, but even so it still gave me a moment's pause. His golden eyes held me with the stare of a predator and everything in me wanted to call up my fire or draw Glimmer. I fought against my instincts; I had to step closer to that beak that could quite literally tear me into shreds.

'How do I climb on?' I was pleased my nerves weren't showing in my voice. I had no doubt he'd picked up on the accelerated heart rate and the suddenly sweaty palms.

Shirdal simply lay down, and I threw my leg over his lion's body before I could think better of it. Hysteria was rising in me. Who rode a lion? No one, that's who. Lions killed people, and so did griffins.

Before I could talk myself off his back, Shirdal was standing. I swore as I hastily grabbed a tuft of fur at the apex of his back and squeezed my legs against his body. He took three steps forward, flapped his huge wings and then we were airborne.

Chapter 12

Flying is a love of mine, normally because it is followed by skydiving. It's still weird to land in a plane, though I had gotten used to landing in a helicopter. Of course, now I had the one crash under my belt, maybe next time I'd expect a jump again. The psyche is a weird beast.

Flying on the back of a griffin is something else – and I suddenly realised why dragons restricted rides to their mates only. It felt incredibly intimate to be astride Shirdal. My heart was hammering and soaring at the same time, like I was one sneeze away from a heart attack.

Thankfully, Shirdal didn't waste time on theatrics but headed straight to the castle's most prominent tower. Despite his assurances that nobody would notice us, he really didn't want us to be seen. He flew us to the top of the tower and landed lightly.

Once we were stationary, he reared and shoved me from his back. I landed with an oomph on my bum. 'You could have warned me before you dumped me on the ground!' I grouched.

Before I could pick myself up, he offered me his hand. He had shifted back into human form and, like Emory always did, he had retained his clothing in the shift. Something to be grateful for. There are some things you can't unsee.

'Do they do astronomy on this tower?' I enquired, looking around to see if there were any telescopes.

Shirdal sent me an amused look. 'You've read too much Harry Potter.'

'You caught the reference,' I pointed out. 'So you've read it too.'

'Everyone's read Harry Potter,' he said condescendingly. 'This way.' Shirdal took the lead. I didn't need his guidance because there was only one door off the tower, but I let him take point. He seemed familiar with the castle, so hopefully he could make sure we didn't stroll into Common realmers who were having a day out.

The building was old, *really* old. It felt ancient, like you could sense the history around you. Even though the walls were thick stone slabs, the corridors we walked down were cold; I guess the eleventh-century Welsh didn't use cavity-wall insulation. However, as we walked inside the castle, the temperature increased noticeably.

We entered another room guarded by a bunch of brethren. They all stood as I walked in and, as one, saluted me. The man nearest to me took the lead. I'd seen him around before; he was part of the brethren gang of soldiers that had rescued Emory from Benedict, the crazy ass fire elemental that had kidnapped Emory. 'Ma'am,' he greeted me. 'I'm glad to see you're all right after the helicopter incident.'

I ignored the 'ma'am'. 'How is Chris?'

'He's fine, ma'am.'

'He landed safely?' I enquired.

'Yes, ma'am.'

Now I was struggling to ignore the 'ma'ams'. I'm twenty-five, not fifty-five. 'And the helicopter?'

'Landed with minimal damage, ma'am.'

'Aside from the rock damage,' I muttered a little louder than I intended.

Huge grins flashed around me and I saw a few nudges. 'Told you she wouldn't be fooled,' one of the brethren soldiers said in an aside to his buddy. I didn't want to tell them that I'd been hoodwinked for a while.

'I shouldn't say this,' the brethren member I recognised said, 'but the Prime was really pissed off when he was given a report into the "incident".' He used air-quote fingers to indicate his disdain.

That would be the surge of anger I'd felt from Emory. Ha. I almost felt bad for the person who'd told him the truth. I hoped Emory wasn't too pissed off at Chris, who was only following orders. Though I'd like to have known *whose* orders.

'What's your name?' I asked.

'Mike Carter, ma'am.'

I was really struggling to quash the urge to tell him not to call me ma'am. If I did become Prima, I'd have to get used to it. 'Mike, I'd better go to see the circle.'

'If you please, ma'am, perhaps you'd like to see Summer first?'

I had no idea why I would want to visit Emory's PA, but the men around me seemed to be on my side so I shrugged. 'Sure, why not?'

'I'll take you to her.'

Mike led me through the castle to a heavy wooden door. He knocked twice and opened it. 'I found her, ma'am,' he said to Summer. Now I felt less special. Maybe Mike 'ma'amed' everyone.

We were in a huge office. There was a solid oak table, which had the usual office accoutrements on top of it, a sofa and a roaring fire. Summer was behind the desk, clicking away on a computer, looking every inch a power secretary. Behind her, was the door to Emory's office. You had to get through Summer to get to him. She guarded it like the dragon she almost was.

Summer Lopez had worked for Emory for more than a decade, but she still looked younger than me. Her brunette hair had fresh highlights, her nails were painted and her makeup was discreet but immaculate. As usual, she wore a fitted shirt and a pencil skirt with skyscraper-high heels. She smiled as she saw me, but it was a reserved smile and I could see she was nervous, especially when she took in Shirdal following me like a lovesick puppy. 'Thank you, Mike. Do leave us,' she instructed.

'Certainly.' He turned to me. 'I'll be outside, ready to escort you to the circle.'

'Thanks, I appreciate that.'

Summer sat on the sofa, still following Shirdal's movements with obvious anxiety. She wasn't thrilled to have a griffin assassin in her office.

'What can I do for you?' I asked pointedly.

She swallowed nervously. 'Listen, you're about to meet the dragon circle. They are Emory's day-to-day advisers. At the moment, if anything were to happen to Emory they would step up into the power vacuum and one of them would be appointed temporary Prime.'

'What's your point?'

'Adding you to the equation takes them a step further away from power. Once you're Prima, if anything happened to Emory you'd be running the show until a new dragon was appointed Prime. The selection process usually takes a year or two.'

'They see me as a threat,' I stated.

'Definitely – because you are. But also they want to assess whether you're strong enough to lead us if you need to.'

I couldn't answer that question. I have never been a leader; I tend to work in the background, doing important stuff but keeping my head down. I don't care much about recognition; I just care about achieving the right results.

And I didn't want to imagine a scenario where I would be the leader rather than Emory.

'So what do you propose?' I asked.

'Appearances are important. They need to see you as kick-ass. You need to dress the part.'

I gestured to Glimmer on my hip. If openly wearing a weapon didn't count as kick-ass then what did?

'That's a good start,' she said approvingly. 'But that shirt is drab.' She said frankly. She wasn't trying to be offensive, though that was the end result. She stood up and went to a cupboard, pulled out a couple of hangers and held out a leather outfit. It would have been perfect for an S&M club.

I shook my head firmly. 'Nope. It's not going to happen.'

She stared at me for a moment before putting the leather trousers back in the cupboard. 'Okay, I'll compromise. We can lose the leather pants but you need something better than that shirt. Put this on.'

She held out the top. All I could see was a lot of leather and metal buckles. It wasn't my thing, but I was happy not to wear the leather trousers so I thought that the least I could do was to try it on. That way, I could reasonably refuse to wear it when I looked ridiculous. 'Shirdal, look away,' I instructed.

He turned his head obligingly. I undid my "drab" shirt quickly before unzipping the leather top and sliding into it. Summer zipped up the back before coming around the front to readjust a couple of the buckles. She stepped back and smiled. 'There,' she said approvingly. '*Now* you look like you can kick ass.'

In any other place, I would have worried about being cold in my skimpy leather top, but I was going to hang out with a bunch of dragons so the heating would be on. And it turned out that leather is surprisingly warm. Despite myself, I kind of liked it.

Shirdal let out a low whistle. 'I don't know about kick-ass, but it's definitely sexy.'

I frowned. I wasn't aiming for sexy.

'You're beautiful,' Summer shrugged. 'It goes with the territory. You look kick-ass *and* sexy.'

'I would do you!' Shirdal agreed loudly. *Lie.*

'No, you wouldn't.' I grinned.

Summer winced. 'That's another thing that I need to talk to you about. Does Shirdal know what you are?'

I opened my mouth to say that he didn't, but Shirdal answered. 'She's a truth seeker, just like Mary was.' My jaw dropped. 'I haven't told anyone,' he said to me in all seriousness. *True.*

'I appreciate that.' My mouth was bone dry.

'The Connection knew what Mary could do, so it's not the biggest leap of logic that you can do the same. It's clear when you question people. You lean into some questions, but not others. You've already got your answer and you believe it because you already know it's true. You don't need to bother with a bunch of follow-up questions.'

I had never even considered that my questioning style could be giving me away. Maybe I didn't have a mole; maybe Stone hadn't betrayed me with a footnote in a Connection file somewhere. Maybe the issue was just *me*. Damn.

Summer cleared her throat. 'I told someone.'

My heart stopped. 'Who?'

'Elizabeth Manners.'

'Greg Manners' mum?'

'Better not to think of her like that because that implies some sort of maternal softness. Elizabeth isn't soft.'

Shirdal snorted. 'The woman is a cold-hearted bitch.'

Great. I glared at Summer. 'And you told her my greatest secret because...?'

'It wasn't long after you'd questioned me, when you suspected I was a mole.' There was a fair amount of bitterness in her tone. 'She ambushed me while I was vulnerable. I wanted to hurt you, emotionally not physically. I'm really sorry. Things have changed between us and I feel bad about it now.' *True.* She spoke briskly, looking at my shoulder.

I'd been working hard the last few weeks to build a truce with Summer. I didn't want acrimony; we were the main women in Emory's life apart from Audrey. I was fully aware that if Summer and I didn't get along, Emory would fire her eventually to make things easier for me. He likes taking care of me and making my life better so exposing me to a bitter PA over and over again wouldn't fit. I didn't want that on my conscience because Summer was a great PA. Personality clashes aren't a good reason to get someone fired.

I gritted my teeth as I told myself that. I wished Gato was there – I could have done with a doggy cuddle. But I could almost hear my mum's voice telling me to be the bigger person.

'It's fine. Bygones. Just – don't tell anyone else. Please.' I couldn't stop myself sighing. These days it felt more and more like I was fighting a losing battle.

'I won't, I promise,' Summer swore sincerely. *True.*

I changed the subject. 'So what can you tell me about the dragon circle? Give me some gossip I can use.'

'Elizabeth oversees our Connection relationships. Fabian handles the court's international relationships. Leonard handles the court's finances. Veronica advises on, and oversees all things brethren.'

I thought of Bentley Bronx. 'Who deals with internal discipline?'

'Emory, of course.'

That seemed a bit shit. If I were ruler, the first thing I'd delegate was dealing with rule breakers. It would be hard to appear a benign ruler if you had to chuck people in dungeons.

Emory had said that the court was occasionally violent and cutthroat, though that had been hard to imagine when the Emory I spent so much time with was civilised and urbane. But he'd warned me time and again that I'd see a different side of him at his court. Forewarned was forearmed, but I still felt apprehensive.

I'd told him that nothing he could do would change my feelings for him, and I'd been surprised when my statement had pinged as a lie. There were evidently lines he couldn't cross or our relationship would be irreparably damaged. But even I didn't know what those lines were.

Chapter 13

I left Shirdal in the anteroom with the other brethren. Taking a bodyguard into the dragon circle would probably send the wrong vibe and suggest that I needed protection. Shirdal argued but ultimately agreed, albeit sulkily.

Emory and his circle of advisers were sitting at a large table as I entered the hall. It was freshly plastered and had cream walls. The many large windows, all with wooden frames, looked sympathetic to the building's age from the outside, but inside they had handles so they could be opened and closed with ease. Nothing about this room said medieval except the table; it was round, and I had to resist the urge to hum irreverently, 'We're knights of the round table' from Monty Python's *Holy Grail*.

Emory stood as I entered, forcing all of his advisers to do the same. He smiled and gestured to the empty chair next to him, drawing it out for me like the gentleman he was. I felt a rush of arousal along our bond so strong that it made me pause mid-step. Emory liked the leather top.

'Jessica,' he greeted me quietly, pressing a kiss to my knuckles. Apart from Emory, I don't think anyone had ever kissed the back of my hand before. It was surprisingly sensual and intimate.

'Hi,' I blurted.

His lips curved up and his eyes warmed. 'Hi.'

I snapped us out of our moment. 'Hello, everyone.' I smiled broadly around the table as I plonked myself down next to Emory. His chair was throne-like and mine was only fractionally less so; the other chairs were plain wood. Emory *did* like his power plays.

'Sorry I'm late,' I said breezily, 'I thought I would teach you all a quick lesson in patience. For future reference, I don't respond well to people downing helicopters that I'm in – though I thoroughly enjoyed the skydive. I've only ever managed one jump out of a helicopter so far, so I suppose I should thank you for the opportunity to repeat the feat.'

It was easy to tell which woman was Elizabeth Manners: she looked like her son Greg in drag. Her jaw was a little softer but otherwise the family resemblance was strong. Surprised at my bluntness, her mouth dropped open slightly. Perhaps it wasn't the done thing to openly talk about the challenges, but if that were the case someone should have sent me the memo.

'You always find the silver lining,' Emory murmured.

I grinned at him. 'I do. I'm a half-full kinda girl.'

'Jessica Sharp,' he said formally. 'Allow me to introduce you to my circle ... '

'No need,' I said lightly. 'This is Elizabeth Manners, Greg's mother, whom I've heard so much about already. And of course I know Fabian – we saw him once at Ronan's ball.' We'd gatecrashed the piper's fundraiser. Ostensibly it had been to raise charitable funds, but the true purpose of the ball had been to persuade rich people to give him their unicorns so he could carry on making the illegal drug Boost. Fabian visibly flinched at my comment and stared wide-eyed at Emory. Oops. Emory hadn't let on about seeing him there, had he? Well, it would make for fun conversation.

'And this is Veronica.' I continued. She wasn't what I had expected. She was a beauty with pale skin and elegant features – but her hair was bright fuchsia pink. She nodded in confirmation, eyes narrowed; waiting to see what bomb I would drop on her. I smiled back; I had nothing – for now. 'And last but not least, we have Leo over here.'

I couldn't resist the nickname. He had been glowering since the moment I had strolled in and now his frown darkened further.

'Leonard, not Leo,' he said abruptly with a glare.

He was wearing wire-framed glasses, which were a clear affectation rather than something he needed. His pinstripe suit was neat but the ruffled shirt was straight out of history. He looked like he had been dragged kicking and screaming into modern times.

'Of course, Not-Leo,' I agreed easily. I wondered how long it would take him to realise that was his new nickname.

'You're well informed,' Elizabeth said tightly, shooting a look at Emory.

'Oh, not by him.' I laughed. 'I'm a PI. Ferreting out secrets is what I do. None of you have any skeletons in your closets that you would like to confess to, do you?'

They all shifted in their seats and exchanged uneasy glances. I'd gotten their names and dates of birth from Summer. After I had found out about their current aliases,

I would dig into their older ones. It would take time – normally I chucked this sort of thing to Mo – but their unnaturally long lives weren't something I could explain to a Common realmer like him. I would have to get my hands dirty. It was a good job that I loved a project.

I'd start it later; Alfie was still my number-one priority. Thinking of him, I slid my phone out of my pocket to discreetly check if Hes had emailed me. Nothing. Damn. Impatience shot through me but I quashed it.

Now I had time to kill, it was an opportunity for some small talk. 'So, how has everyone's morning been?' I asked lightly. 'Mine started out well until a dragon spat rocks at my helicopter. What about you?' I can do small talk with the best of them, but Emory had coached me time and time again that it was a dog-eat-dog realm and I needed to appear tough – rude even – if I could manage it. I couldn't manage rude, mum would roil in her grave, but I could do bluntly abrupt.

Elizabeth Manners met my eyes boldly. 'If you think you're going to make me feel uncomfortable, you're wrong. The consort challenges are there for a reason.'

'I don't disagree with the challenges in principle, but I should know what is a real test and what is a fake scenario,' I argued.

'If you know it's not real, then you won't react in the same way,' Veronica explained patiently.

'No, I won't,' I agreed. 'But I'll still react and deal with it, so you can still sit there with your clipboards and give me marks out of ten. How am I doing so far?' I asked out of genuine curiosity.

Fabian sneered. 'You're failing at diplomacy.'

'Ah, but if I'd known I was being tested on diplomacy, I'd have been more diplomatic. When I deal with Other creatures – when I deal with abused spouses or cheating spouses or missing children – my questions are diplomatic and discreet because the situation demands it. I am flexible and versatile, which you'd know if you'd spent five minutes talking with me rather than spitting rocks at my damned helicopter.' My tone was getting decidedly grumpy.

'We seem to have gotten off on the wrong foot,' Veronica said demurely.

'Just a tad. Next time, don't try and kill me via my helicopter and we'll get on fine.'

'It's not *your* helicopter,' Not-Leo muttered. 'It's the Prime's.'

'What's mine is his, and what's his is mine. We're a team. His helicopter is my helicopter.'

'And is your hellhound, his hellhound?' Elizabeth queried archly.

'My hellhound isn't mine, not really. He's a sentient creature that chooses to hang out with me, and I'm blessed with his presence. Similarly, while Gato chooses it, Emory is also blessed with his presence. Gato isn't a pet, he's a life companion.'

There was a knock on the door and a couple of brethren staff came in carrying trays of sandwiches. They were not the usual slabs of bread I'd have expected for ravenous dragons but delicate finger sandwiches more suited to an afternoon tea. What was impressive was the sheer quantity of them. There had to be hundreds.

Another staff member came in with a tray of fancy wraps, followed by another piled with cakes and scones. We really *were* having afternoon tea.

We started to load up our plates as someone trotted around filling our cups with tea or coffee. We were just digging in when another brethren man entered the room and murmured something in Emory's ear.

I felt his irritation through our bond. 'Excuse me a moment,' he said, pushing back from the table. 'Please, eat without me. I won't be a moment.'

I waited until they'd all taken a bite. 'So what would you like to say to me now Emory isn't here?'

'Are you always this blunt?' Veronica smiled with one eyebrow raised.

'No, not always. I'm a social chameleon,' I explained.

'But right now you think the situation requires bluntness?' Not-Leo said with pursed lips.

'Right now, I'm up against the clock. I'm working a kidnapping case and instead of solving that I'm having high tea with you. I don't have time to waste on chit-chat, so get to the point and we can all get on with our day.'

Elizabeth smiled. 'I've been so looking forward to meeting you.' *True*. Huh. I hadn't expected that. But maybe she'd been looking forward to meeting me so that she could mess with me. My lie detector would be of little help to me in this room. Dragons can't lie, but that doesn't mean they can't do some fancy wordsmithing using implication and omission.

'You're not quite what I had expected based on Gregory's comments,' she continued. I blinked before I realised she was talking about her son, Greg. Elizabeth had bypassed the sandwiches and started on the cake. What kind of monster started with cake? I wasn't sure, but I wanted to be that kind of monster.

I considered her comment, wincing internally at what Greg must have said about me. I had turned Greg's hair pink for a number of weeks, so I doubted he'd had lots of effusive compliments to share about me.

Fabian took a sip of his coffee. 'How much has Emory told you about his child?'

My mind went blank. What the fuck?

Chapter 14

Fabian's smile was a little smug; he knew full well he'd pulled the rug out from under me. Emory had never told me that he had a kid. He'd talked about having kids with a wistful yearning, but it clearly wasn't something he'd done yet.

Something was going on here. They were wordsmithing again, trying to fuck with me. Fuck *them*.

I smiled brightly at Fabian. 'Not a lot. Feel free to tell me more.'

'Well, you know his name, of course.'

'Nope. Do fill me in.'

Veronica looked at me, eyes wide. 'Oh dear.' She bit her lip. 'His name is Evan – with an E for his father, of course.'

I knew what she was trying her hardest to imply, but she hadn't said Emory was the father and I didn't believe it. 'And what was his father's name?' I asked calmly.

That wiped Veronica's smug smile off her face. 'Elliott,' she admitted. Gotcha.

I could put two and two together. 'And how did Evan become Emory's ward?'

A king's ward is a young person placed under the care of a nobleman or the king usually because they have no parents or their parents are unable or unwilling to care for them. Emory had been Audrey's ward, so it made sense that he would assume that role for another child. But dammit, I wished he'd discussed it with me.

Being blindsided like this was no fun. Fabian and Veronica were trying to make it sound worse than it was by implying that Evan was Emory's son, but actually they didn't need to. It was bad enough that Emory had a ward that he'd never told me about.

I tried to bury the sting of that deep down so that none of the dragons around me would detect it. Emory would know because our bond would tell him.

Even as I thought that, he strode back into the room, his eyes searching mine. 'Everything okay?' I asked him.

He sat down next to me. 'A small problem, easily resolved.' He glared around the dragon circle. 'It was not something that would usually require my attention.' He was aware that the dragons had arranged for him to be called away. 'A dragon was seen flying by someone in the Common realm.'

'How is that possible?' I thought of my flight on Shirdal's back earlier on and his explanation about what would be seen. Surely the Verdict would step in and assert itself?

'Most Common realmers simply won't see something like that because the Verdict will pop a more acceptable image into their heads instead. But some have already had glimpses of the Other realm – flashes of lilac skies, that sort of thing. They should have been introduced to the Other realm but, for whatever reason, they weren't. It's a rare occurrence.' Emory explained.

'Will you get the Connection to clear their minds?' I asked.

'No,' Elizabeth said firmly. 'We deal with that sort of thing in-house. We have a wizard on retainer – a number of them, actually. We'll send one of them to clear their minds.'

'If they can only see the dragon flying because they should have been introduced to the Other realm, why don't we simply introduce them to the Other realm?' I queried, genuinely puzzled.

Elizabeth shrugged. 'The older you get, the harder it is to accept an introduction. Older minds are inflexible and struggle to accept a magical reality.'

'How old was the person that saw the dragon?' I asked Emory.

'Twenty-six.'

'That's ridiculous. I got introduced at twenty-five, and I had no problems acclimatising,' I exclaimed.

'That is not the norm,' Elizabeth said firmly.

'How do you know if you don't try? When was the last time you tried to introduce someone slightly older? And besides, if they don't take it well, what would you do? I bet you'd clear their minds anyway. What's the big deal in giving them a chance?' I looked at Emory with pleading eyes. That could have been me.

He studied me carefully before nodding agreement, then pressed a button under the table. The door swung open and Mike Carter, the helpful brethren foot soldier, entered. 'Sir?' he enquired.

'My orders have changed. Arrange for Miss Flowers to be taken to a hall and formally introduced. Have a wizard on standby for a clearing if necessary.'

'Yes, sir!' Mike snapped out a sharp salute and left. A lot of the brethren had military training and, after their four years in the army, the saluting was hard to shake. I don't think Emory tried too hard to shake it; the chain of command was essential to the brethren way of life.

'Introducing her is a mistake,' Veronica said firmly.

'We'll see,' Emory countered. 'Maybe it's time to update our policy. We mustn't allow such things to languish.'

'We must ride the wave.' Elizabeth sighed, her tone making it clear that was something she'd been told on multiple occasions.

Emory laced his fingers between mine under the table. 'Exactly.'

I gave him a squeeze before reclaiming my hand so I could eat. I wasn't feeling in the mood to hold hands. He hadn't told me about Evan. How could he not have told me about Evan? Luckily for him, I wasn't one for airing my dirty laundry in public, though that was what the dragon circle wanted. I would bide my time to question him further, no matter how much being patient killed me.

I am inherently nosy; it's not in my nature to let something rest.

The conversation had moved on. Not-Leo was telling us a story about the treasury hoard that was utterly dull. I waited until there was a lull and excused myself to use the bathroom.

Once there, I double-checked the room. Although it didn't seem like there were any places for someone to listen in to my conversation, I was struck with an extra layer of paranoia. Today I decided to do something I rarely did these days: use the IR. The Intention and Release was a wizard's main magic. To use it, you gather your intention, then focus on what you want to achieve. When you're ready, you release the focus towards the object you wish to affect, usually using a word. Some of the cool kids use gestures but I've never really gotten that far with it.

I gathered the intention, concentrating on the fact that I wanted to have this conversation with Hes with no one listening in, and then I released it with a whispered, 'Privacy.' My magic hummed and I felt the pull that meant it was working. I wasted no more time and rang Hes. 'Hey, I don't have much time. Have you got anything back from the searches you did this morning?'

'Alfie hasn't used a credit or debit card since he was taken.'

'Supposedly taken,' I interjected.

'You don't think he was kidnapped? If he'd walked away by himself, there would be card charges,' Hes disagreed.

'There would *probably* be card charges,' I corrected. 'If he really wanted to disappear, he'd spend cash. Check his statements – were there any regular cash withdrawals?'

There was a pause while she shuffled paper around. 'No, nothing I can see,' she said finally.

'Hmm. We still can't discount it. I expect he gets a good portion of his wages in cash.' I'd have to check that with Farrier. 'Did anything else pop up in Alfie's background check?'

'No, not really. He buys a lot of KFC and trainers, but that's it. No real hobbies to speak of that I can tell from his expenditure. But Ike has some red flags – two Connection arrests for excessive violence. Both times the charges were dropped after the High King, Krieg, stepped in.'

I frowned. If Ike was under the High King's protection for some reason, why on earth was he on the run with the circus? 'How long has Ike been with the circus?'

'He's been on the payroll for three years.'

'You hacked the payroll?' I asked in genuine surprise.

'Yup,' she confirmed smugly.

I was impressed. I hadn't told her to do that; she was thinking outside the box. 'Good work. Talk to me about Bentley Bronx.'

'Bronx is a mean son of a bitch. There have been countless accusations of excessive violence, but the Connection has never arrested him.'

I frowned. 'That seems strange. Normally the Connection is all over any "creature" infractions.'

'Exactly. So I did some digging. He's getting regular payments from Linkage LLP. I did some more digging and it's owned by—'

'Gilligan Stone,' I finished. I knew that Linkage LLP had been owned by Zach Stone's Anti-Crea father. Gilligan Stone had been the wizard symposium member and Linkage LLP had been an organisation that ran a lot of the Connection's black ops to give them extra deniability.

'No, not Gilligan – Zachary,' Hes explained. 'Linkage LLP passed to him when he became the wizard symposium member.'

Well that made sense, but it begged the question – 'Who did it pass to after Zach's death?'

'That's the weird thing. The company was frozen while the estate was in probate but recently it's been unfrozen.'

'Who has taken over?'

'No one. The director still says Zachary Stone.'

I sighed. 'Damned paperwork is always glacial. I expect the register will get updated in six months' time. Okay, so Bentley is getting paid off by the Connection on the sly, but to do what?'

'Be a mole?' Hes suggested. 'Give information on the herd?'

'Likely,' I agreed. 'And Bentley's movements?'

'He's been in Liverpool, just like Roscoe said. There were a few card charges at a bar – Alma De Cuba – on the night his son was taken,' Hes stated.

'With people being able to pay contactless without entering a chip and pin, he could have passed his card to a colleague to help him establish an alibi,' I pointed out.

'Yeah, but the bar has a big social media following. I spotted Bentley in the background of a couple of customers' photos. He was definitely there. If he's involved in his son's kidnapping, then he hired someone else to do it.'

Chapter 15

'Did you get lost?' Fabian asked cattily in his soft French accent.

I had taken longer in the bathroom than I'd intended, but Hes's report had been fascinating. She had emailed it to me and I'd taken ten minutes to skim read it. I'd asked her to start reports on the dragon circle too, and I'd text her their names and official dates of birth.

'Just refreshing my makeup,' I lied, bald-faced.

He raised an eyebrow at that because my makeup was obviously not touched up in the slightest. Let them wonder what I'd been up to. I slid in next to Emory and dug into the cakes that had been piled on my plate. The dragons ate a lot, and the dainty sandwiches had not lasted long.

Elizabeth and Not-Leo attempted some light conversation about the weather, which I dutifully joined in. We agreed that it was unseasonably warm. I let them see that I could do this polite small-talk bullshit, if I wanted to. Mum had drilled manners into me from an early age; I could talk weather with the best of them.

We'd just been served more tea and coffee when my phone started to vibrate, so I pulled it out to see who was calling me. It was Nate. Now that I knew he was trying to get my attention, I concentrated on my bond with him. It was hard to reach him because Emory's bond had taken precedence, but my link with Nate was still there, slow and steady and reassuring.

He was worried so, rude or not, I slid the bar to answer the call. 'Nate? Is everything okay?'

'Not exactly. My father has just called me. There's been a break-in at his office – your office, to be precise.'

I sat up straight. 'Is Hes okay?'

'She wasn't there.'

The break-in must have been timed to perfection. Hes had been in the office all morning, but she'd left as soon as we finished talking to serve those papers for me. In an hour's time she would be back to check on the other reports that she'd started running. 'What happened?' I asked tightly.

'It looks like it was the Anti-Crea,' Nate admitted unhappily. The anti-creature movement had called themselves the AC movement for a time, until they realised it made them sound like they installed air-cooling systems. They now call themselves the Anti-Crea, which always made me think of the Antichrist. Whichever way they spun it, their name didn't have good connotations – and neither did the vitriol they spewed.

I was surprised that they'd risk the wrath of Lord Volderiss. Vampyrs didn't fall under the creature umbrella, despite needing blood to survive. Generally the Anti-Crea tried not to piss off the human side because they needed allies. 'What makes you say it was Anti-Crea?' I queried.

'Well, for one thing they scrawled their insignia on the walls,' Nate said drily.

'That's a pretty good reason for suspecting them,' I agreed with amusement. 'How did they gain entry?'

'Brute force – it's ballsy as hell. It was just Verona manning reception. The security tapes were jammed and Verona was incapacitated. She was struck from behind and has no memory at all about the attack.'

Verona and I did not get on. The vampyr bitch looked down her nose at me and I scowled right back, but still … despite that, I was surprised at a twinge of something that felt like concern. 'Is she okay?' I asked reluctantly.

'She's fine, though her pride isn't. I'll tell her you asked after her.'

'Don't you dare!' I protested.

Nate laughed.

'Was anything taken?'

'It's difficult to tell. The room is a mess – the files have been flung everywhere. There's "dragon whore" sprayed on the wall, too.'

'He doesn't pay me, so that's inaccurate,' I huffed. 'Graffiti should at least be accurate.'

'I'll be sure to remember that next time,' Nate said sardonically. 'Hes is on her way back to the office so she can tell us what was taken, if anything. I'll send some pictures of the scene to you.'

'Okay. Will you be all right seeing Hes?'

'I'll be fine. I'm a big boy. I can cope with seeing my ex.'

Despite his words, I felt a flutter of remembered hurt down our bond. 'Liar,' I sighed softly.

'I'll be fine,' he repeated stubbornly. *Lie.*

I didn't call him on it a second time.

'The break-in was pretty spectacular,' Nate went on. 'They used a potion bomb.' He said it with the same incredulous tone as if someone had used a nuke. 'Someone had already called the Connection before back-up arrived.'

'How do potion bombs work? I've only ever seen potions used in conjunction with runes before.'

'They're rare and very expensive. The witches don't let them out of their sight, or sell them conventionally. Apparently they require specific ingredients and brewing circumstances, it's one of the witches' closely guarded secrets. The existence of potion bombs is one of the reasons why witches aren't bothered by the Other community. One potion bomb and you're a goner.'

'Who has the case?'

'Father pulled strings and got Inspector Garcia on it.'

'Elvira? Well, at least she's competent,' I mused.

'Expect her call.'

'Lucky me,' I quipped.

As I hung up, I wondered for a second whether this was another challenge. It didn't seem likely. Firstly, it was too far away and the dragons couldn't observe how I responded. Secondly, there was the use of the phrase 'dragon whore'. An insult like that was not something a brethren member or dragon would write. It could have been a double bluff, but my gut didn't think so. My gut said this was about Alfie, and my gut was rarely wrong.

'What's up?' Emory asked, frowning.

'There's been a break-in at my office. It looks like the Anti-Creature movement are behind it. They sprayed "dragon whore" on the walls, as well as their insignia.'

Elizabeth slammed her hand on the table. 'That cannot stand. We need a swift and hard reprisal.'

'Against whom?' I asked. 'Until we know who broke in, reprisals are off the cards.'

'You said it yourself – Anti-Crea.'

'I said it *looks* like the Anti-Crea. Those fires are already stoked. Some mischievous soul might be trying to put a light to the tinder, so let's be sure before we take action.'

Elizabeth glared. 'You sound like him.' She gestured at Emory.

'Good. We often sing from the same hymn sheet. We need information, not half-cocked responses. When we know the identity of the culprits, *then* we'll rain hellfire on their heads.'

Elizabeth brightened. 'I knew I was going to like you.' *True.* I frowned a little at my internal lie detector, it had never been wrong yet, but I certainly hadn't gotten the impression from Elizabeth that she had *any* positive feelings about me, let alone that she came here prepared to actively like me.

'Not actual hellfire,' Emory hastened to add. 'Jess is talking metaphorically.'

'Am I?' I smiled a little and made eye contact with each of the dragons around me. Let them wonder what I would do – what I was capable of doing.

Chapter 16

After our somewhat eventful lunch, Emory and I retreated to his suite of rooms. It had everything you could want including a bedroom, an office and, of course, a small armoury. Emory had his own sitting room decorated in a soft and soothing sage green, completed with a brown leather couch and a roaring fire burning in a sizeable fireplace.

Attached to the sitting room was a sumptuous bedroom decorated in earth tones, complete with a mammoth four-poster bed, and an en-suite bathroom. The modern bathroom had huge textured off-white tiles, making it feel a little sterile. Still, it had an enormous bath, complete with fancy clawed feet, and a double shower too. No matter what your cleanliness requirements were, this bathroom had you covered.

Off the sitting room was a cosy study for Emory to work in, though generally he preferred to work in his main office so that he was easily findable. He had an open-door policy. He was a modern dragon. The last, and most interesting, room was his armoury. It felt a little like a museum piece. Swords, daggers and guns lined the walls. The ammo was kept in an easily accessible cupboard, though it had a combination lock on it.

'Any particular reason for the weapons?' I asked curiously.

'Everyone likes a sword on the wall,' he said confidently.

'One or two. This is a little excessive.' I gestured to the hundreds of weapons in the room.

'Says the girl with a dagger on her hip,' he teased.

'I have Glimmer. That's different,' I protested. 'It's being very well behaved.'

'Glimmer is different. Wearing it is *worse*. It's a sentient national treasure.' He grinned at me. 'Did you see Leonard's face when you walked in with it on?'

'No,' I admitted. 'I was busy enjoying your reaction. You like the leather top, huh?'

'I love it. Where did it come from?'

'Summer gave it to me,' I explained. 'She said I needed to look more kick-ass.'

'I should give her a raise,' he murmured as he moved towards me with a certain look on his face.

'Oh no, back you go. Now is *not* the time.'

'Now is always the time,' he countered. 'It's the only time we get.'

Technically, that wasn't true. With a handy hellhound, you could also access the Third realm for a spot of time travel. I could get now and the past; I was lucky like that.

My phone buzzed again. This time it was Elvira. 'Hey, Elvira.'

'That's Inspector Garcia,' she corrected grumpily.

'And how is Inspector Tasty?' I enquired.

She sighed. 'Don't encourage him. I'm ringing you about the break-in. Where were you when it happened?'

I hesitated; I didn't like giving information to the Connection. 'In Wales, with my boyfriend,' I offered finally. There, that was vague enough.

'And he can corroborate that?' She pressed.

'Am I suspected of graffitiing my own office?' I asked wryly.

'Of course not, but I need the information for my file.'

Yeah, I bet you do. 'Yes, he can corroborate that if you need him to. I'm surprised an inspector is on this case.'

'Me too,' she grumped. 'No doubt strings were pulled. This is usually detective-level shit – normally I'm only called in for dead bodies.'

'Lucky you. Was anything taken from the office?'

'Hes has confirmed that one file was taken: Alfie Brown's.' She paused. 'Tell me you were hired by the circus *after* you'd finished your investigation for me.'

Oops. I winced. 'Absolutely,' I said firmly. 'I wouldn't have taken on two cases at the same time that represented a conflict of interest.'

'I hope that's true,' she muttered with an edge to her voice. 'Alfie's file is the only thing that was taken. I've checked our database and no formal report has been made about his disappearance to the Connection.' Her tone was reproachful.

'He's eighteen and there's no sign he's been snatched. No ransom demand.'

'You think he's gone willingly?'

'Yes.' I wasn't surprised when that buzzed *true*.

'I'll note that in my report.' Her tone was friendlier now she believed I wasn't concealing crimes from the Connection. 'The forensics are here for finger printing.'

'You do finger printing?'

'Of course we do. We use all the modern policing techniques *plus* magic.'

'Good to know.'

'I'll let you know the results. I'm getting pressure from on high to get this wrapped up, so I'll put an urgent on the prints. But don't hold your breath – the chances of us having any matching ones on file are slim. This is going to be a cold case very quickly.'

'I appreciate your candour.'

'Yeah, yeah.' She rang off.

I turned to Emory. 'I'd better go to the circus. It was the centaur kid's file that was taken. The rest of the mess was just a smokescreen. I'm willing to bet good money that Bentley Bronx now knows the location of his wife.'

'And presumably he's already got the kid,' Emory said grimly.

'Maybe. I'm not sold on that, but he may have him. You've got to keep an open mind about these things.' I leaned over and gave him a quick kiss. 'What's on your agenda?'

'Leonard has requested an urgent meeting, so I'll see him now and find out what's got his knickers in a twist. Then I have the meeting with the two dryad factions to oversee.'

I gave him a slower kiss. 'Have fun.'

'Doubtful.' His eyes skimmed the leather top again. 'I could cancel ... '

'You could, but I can't. I've got to go – Bella could be in danger. Can I use one of your safe houses if necessary?'

'Of course. My safe house is your safe house,' he said lightly. Then his tone changed. 'And Jess?'

'Yes?'

'Take Shirdal with you,' he requested.

I raised an eyebrow. 'Was it you who asked him to babysit me?' He didn't answer, which was an answer in itself. 'We still need to talk about Evan,' I added abruptly.

'Evan who?'

'The one that's your ward?' I huffed.

He blinked, mouth dropping open in surprise. He recovered himself with a clack. 'Only on paper.' He reassured me firmly. 'I have nothing to do with him really. I think we've only met twice.'

'Ah. Veronica was busy implying that he was your biological child when you stepped out at lunch.'

'She what?' He glared.

'Relax, I knew it was bullshit.' I frowned. 'You were Audrey and Cuthbert's ward. Did they only see you a time or two?'

'That was different. Evan is older. He's sixteen.'

'So?'

'He manifested as a dragon at fifteen, a real late bloomer. His parents were both wizards. He was introduced to the Other at twelve, but he couldn't seem to handle the IR. His parents thought he was a dud, but at fifteen he proved them wrong. They were horrified that they birthed a creature – they're Anti-Crea.'

'I didn't realise a wizard and a wizard could make a dragon shifter. I didn't think that was possible,' I said, frowning.

'It's not. I expect his mum got handsy with a dragon-shifter but if she won't tell us who... Well, we haven't got a father figure in the mix.'

'I know they were Anti-Crea, but surely he was still best placed with his family? They can't be that fanatical that they—'

'They tried to kill him.'

'They what?' I gasped, horrified. 'Their own son?' Just the thought made me feel sick.

'There are some vile humans out there. He was rescued, by Stone actually. He brought him here and the rest is history.'

'The rest is everything else. How did you end up being his guardian?'

'I'm not really his guardian, that's Sophie and Danny. They were sick at the time of the legal hearing so I stepped in and signed some paperwork. It doesn't really matter who is on the documents as long as he's being raised by us.'

'Okay, so you have a kid.'

'I do not.'

'Are you Audrey and Cuthbert's son?'

He paused. 'That's different.'

'Not by much.'

'You can't seriously think that I have a child because Danny and Sophie got a vomiting bug. That's ridiculous.'

'What's ridiculous is you not stepping up to the plate.'

'There was no plate to step up to.' He ran a hand through his short hair. 'I'm going to kill Veronica,' he muttered.

'It was Fabian, too,' I confirmed honestly. It seemed unfair to let Veronica face his vitriol alone. 'We'll talk about it more later. I've got to go. I need to make sure Bella is okay.'

'Be safe. Don't kill anyone I wouldn't.'

'That's not very limiting,' I quipped.

He smirked.

Chapter 17

I rang Lucy as I walked from the castle to the circus field. Shirdal gave me the illusion of privacy by flying above me as I marched on. Lucy was busy, so the conversation was short, but it still made me feel better that we'd touched base.

All the miles between us wouldn't stop her being my sister from another mister. I wasn't the only one facing challenges, and I worried about her, but I let myself be reassured by the happiness in her voice. She and Manners were getting along like the wolf and the moon. Whatever they were facing, they were battling it together – and with her wolf, Esme, too, of course. They could handle it. I squared my shoulders. So could I.

The circus lunchtime show had just finished and the audience was pouring out of the field. Despite the short notice that the circus had arrived, there seemed to be no shortage of people happy to go and watch the performance. I had seen droves of brethren swaggering down to the circus. I suspected that Emory had encouraged attendance, knowing the circus was struggling financially.

I found Gato in a crowd of adoring fans, being patted by a bunch of kids and having his photograph taken. He was wearing a rather dashing black-and-red waistcoat. Somehow, in twenty-four short hours, Gato had become part of the circus. 'Hey boy,' I called him. 'Taking part in the shows now, are we?'

Gato gave a bark and a happy wag. He was living his best dog life and I felt a twinge of jealousy that he was having such a good time without me. I missed him. As if sensing my thoughts, he trotted over and gave me a giant lick. 'I'm glad to see you too,' I said, giving him a kiss on his huge head. 'Do you know where Bella is?'

He turned on his tail and set off; looking back over his shoulder to make sure I was following him. 'I'm coming,' I reassured him.

He led me to Alfie and Bella's caravan. Shirdal landed on the roof so quietly that I doubted the occupants heard so much as a scrape of claws. 'I'll stay out here,' he suggested, looking around from his outpost. 'Holler if you need me.'

If I hollered, he'd peel the roof back like it was a tin can. I nodded before knocking on the thin caravan door. Ike opened it, his expression shuttered. 'Hi,' I said pleasantly. 'Can I see Bella? It's important.'

He grimaced but stepped aside and let me in.

Bella was looking much better. Her black-blue hair had been plaited elaborately and she had on a full face of make-up. She had clearly just taken part in the performance. Today Bella was cheese to her previous chalky appearance, and my alarm bells rang.

She smiled brightly at me before dimming it a little at Ike's warning glare. 'Oh, um, Jinx. How nice to see you again.'

I'd done a kidnapping case or two, and the parents didn't smile like this until *after* their kids were safe. I also noted that she didn't immediately ask after her son.

'I've got some bad news, I'm afraid,' I started. Her too-sunny expression didn't waver; she was certain her son was fine. 'Somebody broke into my office in Liverpool. They rifled through a number of files but only one appears to have been taken – the one that I set up for Alfie. Obviously it contains a number of details, including your current location. I believe there's a strong possibility that Bentley Bronx broke into my office and took your file, so you may be in danger. I'd like to move you into a safe house.'

'Oh, I'm sure that's not necessary,' she said lightly and looked at Ike. *True.*

'I'll keep her safe,' Ike grunted. *True.*

For whatever reason, they didn't think that whoever had broken into my office was Bentley or that he was a threat. Something had changed since I'd met with them before. 'Were you contacted by someone?' I asked bluntly. 'The kidnappers?'

'No, not by them.' Bella's hands flew to her lips in the universal 'I shouldn't have said that' sign. Eyes wide, she tore her hands away from her mouth. She would make a shit spy.

'Were you contacted by Alfie?' I asked evenly.

'That's enough questions. Bella is upset,' Ike snarled. *Lie.* 'You'd best go.' *True.*

'I really think you should be honest with me about what's going on. Have you told Farrier the truth?' Neither of them replied, so I took another stab at getting Bella to a safe house. My gut had a bad feeling about all of this. 'You should think about moving somewhere else. Just for the meantime.'

'We appreciate your concern, but we have the rest of the circus. We'll be fine,' Ike said firmly. 'Let me show you out.'

He manoeuvred around the small space, then held the door open for Gato and me. I had no doubt he and Bella were in contact with Alfie, but I had no idea why they weren't being honest about it. Something else was going on and I didn't have the full picture.

My gut still said Bentley was someone they should be worried about. If Alfie was fine – as I was guessing from Bella's reaction – who but his father would want his file? I supposed the Anti-Crea could want it. Alfie was a centaur and he fell on the creature side of the spectrum so maybe they wanted to get hold of him for some reason, but that theory felt tenuous at best.

Ike followed me out of the caravan, ostensibly to escort me safely off the circus site. As we walked past, one of the tumblers spat on the ground. 'Miscegenating scum,' he muttered at Ike.

I turned. 'What did you say?' I asked incredulously.

'You heard me,' the tumbler said defiantly. 'Mixing the magical races isn't right. He's sinning.'

'My sins are between me and my god,' Ike said calmly.

'You're not going to be seeing your god, you're going straight to the daemon realms.'

'We'll see.'

'Step back, Raul.' Another man stepped forward with a young girl by his side, his daughter I guessed because there was a strong family resemblance. The man rolled his Rs a little, like he was Mexican or Spanish.

'This is nothing to do with you, John,' Raul said, his tone much friendlier. 'Take Emily and go back inside.'

John shook his head. 'Why do you keep on with this nonsense? Haven't we all been through enough?'

'I've got no issue with you, John. You and Mary are law-abiding folk.' It was a jolt to hear Mum's name, though of course he wasn't talking about her. He was talking about another Mary, one that lived and breathed and got to raise her daughter. Lucky bitch.

Grief threatened to swamp me, so I grasped at anything to distract me. 'What's your name?' I asked Raul. I knew it already of course because John had called him by name before, and I was nothing if not an observant soul, but it was an easy question to get someone talking.

'What's it to you, bitch?' He sneered at me. Ok, maybe he wasn't in the mood to get talking, but there are acceptable ways to talk to someone, and this wasn't one of them. The problem with grief is that it often rides in with a helping of anger. I let the latter wash over me. 'Can you not remember it?' I sneered back at him. 'Too many syllables?'

Raul glared and took a threatening step towards me. Suddenly Shirdal moved. It was nothing overt – he didn't flex his muscles or draw a weapon – but all of a sudden he was ... threatening. He was a predator and he was letting this asshole know that he was the prey. The tumbler felt it too and he subsided. With one last hate-filled glare at me and Ike, he stumbled away.

'Towers,' Ike muttered. 'That's Raul Towers.'

'Towers is a twat,' I said.

Ike smiled, the first genuine smile I'd seen on his face. 'He is. Thanks, John, for the support.'

'No problem, Ike. We're family.' John clapped him on the shoulder before wrapping an arm around little Emily and walking away.

'You could squash Towers like a bug,' I pointed out to Ike. 'And just as easily. Why don't you?'

'Bella doesn't like violence. She's spent too much time with Bentley. Most of the circus feel the same. A lot of people are running from dark pasts. John and Mary are dryads; they dislike violence too. If I beat up Raul it would affect more than me and Raul. It would affect the whole community.'

Ike had brought Bentley up, so I felt I could press my point home one more time. 'Talking of violence ... Bentley is a dangerous person and he may be in Liverpool, not too far from here. Keep an eye on Bella,' I requested. 'Everything in me is saying that she is in danger. I know that you don't think she is, and I know that Alfie is safe, but Bentley is dangerous.'

'We appreciate your concern. I will keep Bella safe.'
True.

It would have to do. I hoped he would take my concerns seriously. I noted he didn't deny that Alfie was safe. 'What does Towers do?' I asked.

'Besides bitch and moan? He hangs out with a couple of other race-purity nuts. We avoid them – most people avoid them. Most of the circus troupe are welcoming. Whatever we once were, we're all Common realmers now.'

'Okay. But keep your eyes peeled.'

'I will,' he reassured me. I could see he wasn't worried; maybe he wasn't a worrier and I was worrying enough for both of us.

'Tell me if you don't want me to pry, but your record showed you'd had High King Krieg intercede on your behalf twice before. If you have the might of the High King behind you, why on earth did you run away with the circus?'

'Who said I was running away?'

'Virtually everyone here is running from something,' I pointed out.

'Not me. I'm running *to* something.'

'To what?' I asked curiously. I'm too nosy for my own good, but Ike didn't seem to mind. He studied me for a long moment, and I thought he wasn't going to answer.

He cleared his throat. 'I met a seer priestess once. She told me I'd find love at the circus. I thought it was bullshit, of course, but as loneliness crept in, I began to get the craziest idea.'

'To run away and join the circus?'

'Exactly. Best thing I ever did.'

'And did you find love?'

Ike smiled. 'Love and happiness.'

'You'll keep Bella safe, won't you?'

'With everything that I am.' He promised. He paused. 'Tell anyone about this conversation, and I'll kill them.'

'Not me?' I asked with genuine curiosity.

'No. Not you. You're trying to help Bella, you get a pass.'

'Good to know. I won't tell a soul.'

I gave him a wave as he left me to go and keep Bella safe. I hoped.

As I strode away from the circus, the fortune teller, Victoria, stopped me and grasped my arm. I knew that trick, I'd done it myself. 'Did you see anything helpful?' I asked the seer.

'Fire and death. Illusion and time.'

'An average day for me then,' I joked.

She glared at me and continued as if I hadn't spoken. 'Deception and mistrust. The crown will topple.'

I thought of the newly crowned king in Buckingham Palace. If the seer was right, poor King Charles was in for the shortest reign in history. I dismissed the thought; I'd never been a big fan of prophecy, even though I knew there was one floating about for Lucy.

'Anything about young Alfie?' I asked the seer.

She removed her hand. 'Alfie is an idiot but he's fine. I told the circus master he would turn up.' Despite her words, her tone was warm. She liked the boy.

'And where will he turn up?'

'He's got himself mixed up in dragon business.' *True.* She slid me an amused glance, 'But then you'd know all about that, wouldn't you?'

I struggled to keep my face expressionless. *If* Alfie's supposed kidnapping was the work of the dragons, then I was hip deep in it as well. Someone had taken him when I was working at the circus. The dragons knew his disappearance would be noted, and that Farrier would seize the opportunity to have a PI on his doorstep.

Now I needed to ascertain whether Alfie had been taken to distract me from the challenges – or whether he was part of them.

Chapter 18

'You look grumpy,' Shirdal asserted.

'I'm not grumpy, I'm pissed off. The fortune teller, Victoria, suggested one of the dragons is the mastermind behind Alfie's kidnapping.'

'Which one?'

'Isn't that the million-dollar question? Let's head back to the castle. I've got some questions.'

We had time on our hands so we took the more leisurely route to the castle. At the entrance, we showed the special passes that Emory had given us and the staff let us in, no questions asked. I recognised one of the guys as a brethren member.

Chris, the helicopter pilot, was on his way out. When he saw me, he cast down his eyes and tried to avoid me. Nope, that wasn't going to fly buddy. 'Chris!' I called. 'A moment?'

He grimaced but stepped aside out of the flow of the people to talk to me. 'I'm sorry—' he started.

I waved it away. 'No problem. I know it wasn't your choice to bring down the helicopter, but you chose your words very carefully. Who told you to do that?'

'Elizabeth Manners.' *True.*

'And did she tell you why?' I asked curiously.

'No. She just said it was imperative that I didn't lie. To be honest, dragons have a real thing about lying, so I didn't think too much of it.' But now he was looking at me curiously.

Damn. He hadn't thought too much of it until I started questioning him about it. Shit. Quick, give him something else to think about! 'For my wedding with Emory, I'd like to fly in via a helicopter. Would you fly me?' I blurted. I had no idea why that thought was hiding in my subconscious.

'You'd still trust me to fly you?' Chris asked seriously.

'Of course,' I confirmed. I wasn't surprised when it buzzed true; it wasn't Chris's fault that Elizabeth had drawn him into her machinations. And though Cuthbert had warned me I couldn't trust anyone during the challenges, it didn't mean I couldn't trust them ever again. Hopefully Chris's role in all of this was done.

He hit his chest with his fist and bowed. 'I'd be honoured, Prima.'

I smiled awkwardly and he took his leave. His steps seemed lighter. Job well done.

The castle was crowded with families out for a special day together. As I people-watched for a moment, one young lad stood out. For one thing, he appeared to be alone; no adults went near him, nor any children for that matter. For another thing, he couldn't stop glaring at me. His eyes were locked on me, giving me his evilest stare. I was in someone's bad books, though I had no idea why.

I crossed the distance between us. 'Hello,' I greeted him. He looked like he was in full emo mode, with skinny jeans and a black, oversized hoodie. His long dark hair curled on his shoulders. The glare intensified at my greeting and he didn't respond.

My hackles rose. My mum taught me that politeness was next to godliness so there was no excuse for being rude. I turned to Shirdal. 'Give us some space, please.'

Shirdal raised an eyebrow but stepped back obligingly. He sure was taking his bodyguarding gig seriously. He moved several feet away and leaned casually against a huge boulder, which for some reason, was standing at the side of the courtyard. It looked like it had once been thrown in by a trebuchet, and it reminded me that this castle had seen some action. It wasn't just something pretty to look at – and nor was I.

I turned my attention back to Emo Boy. 'You might not have heard me, but I said hello.' This time my tone was not friendly in the slightest.

The kid raised his eyes sullenly. 'Yeah. And?'

'And it's polite to reply.'

'Whatever.' He shrugged.

'What's your name?' I pushed on.

'What's it to you?'

'When you glare at someone like that, it's a pretty clear indication that they've pissed in your cereal. To my knowledge, I haven't been anywhere near your breakfast food so what gives?' I asked.

'I don't think adults are supposed to say things like "pissed in your cereal" to kids,' he sneered at me.

'I must've missed the memo,' I said blandly. 'Besides, you're hardly a kid. You must be seventeen.' He was actually sixteen, but kids always like it when you think they're older than they actually are. It works with three year olds and teenagers alike.

A hint of amusement showed in his eyes even though his tone was still derisory. 'I'm sixteen.'

'And what do sixteen year olds do for fun around here, Evan?' I asked him lightly.

His jaw clenched. 'If you knew my name, why did you ask it?'

'Because I didn't know it, not for sure,' I explained. 'You're Emory's ward.'

'I'm surprised he's even mentioned me,' he said bitterly, folding his arms. 'He has nothing to do with me.'

'He's a busy man,' I offered lamely, grimacing internally.

'Yeah, apparently so. He's not too busy for *you*, though, is he?' Ah. Hence the glaring.

'What's your story, Evan?' I asked him a broad question, mostly to see what story he'd paint of his past.

'There's not much to tell. I was raised by wizards until I got introduced. Then it turned out that I'm a dragon shifter.' He was giving me the short version. The long version included him being introduced but having no magic. It had to be hard, having a couple of years thinking you're a magical failure.

'I'm guessing a dragon-shifter son is rare from two wizards?' I pried.

'Impossible.' Evan's chin jutted up. 'I'm living, breathing proof that my mum had an affair.' His lip curled.

'That must have been hard for you,' I offered.

The defiance bled out of him and he sighed audibly. 'Yeah, cry me a river.' His words were hard but his shoulders were hunched in on himself and his loneliness was palpable. Poor kid.

'It must have been awkward for your parents too.' I thought his parents' behaviour was reprehensible and inexcusable, but people hated it when you criticised their families, so I offered the excuse.

'Yeah, you could say that. When it became clear that my parents were done with me, I got taken in by dragon shifters.'

'That must've been tough,' I sympathised.

'To be abandoned by the family that raised me because it turns out that I'm something else – something not of my own making? Yeah. Wasn't the best.' His arms were wrapped around himself tightly, giving himself a hug.

'I'm sorry.'

'Whatever.' He shrugged, sighed heavily and looked away, but I caught a hint of tears in his eyes.

I tried to bring the conversation around to something positive. 'The dragons adopted you a year or two ago?' I asked.

'Not adopted. I wasn't *adopted*. I've been legally *relocated*.' The anger was back. Teenagers shift emotions faster than a chameleon changes colours. Evan was back to sneering at me. Better than tears, I guess. 'Emory is my guardian. It was supposed to be Danny and Sophie, but they got sick and couldn't make it to the court that day. Emory attended the hearing instead, and hey presto.'

'Who looks after you?'

'Danny and Sophie, obviously,' he drawled out.

'But Emory is on the paperwork,' I clarified.

'Yeah.'

I tried a different tack. 'Do you go to school?'

'Of course I do. I go to regular school, but soon I'm transferring to the academy when it opens in September.' At the mention of the Academy, he brightened for the first time since we'd started talking.

'What's the academy?' I asked.

He looked at me with genuine surprise. 'Don't you know?' He was delighted to rub my face in my lack of knowledge. 'The Prime Elite is setting it up. It's a boarding school for anyone magical. You'd think the Prime would have mentioned it.'

'You'd think,' I agreed as evenly as I could. First a ward and now a whole academy. I felt a sting of hurt. How could Emory not have mentioned such a huge project to me? How many other secrets was he keeping? 'The academy sounds great,' I managed, despite my own emotional upheaval.

'It's going to be amazing, as long as we can get the other kids to come. But if they don't then it'll just be a creature school, which would still be cool. It would be cool just to be able to learn in a school where you don't have to pretend that you're something you're not.'

'That makes sense.' A thought occurred to me. 'Do you live in the castle?'

'Not in the castle itself. I live out in the village with Danny and Sophie but us younglings come here for lessons at the weekend.'

'Oh.' I deflated a little.

'Why?'

'I was just wondering if you'd seen anyone unusual hanging about.'

He grinned suddenly, happy to be superior again. 'Do you mean Alfie?'

My heart stuttered. 'Yes. Do you know where he is?'

'He's hanging out in Elizabeth's suite.' *True.* He sent me a smug look. 'He's been right under your nose this whole time.'

Motherfucker.

Chapter 19

Before I could track down the location of Elizabeth's suite, my phone blared into life with the Cruella de Vil theme tune. Elvira: I'd allocated the tune in a less than charitable mood. She wasn't that bad, especially now that there wasn't a Stone of contention between us.

I answered hastily, hoping for some news about the break-in at my office. I gave Evan a wave he didn't return as I put the phone to my ear and walked away. 'Hi, Elvira, what's up? Tell me something good.' God knows, I could do with some good news.

'I'm not sure that I'd call it good, but I do have news.'

'Hit me.'

'I wish,' she muttered bitchily. *Lie.* Aww. We really were bonding. 'I got some results on the fingerprints.'

'Already?' I said with surprise.

'I told you, I had it run as an urgent. It didn't take long to ping because we had the comparison on our database.'

'Don't leave me hanging,' I urged. I was dying to know who broke into my office. I was technically under Lord Volderiss's protection so whoever did it was brave, stupid or powerful. Possibly all three.

'We found two sets of prints that we couldn't eliminate as belonging to you, Hes or one of Volderiss's cleaning staff or security team,' Elvira confirmed.

'Okay. I'm looking for two people.'

'You're not looking for anyone,' she countered.

'If you give me the names, I can find some known associates for us to dig into,' I wheedled.

'There's no *us* – this is *my* investigation,' Elvira said firmly.

'Yeah, yeah, I consider myself formally warned off. So tell me,' I entreated.

'Stone.'

I huffed. 'Let's leave our history with Stone to one side for a moment and focus on the case. Whose prints were in my office?'

'Stone's,' she repeated.

What? I frowned as I cast my mind back. 'I don't think he was ever in my office. Do you remember when my car got destroyed while I was at the office with Manners?'

'Yeah I remember,' Elvira confirmed.

'Stone later confessed to being behind the fire. Maybe the prints are from then?' It was a bit of a stretch. The fire had taken place in the garage. But as far as I know, he'd never stepped foot in my office. That was the only time I knew that he'd been in the vicinity of my office.

'Nope, it can't be from that long ago. Volderiss's staff swear that they clean the surface of your desk every single day. Someone is up to mischief,' She mused.

'How?'

'Have you seen the movie *Mission Impossible*?' She asked.

'Yeah.' I had no idea where she was going with this.

'Stone's prints are in the Connection database. Presumably someone had access to them and made silicon fingerprints using his data.'

'That's an awful lot of effort for someone to go to. And why? Why go to such an elaborate extent to implicate Stone?' It seemed a bit insane to go that far, but people demonstrated insanity daily, so it wasn't out of the realms of possibility.

'A big fuck-you, I assume, perhaps from someone who blames you for Stone's death. They want you to feel haunted, or some such crap,' Elvira suggested.

There was a pause while I thought about my response. Finally I said, 'It wasn't you, was it?'

She snorted. 'I blame Stone for his death. I read the report you made. He willingly jumped into a portal to close a daemon dimension. The man is lauded in the Connection as a hero. The Prime Elite let him have that much at least.'

'Emory always lets a man have his due. Stone saved us all, not just me and you but everyone in the realm. Sky was trying to break the Verdict and turn the Other realm into a new daemon dimension. The fact we are all living and breathing is due to Stone. I won't lie; if it hadn't been him it would have been someone else. One of us would have sacrificed ourselves to close that daemon dimension, but it was Stone who did it. He deserves to be remembered.' I sighed. 'He would have liked for someone to remember him as Zach.'

There was a pained pause, then Elvira said softly, 'He never let me call him that, even after we'd known each other for more than ten years.'

I'd put my foot in it again. Elvira and Stone had a sort of quasi-betrothal arranged by their families. Even though I'd only known him for a matter of days, we'd gelled. I'd looked at him as a man and not a meal ticket. I didn't say any of that to her; there was no need to rub salt in an open wound.

I changed the subject back to the break-in. 'So if someone got Stone's prints from the database, then what you're saying is that someone in the Connection either worked with the criminals or broke into my office.'

The silence was heavy as Elvira neither confirmed nor denied it. Warning bells were ringing. Did she know what I was, that I was a truth seeker? I couldn't ask, not without giving myself away like I had with Chris. Fuck.

'I'd better go.' Elvira sighed. 'I just wanted to give you a heads-up.'

'That someone is really trying to fuck with my head? What about the second set of prints? Do you have Bentley Bronx's prints on file?' I asked.

'No,' She huffed.

'What about the Anti-Crea?'

'We've arrested some of their members before,' she confirmed, her tone cautious.

'So you have their prints?'

There was a long silence. Finally Elvira admitted, 'There's been a security issue. The files keep getting ... lost.'

'That makes sense in the days of paper files but nowadays there must be electronic copies,' I insisted.

'You would think so, but no. They've been wiped,' Elvira confessed in a low voice, like she was worried about being overheard.

'I assume there's an ongoing investigation as to who the mole is in the Connection?'

'If there is an investigation ongoing, it's not one that I know about,' she admitted.

'That's ridiculous. How can someone get away with that?' I protested.

'Welcome to the reality of the Connection, the biggest global corporation the world has ever seen. But it still has limited resources. The Other population is far smaller than the Common one, and only a few of them choose to become part of the Connection. Even fewer make it to become inspectors. We're stretched thin.' She sighed.

'Yet my little break-in has become a priority?'

'That's politics for you. Someone has their eye on you.'

She meant it as a reassurance, but it made the cold fingers of dread tickle my spine. *Stay off the radar.* Shit.

Chapter 20

Shirdal was looking at me in a strange way, and I wondered if I'd offended him by asking him to give me space while I chatted with Evan. To show I had nothing to hide, I quickly filled him in on my chat with both the emo and Elvira. We talked about who the second set of prints could belong to as we made our way to the brethren anteroom.

Mike was still there. He gave me a broad grin and a salute. 'How can I help you ma'am?' He ignored Shirdal.

Before I could ask for directions to Elizabeth's suite, Jack Fairglass sauntered in. He was in a suit and his dark-green hair was tied back – it looked almost black in this light. For a moment, you could have imagined that Jack was reputable.

His bright-blue eyes sparkled with mischief and he was smiling widely at me. 'Jinx Wisewords.' He bowed low. 'It's so good to see you. It's been too long.' For some reason he was acting like we hadn't seen each other this morning in the river.

I followed his lead. 'Jack,' I responded cautiously.

'I've missed you. Life has been so boring without you,' he purred. He was being weird and giving me his best smoulder. He even threw in a wink.

'I've missed hanging out with you, too. How is Catriona?' I asked pointedly.

'She is young.' He waved a hand. 'She needs time to blossom. Not like you, you've blossomed already. I love this top.' *True.* His gaze ran up and down me suggestively and for a moment my gut clenched. I'm not a girl who invites male attention and I'm shit at flirting because I never give out the right signals, but for some reason Jack was flirting with me. We'd always been friendly, but this was out of character.

I thought back to our weird chat by the river, the whole purpose of which had seemed to be for him to tell me that he loved Catriona. Alarm bells rang and suddenly I grasped what was going on: this was one of my challenges.

Cuthbert had said the challenges were there to test my moral mettle – did that include whether or not I would cheat on Emory? Because frankly, that was just insulting.

'I've got what you need.' Jack winked again. This wink seemed pointed, but I had no idea what he was talking about.

'Are you hitting on me?' I asked baldly.

'Do you want me to hit on you?' He waggled his eyebrows suggestively. He was also skirting things nicely so my lie detector couldn't ping.

'No. Not even a little bit. I love Emory. Hitting on me is rude and insulting to us both.' I glared and folded my arms over my leather-clad bust.

'I'm hung like a satyr,' he promised. *True.* Well, that was way too much information.

'I'm not interested in how you're hanging.' I glared.

Jack grinned his usual smile and dropped the smoulder. 'Can't blame a guy for trying when you're in that get-up,' he said cheerfully.

'I absolutely can. What a girl wears does *not* mean she is inviting attention.'

'What *does* it mean?' he countered.

'That she likes leather. It's surprisingly warm. To work out if she's open to flirtation, look at her body language not her clothes,' I said firmly.

'Gotcha.' He winked yet again. 'Well, my work here is done. See you around.' He turned and walked away.

'That was so weird,' I commented to Mike. He was grinning broadly. Mike gave me two thumbs up. I guessed the brethren were there to report back on my response to Jack's obscene flirting, and I hoped I'd gotten ten out of ten. I wasn't the world's best actress but I'd really worked hard to get some anger into my voice.

I'd have to give Jack a present next time I saw him as a thanks for his bizarre warning; without it, I might have believed he had the hots for me, which would have been upsetting.

I had now successfully completed two challenges. Hopefully I'd proved myself a loyal future mate for Emory. Now I just needed to pass the third challenge and find Alfie.

Something about the kidnapping scenario had always seemed a bit off. There were no real signs of violence, though there had been a rudimentary attempt to make it look like there had been. The wards didn't appear to have been compromised. Amber was a witch of some repute;

if she said the wards weren't compromised, then they weren't. That meant no one had removed Alfie from his caravan without his consent – yet someone had tried to set it up to look like a kidnapping.

The whole thing had been fishy from the get-go and the stench of ocean creatures had increased when Bella had gone from frantic to completely calm. She'd been let in on the secret that there was no real kidnapping involved. I surmised that the break-in at my office was equally bogus, hence Stone's fingerprints being found there. Elizabeth Manners truly was trying to fuck with me. Now she was going to learn who she was messing with.

At my request, Mike led me to Elizabeth's lair. She had her own rooms in the castle, as did all of the members of Emory's circle. Mike had a key and he was more than happy to let me in. He was definitely on Team Jinx. I liked him already.

Alfie was sitting on a sofa watching a large flatscreen TV that looked at odds with the ancient castle walls. He looked exactly like he'd done in the photographs his mother had shared with me. He looked up as I walked in. 'Nice one,' he said. 'Glad you found me. I was getting bored.'

'We wouldn't want that, would we?' I said dryly. 'Your poor mum thought that your kidnapping was real.' I kept my tone hard and accusing; I wanted him to feel bad about all that he'd put her through.

'I know. That was a dick move but the dragon insisted.' He shrugged. He wasn't too worried about being a dick; he knew his mum would forgive him.

'How much did Elizabeth pay you to put your mum through that?'

'Enough. I'll share some of it with her. She won't mind, and it will just be a funny story one day.'

'Not any day soon,' I snapped. 'She was beside herself when you first disappeared. Who else at the circus was in on it?'

'Just Stu. He helped muck up the room for me.'

His best friend Stu had felt like a bundle of nerves every time I was near him. I had mistakenly thought that he was anxious about Alfie, but he must have been worrying about his part in the supposed kidnapping coming to light. Cheeky little selkie.

'Let's show Elizabeth that I managed to find you,' I suggested.

'You did it a lot faster than she expected. She thought she'd have to hide me for at least a week. I'm glad you found me sooner. I've been sleeping on her sofa and she snores damned loudly for a lady. Let me grab my stuff.' He started shoving his things into a holdall. His clothes were strewn over the whole apartment. I bet Elizabeth had loved that.

I took the time to look around. Her rooms were decorated in keeping with the castle's age: dark wooden panels, red-brocade curtains and thick maroon carpets. I peeked into the bathroom, which had a huge fireplace like all the other rooms. She obviously didn't like the cold any more than Emory did. Her bedroom was neat, her clothes folded and ironed. She probably had someone do all that for her.

Shirdal was standing next to me. I paused my snooping as a thought occurred to me. 'Did you know about any of this?' I whispered, so Alfie wouldn't hear. I didn't need him reporting back to Elizabeth that there was trouble in the ranks.

The griffin shook his head. 'No. They kept me in the dark, like a prostitute in a gimp mask.'

Colourful. 'Lovely image. Thanks.'

'You need to loosen up. You're already halfway there with that top, sweetheart,' he leered.

Ugh. Don't remind me.

'Elizabeth won't like you looking around,' Alfie called out. 'She made me swear I wouldn't go into her bedroom.'

The pissy part of me really wanted to mess up her pristine bedcovers but I resisted the urge. Mum wouldn't want me to be petty.

I went back to join Alfie. 'Come on, then, let's get this bullshit over with.' I could sense Emory's concern through our bond and I guessed he could feel the righteous anger that was roaring through me. It was not okay to kidnap someone for some shitty sort of challenge.

I had worked myself into a snit. I was going to kick Elizabeth's ass, whether she was Greg Manners' mum or not.

Chapter 21

When I stalked into the throne room, Emory wasn't there though the rest of the circle was. No one looked surprised at my presence; they'd been tipped off by one of the brethren.

I didn't bother with a preamble. 'I'll be sending you my bill for the time I spent looking for Alfie.' I struggled not to snarl. Be *polite*, Jess. 'It is not acceptable to kidnap someone as part of some stupid challenge.'

'*Fake* kidnap,' Elizabeth corrected demurely.

I glared at her. 'Shit like this is the reason dragons have a reputation for kidnapping princesses,' I ground out. 'It wasn't fake to Alfie's mother. You made sure of that. You have put her through real psychological distress.'

'She'll be compensated financially.' Elizabeth shrugged, as if it was of no moment.

'That is wholly inadequate. What else will you give her?' I pressed.

'I have given her respite from her annoying son,' Elizabeth ground out, glaring at Alfie. 'He snores.'

'I do not! You snore,' Alfie protested.

Her eyes narrowed and I held up a hand. 'Do not let this conversation degenerate into an argument about snoring. That's not why we're here.'

'Why are we here, Jess?' Elizabeth demanded.

'It's Jinx to you,' I said firmly. Only family called me Jess, like Emory and Lucy. To the rest of the world I was Jinx. She didn't get to call me by my name. 'We're here because you put me in danger by faking a helicopter crash, then you distressed Bella by faking her son's kidnapping.'

'Wonder what else she fakes,' Shirdal muttered lewdly, loud enough for Elizabeth's nostrils to flare in outrage.

I enjoyed the moment, and I appreciated Shirdal's support, but this was my show. 'You also made Jack Fairglass fake an attraction to me that could have had far-reaching consequences for our friendship. Your challenges have been petty and poorly thought out.'

'What would you rather? Some sort of trial by fire?' Elizabeth bit back.

'Yes!' The unwise answer burst out of me.

'Fine, then that's what we'll do. Do you release me from my oath to Emory?' She leaned forward, eyes glowing in anticipation. 'Will you participate in an activity that could cause you physical harm?' She held eye contact with me.

'Of course,' I snarled back. In for a penny, in for a pound.

Elizabeth smiled like the shark that she was. 'Excellent. Done and done. So mote it be. You agree to take part in a true challenge. It just so happens that I have a gauntlet prepared for you tonight at 8pm, when the castle is closed and darkness has fallen.'

I kept my face blank even though my mind was in overdrive. I had walked into her trap and now she had me hook, line and sinker.

I glared. 'Did you really arrange all of that bullshit just to get me to agree to a gauntlet? Don't you think kidnapping people and breaking into my office were all a bit extreme? I know you don't get on with vampyrs, but Emory and Nate Volderiss have come to an understanding. By attacking Volderiss's offices you put that in jeopardy – for nothing.

You could have *asked* for me to take part in your stupid gauntlet without these ridiculous schemes.'

Elizabeth's eyebrow had shot up when I'd said about my office getting broken into. 'I didn't break into your office.' She said flatly. *True.*

I was getting the hang of sneaky wordsmithing. 'But you arranged for it to be carried out,' I asserted.

'No.' *True.* 'To the best of my knowledge and belief, none of us had anything to do with breaking into your office.' She looked around the circle; everyone shook their heads. 'See? That wasn't us.'

If it wasn't the dragons ... my gut clenched. Damn. The break-in was real. That meant I was either looking at Anti-Crea – or Bentley Bronx. The file taken was Alfie's, so everything pointed to Bentley.

I pulled out my phone and rang Hes. The kidnapping might not have been real but it was going to have real consequences.

'Hey, Jinx.' Hes's voice was guarded. I wondered if she was alone or if Nate was still with her.

'Do you know where Bentley Bronx is right now? Is he still with Roscoe?'

'Hang on, let me see. I'll just refresh his bank charges and see if anything... There was a charge half an hour ago.'

Alfie came closer to me anxiously. 'Why are you asking about my dad?'

I covered my phone so I could answer him without confusing Hes. 'When you got kidnapped, I opened a file on your case. Someone broke into my office and stole it.'

Alfie paled further. Yeah, kiddo: actions have consequences.

I removed my hand from the mouthpiece and spoke to Hes. 'Where was the charge?'

'I'm looking. One sec. A £5 charge at the Black Boy Inn.' She paused. 'That's a bit of a racist pub name in this day and age.'

'It refers to King Charles II – he was born with dark eyes and his mum called him that,' I said absently. 'Where is the Black Boy Inn?'

'Let me just ... Oh shit. It's in Caernarfon.'

My heart stopped.

Chapter 22

I dialled the number I had for Farrier but it rang out. My heart started to race. Maybe everything was fine. Maybe Farrier was just busy – but the evening show had ended and there was no reason for Farrier not to answer. If there was an issue at the circus, Farrier would be hip-deep in it. My gut didn't like that he wasn't answering the phone when Bentley Bronx was in the same village. It couldn't be a coincidence.

I looked at Shirdal. 'Can I hitch a ride to the circus?'

He grinned and his eyes lit up with joy. 'All aboard for murder and mayhem.' He shifted into his griffin form before I could deny that there would be murder *or* mayhem. Hopefully.

He padded forward and, as usual, his large form took my breath away. The golden eyes were all eagle and they promised death. Not to me, I hoped. While I wavered, Elizabeth opened one of the ridiculously large windows. Surely, they weren't expecting us to bloody well leap out?

Shirdal stood by the open window looking at me expectantly. Yup, they were expecting me to jump out. I swallowed the urge to ask Elizabeth if this could count towards my 'true' challenge.

Glimmer dug into my leg as I climbed onto Shirdal's back. I was just rearranging it so I didn't stab myself when the griffin surged forward. I grasped desperately at his fur.

'I'm coming too!' Alfie shouted at the last moment.

Shirdal's head swung back and I saw him choose to wait. Alfie vaulted on effortlessly, making my climb on look like a toddler mounting a Shetland pony. Great. He put his hands around my waist to hold on, then I had a moment to regret my life's decisions before Shirdal jumped through the window.

Cold wind snapped into me, taking my breath away, then we were falling. Could Shirdal carry us both? Perhaps that was something I should have checked before letting him leap out of a freaking window.

The griffin's wings snapped out and then we were flying. My eyes were shining and my heart was thumping as adrenaline surged through me. Man, flying is so cool; if the moment had been less dire, it would have been perfect.

We were on a mission and Shirdal wasted no time. In seconds we were near the circus, and we could see the last of the audience climbing into their cars and driving home. At least we wouldn't be adding Common realmers into the mix.

'There!' I tried to shout, pointing over Shirdal's shoulder. I could see a fire at the back of the circus – but this was no metal dustbin fire, it was a whole caravan. Shit – it was Bella's caravan. My stomach tightened, a hard ball taking up residence inside it. If anything happened to Bella, it was on me. Somehow Bronx had caught wind of the investigation, broken into my office, stolen the file and found out where Bella was. If the dragons hadn't 'kidnapped' Alfie, none of this would have happened.

'There!' I tried to shout again, but the wind swallowed my words. I moved, desperately trying to signal the change in direction to Shirdal by squeezing one leg, like I would do on a horse. Luckily, he seemed to understand horsey and turned obligingly to where I was pointing.

He flapped his huge wings faster and with even more purpose; he had also spotted the plumes of rising smoke. We were flying terrifyingly fast and all my pleasure had faded. What were we going to find when we landed? *Please let Bella be okay.* Alfie had a death grip on my waist and I knew he was thinking the same thing. Despite what he'd put her through, he clearly loved his mum.

As we got closer to the flames, I could see horses. No, not horses – centaurs, four of them. And a werewolf and Gato. The shit had hit the fan while I'd been pissing about with the dragons. And there was Ike in ogre form. Gato had been busy sending the circus troupe into the Other realm so they stood a chance against the raging centaurs.

It was easy to tell which of the approaching centaurs was Bentley. Alfie was the spitting image of his father, save for the hair, which was all his mother's. Their jaws and their brows mirrored each other, though there was no familial feeling in their eyes as they looked at each other.

Alfie scrambled off Shirdal and ran towards his father with murder in his eyes.

'Gato!' I shouted. 'Send Alfie to the Other realm! Hurry!'

My hellhound was in full battle form. He was a shade smaller than the centaurs around him, but not much. His black obsidian spikes stood tall and deadly, and his eyes were glowing red. He had been facing off with one of the centaurs but now he changed his path, twisting and turning to try and block Alfie before he reached his father.

Bentley thundered towards Alfie with equal rage on his face. His lips were twisted in a snarl and his teeth were bared. I needed to give Gato time to get Alfie into the Other realm …

I summoned fire to my fingertips. My need was desperate and flames came to my hands, hot and heavy and large. Immediately, I threw the massive fireball towards Bentley Bronx. At the last minute he skittered out of its way and it careened into the caravan that was already on fire.

I looked at the four centaurs. They were all male – so where was Bella? Ike, in his ogre form, was lost in rage. Like Alfie, he had no weapons, but it didn't stop him inflicting damage. The nearest centaur was trying to fend him off, but Ike grabbed his head and rammed him into the side of a neighbouring caravan.

There were squawks from inside and the occupants came out, ready to shout at the commotion. Their exclamations died as they saw Ike battling with four other men. As they were in the Common realm, they couldn't see that they were centaurs – but they could see the rage in Ike's face and they dived in to help him without hesitating. It was John, the dryad, and his wife Mary. Mary sent their daughter Emily to run for help, though probably more to get her out of danger.

'Gato! Send them to the Other too!' I instructed, pointing to the dryads. More people fell out of the caravans. I had no idea what type of creatures they were, but at least with the Other sight they would be able to see that they were facing centaurs.

Gato had sent Alfie to the Other realm while I was messing about with my fireball. Alfie now stood on four legs, a young, lithe centaur, rippling with muscles. All his running in human form had translated to his centaur form. He threw his head back and whinnied a challenge at Bronx.

I ignored the two of them for a moment and looked around desperately. Farrier, in werewolf form, was tangling with one of the centaurs, leaping at him with teeth and claw. The centaur let out a scream of rage as Farrier bit his hind leg and narrowly missed his hamstring, then he kicked back with all his might, sending Farrier tumbling across the field.

I fought to ignore Farrier for a moment. Where the hell was Bella?

I looked into the burning caravan. Vomit filled my mouth when I saw a body lying inside. I ran closer, calling some of the flames to me to try and get the fire down to a manageable level so I could get inside. My mind was blank, working on instinct rather than thought.

The flames were blisteringly hot but I managed to get close enough to the caravan to see the body properly. And then I wished that I hadn't. Bella's chest was bloody and mangled, like it had been stomped on by hooves. Her head hung at an unnatural angle and her eyes were wide and glassy. Her blue-black hair trailed out around her head like a grim halo. She was dead, and it was all my fault.

As I stared into the caravan, her hair flickered and, for a moment, it appeared to be blonde. A trick of the firelight, maybe? I had no time to ponder the aberration because the deadly fight was moving ever closer to me.

The dryad John was touching the ground, calling the grass to grow and twine around the enemy centaurs' hooves, though he carefully left Alfie's hooves unencumbered. Alfie reared back as if he were going to slice his father Bentley with his hooves, but Ike pushed him out of the way at the last minute.

'He's mine!' he roared to Alfie, almost insensible in his rage. 'You killed Bella,' Ike screamed at Bronx. 'And now I'll kill you.'

Alfie faltered. 'Mum?' he said in confusion. He shook his head and looked around desperately for her. His eyes met mine and I shook my head wordlessly.

As I stepped further away from the burning caravan, Alfie recognised the wreck of his home. 'Mum!' he screamed, running towards me and the flames.

I threw myself in his path. 'You can't go in there; the fire is too fierce. She's gone. She was already dead before the fire started. I'm sorry.'

Alfie's equine knees folded and his legs gave way beneath him. He collapsed into a pile on the ground, his eyes as wide and unseeing as his poor mum's. He shook his head, his chest labouring as he struggled to breathe.

'I didn't kill her,' Bronx shouted as he tried to fight off Ike.

The reminder that his mother's killer was still loose was enough to jolt Alfie out of his funk. He surged to his feet and spun to face his father. 'You don't get to have him,' Alfie snarled at Ike. 'He killed my mother!'

'Together then!' Ike offered. Alfie nodded and they both faced Bronx.

'I didn't!' Bronx shouted. 'She was dead when we arrived. I swear!'

'Just like Tracy was?' Alfie spat out.

Who the heck was Tracy?

'No.' Bronx shrugged. 'I killed Tracy.' *True.* 'Your little friend should have minded her own business. She heard something she shouldn't have done. I felt bad about killing her, but business is business. You shouldn't have tried to interfere. Your friend would still be alive if you hadn't interfered.'

'Tracy was only six, and you killed her! It makes me sick to think we're related. Don't you dare blame me for what happened! You're a brute, a monster! And I'm going to put you down!'

'Like you did last year?' Bronx taunted. 'You're not man enough to kill me.'

'*I* am!' Ike interjected. He ripped off part of the neighbouring caravan, and a metal pole, sharp and deadly, glinted in his hands. It was as long as my leg and enabled Ike to reach beyond the centaurs' hooves.

Gato and the two dryads were fighting the other three centaurs and I belatedly realised that they could do with some help. I didn't know anything about the centaurs but they'd come here with Bronx, presumably with violence in mind. Even so, I had no idea whether they deserved death or a light spanking. On the other hand, I had no issue deciding Bentley's fate. By his own admission, he'd killed a six year old, Tracy, and beaten his own son to within an inch of his life. I wasn't going to kill him but I wasn't going to stop Alfie or Ike from doing so.

Rather than call up the flames, this time I summoned as much water as I could hold and jetted it forcefully towards two of the centaurs. It came out like a geyser, sending them sprawling.

Gato crashed into the third centaur and knocked him off his feet. As he fell, John wrapped tree roots around him to secure him to the ground where he lay. Mary did the same to the other two centaurs. We turned back to the fight between Bronx, Alfie and Ike just in time to see Ike drive the metal pole through Bronx's heart.

'Here, son,' he said calmly to Alfie. 'You can twist it and pull it out.'

Alfie smiled. 'Thank you.' He grabbed hold of the pole and wrenched it from his father's chest. Blood poured out and Bentley staggered forward two hesitant steps before falling heavily to the ground.

I hoped that in the years to come Alfie wouldn't regret patricide, but it had been a team effort. Perhaps he wouldn't lay his father's death solely at his own door.

I flicked my eyes back to the caravan. It was so much ash and tinder. I thought again about the flash of blonde, and the seer's words rang suddenly in my ears again: *Fire and Death. Illusion and Time.* It hadn't been a prophecy; it was an instruction.

Because the funny thing was that Bentley Bronx was telling the truth when he said that Bella had been dead when they arrived...

Chapter 23

Now that I had belatedly remembered that I could control water, I used it to put out the flames before they spread to any of the neighbouring caravans. The fire had already done significant damage to the one next to it, but that was the extent of the destruction so far.

I poured out a river of water and eventually there was nothing left but the stench of acrid smoke. The fire had gotten hot very fast – probably helped by the extra fireball that I'd accidentally tossed its way. The body in the caravan had long since disintegrated. There was no evidence of trickery, but that flash of blonde just wouldn't leave me be.

I knew what I needed to do. Victoria's words wouldn't stop ringing in my ears. *Fire and Death. Illusion and Time.*

We'd had the first part, now for the second. Luckily, I had a hellhound who had mastery over time. I'd just have to pick an opportune moment to slip away and find someone to deal with the *illusion* part.

Farrier was back in human form; naked as the day he was born. He had press-ganged members of the circus into guarding the centaurs, and Gato had sent the centaurs back to the Common realm; they were slightly weaker and more vulnerable in 'human' form. They were put inside one of the caravans while the herd master was summoned to deal with them.

We had no idea if the centaurs were simply obeying Bronx's commands or if they had come here with their own deathly intent. Whatever, it was the herd master's job to deal with them. The only other option we had was administering vigilante justice, which was difficult when we didn't know whether it was warranted or not, or summoning the Connection. And we couldn't summon the Connection to the circus when the circus was trying to stay hidden from the Connection's eyes. Completing a crime report, reporting a dead body and Bentley Bronx's demise just didn't cohere with keeping the circus hidden.

The rest of the circus members had come out of their caravans, some still dressed in costumes from the performance they'd recently finished. They crowded around Ike and Alfie. To my surprise, I saw Raul Towers wade in and wrap a blanket around Alfie as the boy started to shiver and shake beneath Ike's protective arm.

The herd master wasn't long in coming to remove the three surviving centaurs and deal with them under herd law. The deaths of Bella Bronx and Bentley Bronx were reported to him and duly noted.

The herd master said nice things about Bella and offered comfort to young Alfie. With Bentley gone there was no reason for Alfie to hide any longer, and the herd master offered to let him return to his herd.

Alfie looked uncertainly towards Ike. 'It's your life, kid. You've got to do what's right for you,' Ike said with a shrug, one arm still draped around the boy's shoulders.

'There's always a place here for you,' Farrier offered. He looked jittery and his hands were shaking a little. Luckily, someone had fetched him a pink bathrobe, though it did nothing to lessen the silver fox's appeal. If anything, his ability to wear pink while naked made him seem even more masculine. I caught the look of longing that one of the dancers threw his way.

'Can I think about it?' Alfie asked finally, chewing on a nail.

'Of course you can, Arthur,' the herd master said.

'It's good to hear my real name again,' Alfie murmured.

'No doubt.' The herd master's eyes twinkled. 'We'll remove these three and deal with them. You take your time. If you decide you want to come home, pack your bags and we'll come back for you.'

Alfie's caravan had been destroyed; the only belongings he had were the ones he'd shoved into his duffel bag before he went to Elizabeth's suite. As Ike led Alfie to his own caravan, I took the opportunity to speak to the herd master. 'Can I have a moment with the other three? I have a question.'

'Of course, Prima. They've been loaded into my car. This way.'

'Um, I'm not Prima yet.'

He waved that away. 'A formality only, Prima. I have spoken with the Prime Elite about you and it is clear how he feels. Your union will bring strength and honour to the herds.'

'Um ... thank you?'

He grinned. 'You'll get used to it.' I wasn't sure that I would.

His car was a Land Rover Discovery and the three centaurs were still in their human form, sitting in the back of the car with their arms bound behind their backs. They didn't look comfy but I had very little sympathy for them. Following orders or not, they had come here to kidnap Alfie and Bella. But for now, it wasn't their motivation that interested me.

The herd master opened the back door of the car. 'This is our Prima-to-be. Answer her questions,' he ordered firmly. 'You will not disgrace this herd further.' All three looked down at the floor.

'Can I just have some privacy for a moment?' I asked. The herd master raised an eyebrow but, after a moment's hesitation, he stepped away. 'How did Bentley break into my office?' I demanded.

The centaur nearest to me licked his lips nervously. 'We didn't break into your office ma'am.' *True.* Perhaps Bentley had done it alone? Or with a different crew?

'How did you come to have the file about Alfie?' I asked the question in a different way.

'The file was posted to us anonymously.' *True.* Shit. That means some unknown third party had broken into my office. I hoped that the fingerprint search Elvira was running would turn up something.

'Was Bella dead in her caravan when you arrived?' I questioned.

'Yes ma'am.' *True.*

'Did you come here to hurt Alfie and Bella?'

For a moment the centaur didn't reply. He looked at his comrades; all of them were young, not much older than Alfie himself. He met my eyes again. 'Bentley Bronx was a scary man. You don't say no to Bentley.'

The fact that he'd sidestepped the question was answer enough. I closed the car door, leaving them to the herd's justice.

Chapter 24

Night was falling and I was conscious that I had agreed to some sort of 'true' challenge. I probably wasn't making sensible choices, but I couldn't get the seer's words out of my head.

I waited until everyone was occupied then sidled up to Gato. 'Are you up for an adventure, pup?' I asked. He gave me a big dopey grin. He was always up for an adventure.

'I need you to send us to the Third realm.' I considered. 'Give us a few hours there at least.' Behind me, Shirdal cleared his throat, making me jump. 'I know you're taking this bodyguard thing seriously but you can't come with me,' I said in a voice that brooked no argument.

'I know. Since I wasn't with you before ...' He trailed off.

I frowned at the weird comment. 'What?'

'Not what – when.' He said with a wink. 'By the boulder when you were talking to Evan.' He smiled at me before sauntering off, like we'd just had a normal conversation. Sure.

'Come on, let's go,' I said to Gato. 'We need to be discreet.' Even in Great Dane mode, he was anything but discreet. He jumped towards me and touched his cold nose to the triangles on my forehead. Gato tossed us effortlessly into the Third realm. A moment later we were back in time and, the sun was once again back in the sky.

I pulled out my phone and dialled Amber's number. 'I need a favour,' I said when she answered.

'Everyone always needs a favour,' she groused.

'It's not for me; it's for the circus. I need to help someone disappear – forever.'

'What are you thinking?' Amber asked tensely.

'I'm taking inspiration from my parents. I want to fake a death.'

She sighed. 'Illusion potions are difficult to make and even harder to apply.'

'Too difficult for you?' I asked, knowing the implication alone would push her to help me.

'Of course not.' I could tell she was speaking through gritted teeth. She didn't like having her competence questioned.

'So what do I need to make this happen?' I asked.

'Money and a dead body.' She said the items like they were on a shopping list.

'The first thing I have, the second thing I need to acquire.' Where did one get a dead body from?

'You sort the body; I'll sort the potion. Give me a call when you've got it. I need at least an hour to prepare, then I'll come to wherever you are to apply it to the body.'

'I'm in Caernarfon still.' I confirmed.

'And how are you enjoying your challenges?' she asked, sounding amused.

'They're total bullshit. But Elizabeth goaded me and now I've agreed to a true challenge,' I admitted.

Amber let out a low whistle. 'Well, it was nice knowing you.' She laughed. *True.* Ah, wasn't that reassuring?

'Thanks for the vote of confidence,' I said dryly.

'You don't need confidence, you need a miracle. The last true challenge was held centuries ago and I believe it involved a ravine of phoenix fire. Being immune to fire, dragons like to use fire as often as possible.'

'I've got a bit of a head start when it comes to fire,' I said, feeling more hopeful.

'A bit,' she agreed. 'Let's hope it's enough.' She hung up abruptly.

I turned to Gato. 'We need to find a dead body. Any ideas?'

Gato shook his head. Then I remembered Shirdal's weird comment about not going back in time with me since *he hadn't been with me before...* Perhaps Shirdal could help. Surely assassins had dead bodies on tap? Maybe I'd already had this conversation with him.

I didn't know quite what time Gato had sent us to, so I decided we should make our way to the castle's courtyard. We had to walk a long way from the circus grounds, and we needed to get moving. As I moved to the edge of the field, I saw the fortune teller, Victoria. She didn't say anything but she gave me a knowing grin and a nod. It gave me confidence that I was doing the right thing, messing about with time.

As we walked back over the bridge to the castle, I called the Black Boy Inn. 'Can I speak to the manager please?' I asked politely.

'Speaking.'

CHALLENGE OF THE COURT

I was back in time, and in this time, Bentley Bronx still lived. I cleared my throat and prepared to set him on the course that would ultimately change that. 'Umm. Hi. My friend Bentley and a couple of his mates are at the inn and I want to surprise them. Can I buy them a bottle of champagne? The only thing is, Bentley is really funny about accepting gifts. If I pay for it now over the phone, could you tell him that he's won a prize or something and all he has to do is to pay £5 towards it?'

'That's certainly not the weirdest request I've ever heard. Our cheapest bottle of champagne is £50. Is that okay?'

'That's brilliant, thank you.' I reeled off my card details for her.

'That's gone through for you. I can see your friend, I'll go over in a few minutes and explain about him winning the champagne for the cost of only £5.'

'Thank you so much.'

'I hope he appreciates what a good friend you are.'

I hung up. My gift was the first step in steamrollering Bentley to his death, so I wasn't sure he'd think that I was much of a good friend. I wanted to leave nothing to chance. It was the £5 transaction that had raised the red flag in my mind. Now Hes would have a transaction to track to tell me that Bentley was at the Black Boy Inn.

When we arrived at the castle gates, a member of the brethren – Joe? – at the turnstiles frowned at me. 'I didn't see you leave, ma'am.'

'Secret tunnels,' I joked.

'They're not too secret if someone told you about them.' His frown deepened. 'Did you use the boulder exit or the kitchen one?' Oh man! There really were secret tunnels. Every inch of me did a happy dance. I *love* a secret entrance.

'Boulder,' I lied smoothly.

'Did someone pass you one of the keys?'

'No, sorry.'

'I'd best go lock up,' Joe said with a frown.

'No, don't worry. Just pass me the keys and I'll see to it.' I gave him my widest smile. He wasn't buying it, so I reached out a tendril of my magic and gave him a tiny push to trust me.

How the mighty had fallen. Stone had once done the same thing to me and it had signified the end of our relationship before it had even had the chance to get going. Morality is an ever-growing thing. And the thing was, I was about to get my ass handed to me in some sort of super challenge so I needed every advantage I could think of, including knowing about – and having keys for – some super-secret tunnels.

Joe gave me the keys.

'Thanks! I'll hand them in to Mike later,' I promised breezily and strode away before he could object. 'Come on,' I said to Gato. 'Come with me and do your best job at looking like a normal dog.' He trotted forward obligingly, walking nicely by my heels.

I spotted the boulder in the courtyard. I walked all around it but I couldn't see any hidden entrances. I suppose the clue was in the name: hidden. 'I don't know what I'm looking for,' I confessed to Gato.

I put all of my weight on the boulder as if expecting it to move somehow. Gato grinned and shook his head, then padded back a few steps towards the wall. He looked back to make sure I was watching him, then walked into the wall by the boulder and disappeared.

'What the fuck?' I headed back to the spot where I was pretty sure he'd disappeared. I'd dealt with an illusion like this once before, when Stone had appeared to drive directly into a wall to gain access to the Connection headquarters at the Hard Day's Night hotel. I decided to do as I had done then: I closed my eyes tightly and I strode forwards.

I was bracing for the stone wall to slam into my face, but after a few steps I opened my eyes. Gato was grinning at me.

I could see locked metal gates ahead of me; presumably those were what the keys were for. I turned back to look at the illusion but apparently it only worked one way. From this side the stone surface looked a bit like tinted glass, like a one-way mirror. I guess it was a one-way illusion.

As I stared through it, I caught sight of my other self. I watched as I strode across the courtyard to find Evan. Man, I *did* look good in the leather top.

I watched as other-me sent Shirdal away for some privacy so I could chat with Evan. Shirdal sauntered back to the wall by the boulder and leant against the wall just next to where the illusion had started. That couldn't be a coincidence. I remembered his weird comment earlier, *'I know. Since I wasn't with you before...'*

I crept forward as close as I dared to the illusory wall, and whispered, 'Hey Shirdal, it's me, Jinx.'

He didn't turn to face me. 'I know,' he said, his lips barely moving. 'I could scent you. What are you and Gato doing, playing with the Third realm?' His voice held no censure, just curiosity.

'Saving someone's life. I need a dead body to do it. Do you have one?'

He laughed. 'Surprising as this may be, I don't actually carry dead bodies around with me. I *create* the dead bodies when I arrive.'

'I don't want to kill anyone.' I huffed.

'Then your best bet is to speak to the mermaid.'

'Jack Fairglass? Why?'

'The sea, or the Seiont, will have one for you.'

'The Seiont?'

'It's the name of the river that flows past Caernarfon.'

'And it's full of dead bodies?' I said in horror.

'I didn't say that. But if there's someone sleeping with the fishes, the mer people can bring it to you. Voilà, one dead body that I haven't had to kill for you.'

'Will it be bloated and gross?'

He sighed. 'You asked for a dead body. You didn't specify it had to be in good condition.'

Then again, nor had Amber. 'I guess that will be fine,' I said dubiously.

'So you'd better ring Jack.' Shirdal suggested again.

I dialled Jack's number. I had to step even closer to the illusion so the castle walls didn't interfere with my phone signal. Phone signal was bad enough in rural Wales, let alone adding in several feet of solid stone into the mix.

'Jinx?' Jack's voice came down the line.

'I need a favour – and it's a really weird one.'

There was a pause. 'You helped me with Catriona, so I'll do anything I can to help.'

'I need a dead body. Can you get one from the sea or something? I don't want anyone killed, I just want a pre-existing cadaver,' I clarified, because you can never be too careful in the Other realm.

'As it happens, I know a guy in a mortuary. Let me see if I can find you a John or Jane Doe somewhere locally.'

I thought about what I'd seen in the caravan before the fire had consumed the body. The flash of yellow gold hair. 'A Jane, if possible. A blonde.'

'Being specific makes things trickier, but I'll see what I can do. The community of morticians is tight, but hopefully they can help.'

'It's to save a life; it's not for anything weird. The body is going to be burned, nothing hinky,' I promised.

'Noted. I'll pass it on and let you know. If that doesn't work ... well, the ocean provides. But I'd rather leave the bodies there for the fishes if we can. Fish need food, too.' Jack said lightly.

That turned my stomach. 'Uh-huh,' I managed.

'I'll tell you when I've got one.' He hung up.

My life had turned really weird. I used to investigate people accused of insurance fraud, and now here I was carrying out a spot of fraud myself. But it was for a good cause. 'He's got it in hand,' I said confidently to Shirdal.

'Good. Explore the tunnels thoroughly but carefully. There's something in there that smells of brimstone.'

Brimstone? Of course there was.

Chapter 25

I turned to Gato. 'What do you think? Are you up for exploring some deep dark tunnels under an ancient medieval castle? It seems like a good use of our time.' Plus, who could resist secret tunnels? They were on a par with secret rooms and secret compartments for me. I got a visceral thrill at the thought of exploring them. Besides, I was in a dangerous environment with few allies; I needed every advantage I could get, maybe knowing these tunnels would tip the scales in my favour.

Gato snuffled with laughter and gave a wag. He was laughing at me. Without hesitation he plunged into the tunnels.

'Wait up! Not all of us have night vision!' I bitched. I was about to turn on the torch on my phone, before belatedly realising that it would alert anyone else creeping around the tunnels to our presence. Instead, I pulled the intention and release towards me, gathering it inside me so that I could give my eyes night vision. 'Night vision,' I said aloud as I released the magic. It was like someone had flipped a switch in the tunnels; suddenly I could see every rock and pitted hole.

The corridors hadn't been an afterthought. There were great flagstones laid on the floor, worn and shiny in some parts – clearly they had been used regularly. The corridors were chilly but not damp. These tunnels were well preserved – and they were also gargantuan. Clearly they had been designed so that the dragons could walk down here in either of their forms. Having several feet of air above me made me feel a little less claustrophobic.

I caught up with Gato. After a few minutes, he turned pointedly to me before lowering his body down to the ground to creep forward. Right, covert mode was needed. I copied him as best I could, slinking forwards and wishing I was wearing trainers instead of boots.

Together we moved forward. Light was pouring in ahead of us from a gap in the walls. There was a small chamber adjoining the underground tunnels – and someone inside it was humming.

I swallowed hard. We weren't alone in these tunnels, and the smell of brimstone was thicker here, too. What manner of creature were we about to encounter?

Gato and I crept forward and peered around a corner. A grubby-looking man was humming to a lizard. His hair was matted and his clothes were filthy – he made Shirdal look tidy. I wasn't sure where the bad odour was coming from, him or the lizard.

Truthfully, it wasn't fair to call it a lizard because it was a huge beast, nearly as tall as me. The other distinctive thing about it was that it was covered in flames, although it didn't seem bothered by the flickering flames all over its body. I presumed that the fiery lizard was the source of the brimstone scent. It looked like the Komodo dragon I'd seen at Chester Zoo on a day date with Emory.

'Come on, stop being silly,' the man said to the lizard. 'You have to eat. I know you don't like the underground, but you're a lovely surprise for the Prima-to-be so you'll just have to cope for a few more hours, Salasbara.' He pushed forward some flowers.

The lizard stared at him, unblinking, then suddenly she shrank to the size of a gecko. I bit back an exclamation as Salasbara darted forward, buried herself in the pile of flowers and started munching.

'That's better. Good girl.' The man stroked her. 'You're the best salamander in the world.' She flicked her tail happily and extinguished her flames.

Gato nudged my shoulder to make sure I was watching, then popped his head around the corner. He wagged his head at the salamander. Salasbara stopped eating, looked at us both, then she went back to her food. Gato shrugged his shoulders and pulled back. The man had his back to us; he was still humming, unaware of the interaction between Gato and Salasbara. She was evidently not a guard salamander.

I took a deep breath and, with Gato just in front of me, sneaked past the open door. I waited until we were several corridors further along before I whispered, 'what was that? Waggling your head at a salamander. You nearly gave me a damned heart attack!'

Gato grinned, tongue lolling, unrepentant. He gave me a giant lick then trotted on. There were numerous other corridors off the main one, but he never hesitated. Either he had prior knowledge of the tunnels or he could smell where we were going.

The main corridor started to slope upwards and we followed it until we came to another locked gate. I used the same key to open it then slid it shut behind us. There was another illusory wall in front of us but this one led to a corridor in the castle. We crept down it and opened the nearest door, which led to the kitchen. Bingo. That was what Gato had been heading towards: the smell of food.

The kitchen was a-bustle but all of the occupants paused as I poked my head in. 'Hello,' I said to the room at large.

'Prima!' one of the chefs greeted me.

'Almost-Prima,' I corrected. I was getting sick of making that particular correction.

'Can I get you something to eat?' she offered.

Not wanting to be any trouble, I opened my mouth to refuse but before I could speak my tummy rumbled. Loudly. The delicious smells had already worked their magic on me. 'Just a little something, if it's not any bother,' I said instead.

'Not at all. How about a bacon sandwich?' the chef offered.

I brightened. 'That would be great. Could I bother you for a cup of tea as well?'

'Of course. Sit yourself just here and I'll get everything made for you.' The chef started moving around the kitchen. 'What are you all doing? You have dinner to prepare! Get!' she said pointedly to the rest of the staff.

The kitchen exploded into sound and movement once more. The chef turned to Gato and bowed. 'Lord of Time, can I give you some sustenance?'

Gato gave a bark and a two tail taps, looking happy.

'Lord of Time?' I asked, raising an eyebrow at Gato. 'Lah-dee-dah!' He grinned and licked a paw smugly.

'One of the names for a hellhound – an old name.' She gave me a friendly smile. She turned back to Gato. 'Sausages?'

He barked and tapped his tail again. 'He says "yes please",' I translated.

The chef whipped up a storm and it wasn't long before I'd devoured two bacon sandwiches. Being around dragons is bad for my portion control. Gato, meanwhile, ate twelve sausages without batting an eyelid. Greedy pup.

The door burst open and in strode Jack Fairglass. 'Mrs Jones,' he greeted the chef who'd been serving me. 'The finest of women. Can I bother you for a snack? Something fishy? I'm starving.'

'Of course, Jack. How about anchovies?' Mrs Jones offered.

'That would be perfect.' Jack stopped abruptly when he saw me. 'How did you beat me here?' he asked, looking behind him. 'You were just out there.' He pointed backwards.

I winked. 'I can move fast.' Especially when I'm using the Third realm.

'Apparently so.' Jack frowned in confusion.

I wanted to ask whether he'd found me a dead body, but it wasn't really the sort of conversation you could have in a room full of kitchen staff so I murmured, 'Did you manage to find that thing I asked you for?'

'I just told you that I did, remember? I told you that I've *got what you need*.'

'Oh!' Oh indeed. I hadn't understood what he'd meant at the time. 'I was confused by all the bad flirting. I didn't get that you'd managed to acquire the item for me,' I explained.

'Well, I've got it. And to the specification that you ordered.' Female, blonde.

'Thanks. That's a real weight off. Is it local?'

'Yes. I'm having it driven in now. It'll arrive in about thirty minutes,' Jack confirmed.

'Great. Do you have a property I can use somewhere around here?' I didn't want to drag the body to a hotel, nor did I want to bring it into the castle. The dragon circle's eyes were already fixed on me and there would be too many questions.

'We have a small property in Caernarfon that we keep for any of the mer on shore leave. You can borrow that,' Jack offered.

'Great, thanks. Can you text me the address and I'll send it to Amber?'

'Amber DeLea? The witch?' Jack raised an eyebrow.

'That's the one.'

'She's a bit of a wet lettuce.' He grimaced.

'She's nice,' I said defensively. 'Just a bit thorny – like a rose.'

He sniggered. 'Beautiful and prickly and won't hesitate to make you bleed?'

'Yeah. And expensive. Let me update her and see where she's at.'

I gave Amber a call and, as usual, she answered with a huff. 'I'm on my way. I couldn't get ready any quicker. Potions take the time that they take.'

'I'm not calling to harass you; I'm calling to update you. I've managed to secure the second thing that you asked for. I'm going to send you an address. It will be there in half an hour.'

'Perfect. I'm about half an hour outside of Caernarfon, so we should arrive about the same time.'

'I'll meet you there,' I promised.

'Let's get this grisly show on the road.'

Chapter 26

Jack was being modest when he said the property in Caernarfon was small; it was an enormous place on the riverbank. Luckily it wasn't being used by any of the mer so we had free rein to do all sorts of diabolical things, like cast illusion spells over dead bodies so that we could fake someone's death. Life had certainly changed since I'd entered the Other realm.

Someone had meticulously laid a cloth over the dining-room table and put the dead body on it. Now, I consider myself to be a woman of the world, not sheltered in the least, but even for me it was a bit gross having a dead body in the middle of a dining table.

'She's been kept refrigerated,' the delivery man explained. 'But she'll start to smell if you leave her here for too long.'

'Thanks, Jacob.' Jack shook his hand. 'We'll take over from here. Please thank Noah again from me.'

Jacob shrugged. 'Tell him yourself. Just because he works in the Connection's morgue he acts like he's the bee's knees. My brother looks down on me for being a lowly mortician while he's a coroner.' He snorted. 'Dead bodies are dead bodies.'

I gave an awkward smile; family politics can be murky. Jacob was driving a mortician's truck with a slogan along the side of it: *Respectful death for respectful people.* I guess that meant they didn't deal with dead gangbangers. It seemed that everyone had a line in the sand.

We weren't left alone with Jane Doe for long before Amber arrived. Her driver parked on the drive and she climbed out of the car. As usual, she was dressed in a long flowing skirt and a peasant blouse. Unusually for her, today they were both black. 'Feeling funereal?' I asked.

'Dealing with dead bodies has that effect on me,' she snarked back. 'Besides, I wasn't sure if there'd be blood. It stains your clothes horribly. Always best to wear black when you think you might be dealing with blood.'

'Is that why the Other realmers are always dressed in black?'

'Of course.'

Lovely.

She was carrying her ever-present tote bag over her shoulder. Once she'd put it down on the table, she gently drew back the sheet over the body and immediately got down to business – time is money to Amber DeLea.

She pulled out several jars of gloop and a bunch of paintbrushes and got to work. I'd seen Amber do some complex rune work in the past, but this was something else.

Finally she turned to me. 'You know what the person looks like – the one you want the body to look like I mean?'

'Yes,' I replied.

'Okay, you need to picture her in your mind. Close your eyes and think of nothing but her. I'll tell you when you can stop. Brace yourself for some cold potion on your cheek.'

I closed my eyes and thought as best I could about Bella Bronx. I pictured her pale skin and dark blue-black hair, the sadness in her eyes when she thought her son had been kidnapped and the warmth in her smile when she knew he hadn't been. I pictured her turning to look at Ike, imagining her profile as well as how she looked from the front.

I started as I felt something cold and slimy on my cheek, but I managed to keep focusing on the image of Bella. The rune that Amber was painting seemed very large. I kept my eyes closed as she worked across one cheek, over my forehead and back down my other cheek.

'Okay,' she said finally. 'You can stop thinking of the person we're trying to change the body into. Open your eyes.'

I did as she told me and saw to my shock that the body before me now looked exactly like Bella as I had recalled her. I suspected her son might be able to tell the difference, but to any passers-by the resemblance would be more than enough. 'Wow, that's amazing.' I exclaimed.

'It won't last long,' Amber cautioned. 'The next hour or so at most.'

I checked the time; it was just past 6pm now, we still had a couple of hours left in the Third realm, it had been gone 8pm when we'd gone back in time. The last circus-goers would leave at around 6.30, so that was perfect timing. 'I don't need it to last any longer than that,' I assured her. 'Thank you. I promise that this is for the best.'

Amber gave an abrupt nod, like she didn't care about the morality of what we were doing, but I'd seen through her façade long ago. She definitely gave a shit. 'I'll send my invoice,' she said evenly.

I grinned. 'Yeah, I know the drill.'

'I'm going to leave now so I have some plausible deniability left. I hope all goes well.'

'Thanks. And Amber? The kidnapped kid from the circus? He wasn't kidnapped at all. He went willingly. There was nothing defective about the runes.'

Her shoulders dropped as the tension drained out of her. She blew out a long breath. 'Thanks. That's been worrying me,' she admitted. 'I thought I'd mucked up somehow, though I couldn't work out how.'

'The great Amber DeLea mucking up? Never,' I teased.

'We all make mistakes from time to time, Jinx, even me. I'll see you around.'

A thought occurred to me. 'Actually, if you don't have any plans for this evening, do you mind sticking around? The dragons are holding a true challenge for me, and having a healer on standby might be useful. Plus, it would be nice to have someone in the stands cheering for me.'

'You're very popular with the brethren,' Jack assured me. He'd been so quiet while Amber worked that he made me jump when he spoke. 'They're all rooting for you.'

'And the dragons?' I asked cynically.

'They want you to fall flat on your face or have a horrific death,' Jack said cheerfully. *True.*

'Thanks,' I said flatly.

'You asked,' he smirked. 'You'll smash it and drag those ancient worms kicking and screaming into the future.'

'Emory has already done a lot of the dragging,' I pointed out.

'A bit – but most of them still don't even have their own mobile phones.' His tone was incredulous. Technology had come a long way, I guess even the mer could have phones these days – a lot of them were waterproof to certain depths. I pictured a bunch of the mer sitting around and texting each other in the depths of the ocean. I wondered what the signal was like?

'Yeah, that's nuts,' I agreed. I couldn't imagine not having a phone. It was your Internet, your telephone, your entertainment. You were never bored as long as you had your mobile phone next to you. Rightly or wrongly, it had become as indispensable as one of your hands.

Jack was right about the dragons' attitude to modern technology. It seemed crazy to me. Emory had certainly done a lot to get the dragons to be more progressive – but there again, Emory still didn't drive. I supposed they all had their foibles.

'Have you got a car? To transport the body?' I asked Jack.

'No, sorry.' He paused. 'We should probably have thought about that before the mortician left.'

'Shit. I arrived by helicopter.'

'Of course you did.' Amber rolled her eyes. 'The Prime Elite is obsessed with helicopters.' She sighed. 'It looks like we're using my car then – but you can pay for the boot to be professionally cleaned afterwards. And I refuse to move the body.'

'Deal.' I looked at Jack. 'You'll help me move the body, right?'

He grimaced. 'You sure know how to show a guy a good time.'

'You're not here for a good time; you're here to do the right thing. Congratulations on your moral victory.'

'Thanks,' Jack said flatly. 'Come on, we'd better get this over and done with before the body starts to smell. I'll take her arms, you grab her feet.'

'I'll go and tell my driver to expect a dead body in the boot of his car,' Amber said as she swept out.

'I suppose that's the sort of thing you should get permission for,' I agreed. I looked at the body. 'There's one more problem.'

'What?'

'When I saw it, the body was all smashed up – it looked like it been trampled by hooves. That's why initially I thought that Bentley Bronx was to blame. It's probably why Ike reached the same conclusion.'

'Let's take one problem at a time,' Jack suggested. 'Let's get her in the boot and then we'll worry about smashing up the body when we've got it in place. At least that way there won't be blood all over Amber's car.'

'Good point. She might be grumpy if we did that,' I agreed.

It was disconcerting to move a dead body. Thankfully, because the house was a large one, it was surrounded by a driveway which had solid gates. There shouldn't be any nosy onlookers to see us manoeuvre a corpse about.

We carried it awkwardly between us. Rigor mortis had long since gone so the body was flexible and heavy. I told myself that the person we were carrying had just passed out but the chill of the limbs belied that. 'Amber!' I called. 'Can you open the boot?'

Grumbling she popped the boot and lifted it so that we could manoeuvre the body inside. It was difficult and not very dignified and I was feeling all sorts of awkward, but it couldn't be helped. Once we'd stowed Jane Doe, we slid into the car. Amber rode in the front beside the taciturn driver. He must have been in his sixties and he didn't bat an eyelid at having a dead body in his car. I guess he's seen his fair share of weird shit as he ferried Amber around.

'You didn't want to join us in the back seat?' Jack teased Amber.

'Firstly, it's a bit cosy with three adults and a hellhound in the back, and secondly, you have death on your fingers,' she said primly.

'You touched the body, too.' Jack pointed out.

'I was wearing gloves and using paintbrushes,' she argued.

'You've got a point,' I admitted. 'Do you have any hand sanitiser?'

She wordlessly passed a bottle back to us, but I wasn't sure if all the hand sanitiser in the world was strong enough to wash off death cooties. Next, Amber passed me some face wipes. 'For the runes,' she explained.

I'd forgotten about the goop on my face. Nothing said 'mischief' like strolling in all runed up.

Chapter 27

We drove slowly and carefully to the circus; it wouldn't have done to be pulled over by the police for speeding while we had a dead body in the boot of our car. I have the gift of the gab but even I would have struggled to explain that one away.

Finally, we parked close to Bella and Alfie's caravan. 'You stay here for a minute while I make sure that the coast is clear,' I suggested. Gato ignored me and climbed out of the car too. I rolled my eyes but let him come with me.

I knocked firmly on the door, wondering if Bella was in or if she was at Ike's place. It swung open and a smile blossomed on her face as soon as she saw me. 'Hi Jinx,' she said brightly.

'I don't have time to go through things properly with you, but I know that Alfie was kidnapped by Elizabeth Manners, one of the dragons in the castle. I know that they're paying him a lot of money to disappear for a while, and it's all of part of a challenge for me.'

'Oh! I'm so glad you know about it now.' She clapped a hand to her heart. 'I felt awful lying to you, but Alfie said that I had to or he wouldn't be paid and it would all have been for nothing.'

'Never mind that. The problem is that Bentley Bronx really *is* after you. He's on his way here so we need to get you out before he arrives. And here's the part that might confuse you – we need to make Bentley think that you've died.'

'What? Why?'

'It's hard to explain—' Almost impossible if I wasn't allowed to talk about the way the magical Third realm played with time. I couldn't tell her that I'd already seen it happen in my past, and that Ike had thought that she was dead. Because it had already happened, it couldn't be undone. The fixity of the past. Impossible to explain without referring to time travel, so instead I just stuck to some simple logic. 'If Bentley thinks you're dead, he and his cronies will leave you alone,' I promised.

I could see that she was thinking about it. I pressed on. 'Then you'll be free to stay here, to be with Ike forever, if that's what you want.'

That decided it. 'More than anything.' She smiled softly. 'Okay, let's do it.'

'Don't freak out, but I had a witch cast an illusion spell over a dead body so it looks just like you. The only problem is it's not perfect, so we needed to rough it up a little. Preferably, with hooves.'

'I can do that. Have your hellhound shift me back to the Other realm and then I'll stomp all over the body.'

Relief rushed through me. I'd been wondering how I was going to manage that; in all of the stress, I'd lost sight of the fact that she was a centaur, too. 'Perfect. Gato? Do the honours, please.'

'Wait!' Bella said. 'I need to get out of the caravan before you shift me into centaur form. I don't want to damage it.'

'Good point.' I grimaced internally; now wasn't the time to reveal that the caravan was going to be set on fire.

She stepped outside and Gato touched his snout to her forehead to shift her to the Other realm. Instantly she had four legs and a thick black coat. Her long flowing hair became mane-like. She was a beauty – and she was also buck-naked. I'd seen a bunch of male centaurs before and frankly it had been distracting having their schlongs hanging out. Now here was Bella, tits out, and I didn't know quite where to look. Then I met her eyes and felt ridiculous for being diverted by her lack of clothing.

There were tears in her eyes as she looked down at her four legs, and regret twisted her features. She missed being herself, being in her natural form. 'Sorry,' she whispered. 'It's just ... I made myself forget what it was like.' She blew out a long breath, swiped at her eyes, then trotted off around the caravan. When she came back, she was smiling.

'I'm sorry,' I said regretfully, 'I didn't think about how hard this would be for you.' For an empath, that had been particularly short-sighted of me.

'It's okay; it just took me by surprise for a moment. Sometimes you forget to be grateful for what you have until it's gone. And then it's too late.'

'It's never too late to be grateful,' I said softly, thinking about my mum. I gave a tight smile. 'Come on.'

She followed me around the side of the caravan to Amber's car. Jack slid out, popped open the boot and helped me to manoeuvre out the body. We laid it carefully on the field.

'That's a bit weird,' Bella said, looking at her own face on the dead body.

'I know, sorry. Can you smush it up, though?'

Her lips curled in distaste but nevertheless she trotted forward and started stomping. I winced at the sound of her hooves cutting into flesh. Eww.

Bella danced back and forth over the body until it started to resemble the horrific wounds that I remembered. 'That's enough,' I said hastily. 'Thanks. Now we need to put the body inside your caravan and get the hell out of here.'

'I'll carry her,' Bella offered. 'It's the least I can do considering she's setting me free.' She was exceptionally strong in her centaur form. She picked up the body easily in her forearms, then clipped over to her caravan and pushed her poor doppelganger through the door.

I climbed into the caravan. With some difficulty, I pulled the body onto the bed, where I knew that I would be able to see it from the window. In the future. In the past. In whatever-the-heck time it would be.

Several people, including Ike, would be arriving shortly, so we needed to get the hell out of Dodge. After a moment of indecision, I called a small flame to my hands and touched it to the sofa at the other end of the caravan. The place had been on fire when I'd arrived in the future, but not so badly on fire that I couldn't see the body. Hopefully that small fire would spread slowly.

I climbed out and shut the door carefully behind us. Bella didn't need to see the fire just yet; she had enough stuff going on in her mind. 'We need to go,' I said urgently. 'Now!'

We ran back to Amber's car. Gato sent Bella back to the Common realm so that she could squeeze into the car with us, and thankfully her clothes reappeared with her human form. Now there were three adults and a hellhound on the seat, but we squeezed in because we had no option. Gato sat along our laps.

'Where shall we go?' Amber asked.

'Back to Jack's house,' I suggested. 'We need to hide out for another hour or so until the herd master leaves and the other me decides to take a jaunt to the Third.'

'What's the Third?' Bella asked.

I smiled broadly. 'Oh, nothing. I'm talking nonsense.' Damn, I was bad at all of the secret keeping that was necessary in this realm. It's like Fight Club; you're not supposed to talk about the Third realm to anyone who doesn't already know about it.

It didn't take us long to wend our way back to Jack's house. We piled into the kitchen, leaving Amber's driver sitting patiently in the car. Then we all stared at each other; it had been a long, crazy-ass day. I blew out a breath. 'So ... anyone want a brew?'

Tea solves everything, including residual faking-a-death-together awkwardness.

Chapter 28

We hid out at Jack's house until that itchy feeling of two of me existing at the same time disappeared. It was always a relief when there was only one Jinx running around on Earth. I caused enough trouble when there was just one of me.

When we were certain that Bentley was dead and the herd master had left the circus with the remaining centaurs, we decided it was time for Bella's dramatic return to life. She didn't want Alfie and Ike to think she was dead for too long.

As we approached the circus, it was clear that they were holding some sort of ceremony for her. Everyone was standing in the huge space next to the big top, their faces sad and solemn. Somebody had started a fire in a metal dustbin. Ike was standing next to Alfie with his arm around him. Apparently all they had needed in order to bond was to lose Bella suddenly and irrevocably. Luckily for them, nothing is truly irrevocable in the Other realm.

I felt an ugly twinge of envy as I saw Alfie look up and see his mother striding towards him. 'Mum?' he said in disbelief.

Ike looked up and froze. 'Bella?'

Bella broke into a run and threw herself towards them. Alfie started to cry. He'd been holding it together when he'd thought that she was dead, but now relief was crashing through him and the tears came thick and fast. He no longer gave two shits about his street cred or about appearing strong in front of the crowd.

My heart broke a little. I never got this moment with my mum; she was gone, truly and forever. Gato stepped closer to me and leaned his full body weight against me. I reached down and stroked him, but that wasn't enough. I knelt down and wrapped my arms around him. 'It's okay. I'm okay,' I whispered into his soft ears. *Lie.*

Lie though it was, I had my father and I was thankful for that small mercy.

Ike was waiting patiently but, once Alfie finally stopped crying, he pulled Bella to him and kissed her passionately. Someone from the circus wolf-whistled then cheers broke out. I heard the pop of a champagne cork and within seconds the sad wake turned into a celebratory party. The circus folk didn't care about the deception, just the miracle. Explanations would wait.

Farrier found me. 'Thank you for finding Alfie and doing whatever the heck you did with Bella.'

'She's dead, as far as Bentley Bronx's men are concerned. She'll never be a target again. She can stay with the circus as long as she wants with no fear of being discovered. And Alfie can go back to the herd an orphan, if that's what he wants.'

The circus master nodded. 'Circus life isn't for everyone. Some stay with us for a short time before they move on and find another way to conceal themselves. Alfie is finished with hiding. He'll go back to the herd.'

I agreed. Alfie had run because Bella had forced him to, but without the threat of his father looming over him he would find his own way. 'What about you?' I asked Farrier. 'Aren't you tired of being Cain Stilwell?'

'I've been Cain for almost as long as I was Clark. Both names are mine now. And now I have a different cause.'

'Don't you miss your wolf?' I inquired.

'Now more than ever,' he admitted, sadness in his voice. 'To be with him again, after so long ... We were so in tune, more than we'd ever been. He was so happy to be with me – we hardly even had to wrestle for supremacy. It was ... ' He shook his head as words failed him.

'The werewolf landscape is changing, you know,' I told him. 'My friend Lucy is an alpha werewolf. If ever you change your mind about going back, I'm sure she could help you.'

'Thanks. I appreciate that. But for now my life is the circus – saving others, giving them a home. It gives me a purpose.' He grinned and the years melted away from his weathered face. 'Besides, I just enjoy that my current life is one big fuck-you to the Connection.'

I thought of Elvira. 'They're not all bad.'

'Maybe not, but they're not all good and they're supposed to be.'

He had a point. 'I'd better be going, I'm due at the castle,' I said reluctantly.

'So I hear. There's going to be a real challenge!' He sounded excited. 'I've not heard of a proper one taking place for years, centuries maybe. My grandfather used to tell tales of the dragons' challenge. Something for your head, something for your heart and something for your courage.'

'What does that even mean?'

'I have no idea,' he said cheerfully, 'but expect at least a few things to trip you up. It won't be just one thing, it'll be a series of mini challenges and then something that should kill you at the end.'

'Do the dragons not want their Primes to be happy?' I asked, exasperated. 'Why are they so hell-bent on killing the prime's mate?'

'It's not that, they just get obsessed with their Primes. They want the Prime's partner to be their equal and if you can't pass the challenge, you're *not* their equal. The challenges will reflect Emory in some way.'

'God help me if I have to pick out the finest wine or the best suit. I'll be doomed.'

He laughed. 'Nothing so prosaic, I'm afraid. From the tales, there's usually fire.'

I thought of the hidden salamander in the tunnels. 'I can do most fires.'

'So I saw.'

'Is there anything special about salamander flames?' I asked casually.

'Besides the fact that they are the hottest?' he replied, amused. 'No, nothing. But salamanders are related to dragons, so they're treated with great respect. They can shift in size from as small as your little finger to as big as your entire body. And their flames don't only come from their mouths, like dragons. When they're threatened, they set their whole bodies on fire.'

'Great. Any sure-fire way to make them feel *not* threatened?' I was starting to really worry.

'They usually bond to a dragon. Their bonded can always calm them down.'

'And if they're not bonded?'

'Then the whole place will burn until they calm down. Salamanders usually live in Australia and America because they like warmer climates. That's why you often get grass fires there – someone startled a salamander at the wrong moment.'

I swallowed. 'Can I use my fire-elemental powers to stop a salamander's flames?'

'I have no idea.' He paused. 'You think the dragons have a salamander?'

'I *know* they have a salamander.'

'Best of luck,' he said, but he was grimacing. He didn't think I stood a chance. I wasn't sure that I did, either.

I was walking back to the castle when Shirdal landed next to me with a whoomph. He shifted into human form and glared at me. 'Just so you know, it's rude to give your bodyguard the slip so you can jaunt around in the Third realm and cause havoc.'

'I didn't cause havoc,' I protested.

'Sweetheart, you almost started World War Three.'

'I did not! I got a few centaurs arrested, that's all.'

He snickered. 'And destroyed a few homes while you were at it.'

'Home is where the heart is. I only destroyed some caravan walls,' I said defensively. 'They can buy new walls.'

The evening was running away from me; I only had an hour at most before the challenge was due to start and the shit would probably hit the fan. 'Have you got any advice for surviving the challenge?' I asked Shirdal.

'Start running now?' he quipped.

I glared. 'That's not helpful.'

He stopped walking and grabbed my arm. He turned to me, his expression serious and earnest for the first time that

I could remember. 'You don't need me to make you feel better about this. You've got this. You are Emory's equal and I'm going to be proud to have you as my Prima. You already have everything you need to succeed. Believe in yourself and nothing will stop you, not even a salamander.' He cleared his throat. 'And if you ever tell anyone I said anything so mushy, I'll kill them.'

I grinned. 'Not me?'

'No, kid, not you. You've grown on me.'

'Like poison ivy?'

He grinned. 'You do make me itchy for some reason.'

I snickered and gave him a playful shove.

'While you were off on your holidays,' he continued, 'I took a trip to the library here.'

'There's a library in the castle?'

'Two actually – a Common one and an Other one.'

'Did you have to get permission to go to the Other one?' I asked curiously.

'Maybe I should have asked, but I snuck in when no one was looking,' he said lightly.

'Did you find anything helpful?'

'Of course. Never underestimate the value of a good book. I love a good tale, enemies to lovers preferably. Especially if there's only one bed to share at the inn.'

I sighed. 'Could you be serious please?'

'I'm deadly serious. I love staring at the bodies of dead trees and hallucinating wildly. It frees the mind from the shackles of everyday life.'

I pinched the bridge of my nose. 'Did you find a good book in the library? A helpful book?'

'I found a *great* book – an old textbook on challenges that precisely set out the rules. There were a lot of guidelines. Probably, you won't need to know most of them. Hopefully. But one of the most important rules is that you get to select a "tool of your choice".'

A tool of my choice? Glimmer, maybe?

'Your friends, sweetheart,' Shirdal advised. 'Select your friends.'

'They're not really tools … '

'Allies are tools – of course they are. I read the small print and nothing says your tool has to be inanimate. Summon your friends.'

'You wanna do some challenges with me?'

He grinned. 'I thought you'd never ask.'

That wasn't a bad idea: at worst, it wouldn't work, and at best I'd have friends I trusted at my back. I pulled out my phone and started dialling.

Chapter 29

By the time we walked into the castle, I was forming my team. Nate was coming from Liverpool, but thankfully he could phase. He assured me he could step into a shadow in Liverpool and step out into a shadow in Caernarfon. He would join us if and when the challenge took us outside of the castle. Dragons and vampyrs are a big no-no and he didn't want to add any additional tension into the mix. I appreciated his sensitivity. As for the rest of my team, I already had Gato and Shirdal by my side, but I would need more than that to see me through.

Hauling around dead bodies had given me some bonding time with Amber and Jack so I cheekily asked them if they'd stand with me. To my relief, they both agreed. Amber made some comment about sending an invoice, but I knew that she wouldn't. We had been acquaintances but as time passed we were definitely moving towards the road of friendship. Hell, she was standing with me for the challenge, so I guessed we were already there.

As I approached the castle, one of the brethren gave me a low bow. 'The Prime Elite requests your presence.'

I bet he did. 'Lead the way.'

He bowed low again then led me through the winding corridors until we came to a section of the castle I didn't know. Once again, Emory had been modernising. Everything was light, airy and warm.

Summer was sitting behind her large desk in the antechamber. Her office was nicer than my Liverpool one; for a start she had real plants rather than fake ones, and her chairs were designed for comfort. Mine were utilitarian and painful to sit on for any length of time because I didn't want to encourage clients to linger. Once I had information from them, I wanted them out so I could get started on their case.

For a second, I wondered whether I would ever have a case again. Man, Emory would be pissed if I died in this stupid challenge.

Summer smiled at me. 'The top still looks good. For the challenge, you'll let me put you in leather trousers, right? I've got some with special properties.'

'What kind of special properties?'

'Protection ones. A certain witch has painted runes all over them.'

Even if leather wasn't usually my look, I wasn't going to say no to being secretly covered in protection runes. 'Sure. Thanks.'

She looked relieved. 'Tell *him* that. He's been wearing a hole in his carpet with his pacing.'

I knocked on Emory's door once then let myself in. I held the door open for Gato and Shirdal to join me, but they both plonked themselves down with Summer. Presumably they were giving Emory and me some privacy for a goodbye. It felt rather like they didn't have faith in me to survive, but maybe I was being unfairly touchy. I was pretty sure that the only one that didn't have faith in me was me.

Emory looked stressed. Usually his hair was perfectly coiffured, but today it was a mess. Sometimes he is clean-shaven and sometimes he has a five o'clock shadow dusting his jaw; today was a shadow day. His black shirt was undone at the top, and he'd thrown his suit jacket carelessly across the desk.

He stood up as I walked in and closed the distance between us. As he pulled me into his arms, I could feel his distress. 'Why on earth did you agree to a *true* challenge?' he growled. Anxiety rolled down the bond, but also a fair amount of anger. He wasn't thrilled with either me or Elizabeth.

'Two reasons. One: Elizabeth Manners pissed me off. Two: I didn't know much about the true challenge or what it might entail. So ... I made a poor decision.'

He rested his forehead against mine, 'Bloody hell, Jess. We can fix this.'

'No, we can't, not without you losing face, and you're always saying that's a big deal in the dragon court.'

'It is, but I'd rather lose face than lose you. I'll lose my primeship if it will keep you safe.'

I felt a sting. 'I know you mean that in a nice way, but all I'm hearing is that you don't believe in me.'

'I do, utterly. I swear it.' *True.* 'But I also know that Elizabeth Manners is a vindictive bitch, and you stabbed her son and made him a werewolf.'

I blinked. 'But that saved Greg's life!'

'I know, but he's on the human side now. It's a rift, and a choice she would never have made for him.'

'She'd rather he were dead?' I asked incredulously.

'He's brethren. She's braced herself for his death since the moment he was born, but she wasn't braced for this. I'm inferring – she's never said anything directly – but I've known her for two centuries. I can't imagine her feeling all sunshine and rainbows about you becoming Prima.'

'And now you think she'll try to kill me?' I said incredulously.

'Maybe. Maybe I'm being unfair and she just wants to test you. Dammit, why did you release her from her oath that she wouldn't cause you physical harm? I had to do all sorts of political manoeuvring to get her to agree to that.' Emory's frustration poured off of him.

'Not my best move, huh?' Hindsight was such a bitch.

'No.' Emory's anxiety ratcheted up. 'I can't keep you safe,' he whispered in defeat.

I pushed back from his arms. 'I don't need you to. I'll keep myself safe and prove myself worthy to any doubters.' Including you. 'What did Not-Leo want with you?'

He snorted at the nickname. 'Do you *want* them to hate you? Leonard isn't the nickname type.'

'Leonard needs to loosen up. So what gives?'

He sighed. 'As if there isn't enough going on, someone has stolen the Eye of Ebrel.'

'The what?' I asked blankly.

'A very important artefact to dragons,' he explained. 'It's a sapphire about the size of your fist set in diamonds and gold.'

'And worth a small fortune, I bet,' I noted cynically.

'It's more than the money, it's a symbol of our species' prosperity. While we have the Eye, everything will be okay,' Emory explained. 'It's supposed to usher in a new age when the Revival Prophecy comes true.'

'The Revival Prophecy?'

Emory shrugged. 'It's Elizabeth's thing. A prophecy about the golden age of dragons.'

'Hasn't that already passed?' I teased. 'You know, back when there were knights and things when you were a young lad?'

'Cheeky girl,' he jokingly chastened me.

'What happens when you don't have the Eye jewel thing?' I asked curiously.

'Doom.' He sighed. 'Lots of doom.'

'Damn. No one likes doom. And the Eye has definitely been stolen?' Could you accidentally misplace a sapphire as big as your fist? Probably not, but I'm an optimist at heart.

'Well, the Eye has disappeared from the Treasury. Leonard can't find it.'

I suppressed the urge to say that Leonard couldn't find a hen in a chicken coop. My gut just didn't like something about the man, and I'd long since learned not to ignore my gut. When I did, something horrendous happened.

'Surely it won't be too hard to find who took the Eye? Dragons can't lie,' I pointed out.

'No, but the brethren can,' Emory uttered grimly.

He wasn't wrong. There were a lot of brethren wandering around the castle. That was a *lot* of suspects. 'Hmm. Who had access to the treasury?' I questioned.

Emory ran his hand through his hair. 'Look, forget about the Eye, I shouldn't have told you about it. Leonard and I are going to keep it under wraps and do some discreet digging. We can't let it be known that it's been taken – there would be uproar and we need stability just now. You need to focus on the Challenge.'

I felt another sting of hurt and I pushed Emory further away. 'I'd better get ready then,' I said briskly.

'Jessica ... ' He reached out to me.

I didn't want to leave things like that, just in case the worst did happen, so I stepped forward and gave him a kiss, a proper one with tongue and enthusiasm. 'I love you, Emory. I'm going to be absolutely fine.' *Lie.* Damn it.

Chapter 30

Thanks to Summer I was dressed in leather trousers. I thought that they would be difficult to move in but they moulded to me so nicely that I had no issues. I was grateful that there were no witnesses to watch me lunge across my room like an idiot, checking that the leather would hold up to strenuous movement. I even did a few roundhouse kicks, just to be sure. Yup. I could still kick ass if I needed to.

I swapped my boots for trainers; I had the feeling that running was going to be involved. Night had truly fallen and the cold air was nipping at me, so I added a leather jacket. I was now dressed head to toe in leather, and I felt about ninety percent cow, but hopefully it would give me some protection from stray sparks.

I was glad of the bacon sandwiches that I'd snaffled earlier from Mrs Jones in the kitchen. It had given me some energy to keep going. I couldn't have eaten a thing right now, as I waited for the challenge to start, because nerves were chewing at my gut.

The moon was high and full, and it made me think of Lucy. I hoped that she was having better success with her werewolf pack than I was having with the dragon court. I'd ring her later when I was safe; if I rang now, she'd know I was in danger. I wouldn't be able to keep it out of my voice.

There was a knock at my door and Elizabeth Manners strode in without waiting for me to respond. Rude. 'Jinx,' she greeted me. ' Are you ready?'

I smiled calmly even though my knees were knocking. 'Of course.' *Lie*. Fuck off, lie detector. Sometimes it was the most inconvenient thing.

'You are allowed to take one tool with you. Are you taking that?' She gestured to Glimmer on my hip.

With regret, I removed it from my belt loop. 'No. I'll be selecting something else.'

She looked at me sharply, eyebrows raised. Her lips pursed in disapproval. 'The Prime Elite should not have told you anything about the challenge, including the fact that you can take a tool with you.'

'The Prime Elite didn't,' I said firmly. 'I have other allies here.' I met her eyes. 'Like you, of course.' *Lie.* Ha.

She smiled tightly but didn't respond; of course she didn't, because dragons can't lie. 'You have selected something else to take with you?' she inquired flatly with an unfriendly stare.

I nodded.

'This way, then.' Elizabeth said briskly, changing gears. 'There will be a brief ceremony to start things off.'

She led me through the castle back to the huge open courtyard. I gaped at the number of people who were there. For her to have gathered such a crowd, she'd clearly been planning the challenge for a long time.

Someone had set out two thrones in the courtyard. Emory was sitting on one of them, but the other was bare. The Prima's throne.

There was a time when the thought of being the queen of the dragons had filled me with fear, but having Elizabeth doubt my ability to take on the role was spurring me on. No one dictates my future but me.

The crowd and the thrones weren't the only differences to the courtyard. A huge wicker structure, some twenty-feet tall, towered above us all. Naturally it was in the shape of a roaring dragon.

Elizabeth and I walked slowly and solemnly to the thrones. Her voice when she spoke was loud and clear and ringing with purpose. 'I bring Jessica Sharp before you. She entreats us to accept her as the mate of Emory Elite; if we do so, she will become Prima of us all. It is right that she be tested, that her strength, skills and her moral mettle be proved before us all. It has been agreed by the participant that this be the first true challenge in more than five hundred years.'

The crowd roared its excitement, cheering and whooping. I was feeling slightly less cheery. What had I agreed to?

I spotted Evan in the crowd next to some other kids. He met my eyes, mimed his throat being cut and stuck his tongue out like he was dead. Lovely. I gathered fans wherever I went. Oddly, I felt a bit disappointed; I thought we'd gotten along all right.

Elizabeth shimmered and leapt into the air, drawing all eyes to her. In a moment she had transformed into an emerald-green dragon with golden wings and was flying above the castle. She circled in a dizzying aerial display that I would have admired if she hadn't been such a stone-cold bitch.

I was left standing alone. Veronica, from Emory's circle, sidled up to me. 'Good luck. Trust your instincts.'

I looked at her in surprise and she flashed me a smile. 'We're not *all* hoping you die.'

Marvellous. 'Just a few of you,' I responded drily, glaring at Evan in the crowd.

'You get some bad apples in every family.' She followed my gaze. 'He doesn't want you to die really, he just wants Emory to acknowledge him properly.'

'What's that got to do with me?' I asked in exasperation.

'What is logic to a teenager? Emory is giving you all his spare attention, so Evan is jealous.'

'Emory is only his guardian because of a mix-up with the paperwork,' I pointed out.

'Nonetheless, he *is* Evan's guardian,' she confirmed firmly, her tone a little disapproving.

She was right; maybe Evan was justified in feeling a bit hard done by. He'd thought he was going to be raised by the king of all the dragons and instead he was getting ignored by him. I'd probably hold a bit of a grudge in those circumstances.

When Elizabeth finished showing off, she landed with a whump. She stayed in dragon form, towering over the assembled crowd. 'Jessica Sharp, what do you choose as your tool to use in these tasks?'

'I choose my allies.' I gestured to my friends at my back: a mermaid, a witch, a griffin and a hellhound. It was the start of a bad joke – the story of my life.

Nate was still conspicuously absent, but I knew he was watching from the shadows somewhere. His proximity buzzed through our bond, and his readiness. He was eager to get things started. At least one of us was.

Silence greeted my announcement. Elizabeth conferred with Leonard and Fabian, then Leonard hauled out an ancient-looking book – no doubt the one that Shirdal had already pawed through – and we all waited while they read.

Finally Elizabeth cleared her throat and belched out a small flame; it was the only sign of her unease. 'An unusual choice, but the rules have been checked and your choice is valid.' There was grumbling and cheering in equal measures from the crowd. Some people thought I was cheating – hell, *I* thought I was cheating – but I'd use anything to get out of this alive.

'The challenge comprises a number of tasks. Each one must be successfully completed before the next can be attempted. For the first of the tasks, Jessica Sharp must set this wicker dragon alight—' she paused dramatically '—using only magical fire.' She gave me a triumphant, toothy grin.

I looked at Emory in confusion. He was grinning too, a shade away from laughing. Did Elizabeth not know I had a fire elemental's powers?

'To be clear, you may not use the IR to grow a regular fire into a bigger one,' she clarified, still smirking. That had been an old trick of Stone's; he was a wizard with an affinity for fire. But Stone couldn't create fire from nothing using his magic alone and he'd carried a lighter in his pocket, ready to use its spark to grow a sword of flames. Elizabeth knew I was a wizard and thought I was hindered by the same limitations. I was going to blow her mind.

I gestured for my allies to stand back and strode to the gargantuan wicker frame. It was beautiful, and I almost felt bad for what I was about to do. I called flames to my hands and an audible gasp ran through the crowd. Ha! I might not be a dragon, but I did have fire. I gathered and grew the flames until I had a huge fireball roaring in my hands. I thanked my lucky stars that I'd once been hired to spy on Samantha and Bianca's blossoming relationship; it may have ended a marriage, but it would allow me to have mine.

Once the fireball was nearly as big as me – I was going for drama – I thrust it towards the wicker structure. It went up in flames so quickly that I realised it had been doused with accelerant. That made me feel a bit better; I must have a secret ally. Maybe I would make it through this.

Chapter 31

If Elizabeth was nonplussed by my success, she didn't let it show. 'The first task has been completed!' she called to the assembly. 'Now on to the second.'

Oh great, I didn't even get a toilet break.

She hooked a long, deadly-looking claw into some fabric and ripped it away to reveal a small metal cage about a foot square. I looked at it curiously.

'For the next task, you must get the creature into the cage.' She smirked. 'Bring in the creature!' The crowds parted as Salasbara the salamander was led into the arena by the man I'd seen beneath the castle.

Salasbara was in her largest form. She had a chain around her neck and she was being tugged into the courtyard.

She didn't look happy. Her handler dragged her into the centre, then removed her chain necklace. Something in me relaxed when she was freed; it wasn't right to keep anything in chains.

Before the handler stepped back, he pulled out a knife and regretfully plunged it into her tail. Salasbara screamed and whipped around to face him. Instantly she set her whole body aflame and spat a fireball at him, though it hit him with no visible effect. Dragons are immune to fire, after all.

'Sorry, Sal,' he muttered and melted back into the crowd. Looking dejected, Salasbara watched him go. Poor thing, to be betrayed by her handler like that.

Flames or no flames, I stepped towards her and pitched my voice softly, just for her. 'That was a really shitty thing for him to do – it must have hurt like a bitch. Can I take that out for you?'

She swung towards me, chittering with agitation, flames leaping higher up her body. She fixed me with her golden eyes and clacked her jaw in warning. I got the message loud and clear: *Don't come any closer.*

'I can't take that dagger out from here,' I tried to explain. I had no idea how sentient salamanders were, but if there was anything I'd learnt about the Other realm it was to underestimate the creatures within it at your peril.

'Please let me help you,' I entreated. I'd forgotten entirely about the stupid task and was focused on helping her.

I had no idea what to do. She was too angry, too upset and untrusting. Suddenly I thought of Audrey's words of advice, her hints to use my empathy. I closed my eyes and concentrated on the ocean, then let it recede. For a moment, I was overwhelmed by the discordant minds of the crowd. Anticipation, excitement and, yes, malice; some here wanted me to fail. And then love found me again and I was filled with affection and trust, not just from my hound but from all of my companions. It warmed me. They believed I could do this – *I* believed I could do this.

I pictured snow just around me but no further. I didn't want to affect the crowd; I just wanted to calm the poor, wounded salamander. I let the snow fall and place a comforting blanket out around me. Slowly Salasbara stilled and her tail stopped whipping from side to side. I moved closer.

'Hello, Salasbara. I'm Jinx. Salasbara is a bit of a mouthful, isn't it? How about I call you Sally?' She blinked and I took that as a yes. 'Okay, Sally, I'm going to take the knife out. It'll hurt for a moment,' I crooned, 'but everything will be all right.'

She tracked my every moment, following me as I inched closer to her tail. The dagger was jewelled and pretty. Finders keepers, I thought grimly; that twat wasn't getting his blade back, not when he went around stabbing salamanders willy-nilly.

'Ready?' I asked Sally. She stared unblinkingly at me and I had no idea if she understood. With shaking hands, I reached out to the knife. One snap of her jaws and I'd lose my fingers for sure. Amber wouldn't be able to re-attach them if they were in the salamander's stomach. I swallowed hard, my mouth suddenly dry.

Sally let me touch the knife. I waited until she was watching before I wrapped my hand around it, ready to wrench it upwards and pull it out. I counted to three in my head and then I yanked with all my might – it would be awful if I pulled and caused her pain but didn't get it out. Luckily, the dagger sprang free from her flesh.

She let out a roar of pain and flames leapt up her body. I was too slow in jumping back and the flesh on my right hand suddenly felt hot – too hot. Luckily my arm was covered by the leather jacket, so hopefully it would be okay. Now wasn't the time to focus on my injuries. Sally's flames were hot and her emotions were high; she was a danger to everyone around her, including the crowd.

'I'm sorry, Sally, it's all done now. I'm sorry,' I repeated. I closed my eyes again and let it snow until the flames slowly receded.

'Amber,' I called without looking behind me. 'Can you heal salamanders?'

'I can try,' she offered, with none of her usual certainty.

I turned to her. 'What's up?'

'I'm not a fan of lizards,' she admitted, biting her lip.

'She's hurt,' I entreated plaintively.

'Yeah, I know.' Amber came closer but she was visibly trembling with fear.

I moved to Sally's head and looked into her eyes. 'This is Amber. She's a witch, and she can do all sorts of clever things to heal you. If you'll let her, she'll make you better.'

Sally watched us, but she didn't move away. 'I think you have permission,' I said to Amber. 'Go for it.'

'You *think?*'

'I don't speak salamander.'

Amber opened a pot of potion and started painting runes on Sally. Almost instantly the tension drained out of the salamander's scaly body. She made another chittering noise, but this one was much happier. After a minute, Amber closed her jars and stepped back. 'She's all good.'

The wound on Sally's tail had closed up and was all but gone, leaving nothing but the faintest scar.

Now she was all right, I could focus on the task. Fitting Sally into that tiny box would have seemed impossible if I hadn't seen her shift during my time travels. I knew she could shrink – now it was just a matter of persuading her to do so. Piece of cake. Man, I could really have done with some cake just then.

Before I could ask Sally nicely, I noticed that she was shivering. I touched her skin. It was dry and very cold. If she was anything like Emory, she wanted to be warm. 'You're a bit chilly. Here, I'll warm this.' I summoned my fire and held it over the metal box. 'Why don't you shrink and hop in there? It'll keep you nice and warm,' I said when I'd extinguished the flames.

She looked at me, then back to the cage. She was hesitant and I couldn't blame her; the last person who'd tried to force her somewhere had stabbed her. 'I won't hurt you,' I promised.

She looked at me for a beat longer before she started to shrink. Finally, she gave a pitiful squeak and climbed up my leg and onto my arm. Luckily she stayed off my hand, which was red and throbbing like a son of a bitch. I tried to put the discomfort out of my mind.

Looking around, I spotted a few daisies in the grass. I picked a handful and put them in the cage. It wasn't much, but it was something. Sally happily hopped in, dived onto the flowers and rolled around in the warmth. She gave a happy purr. Who knew that salamanders could purr?

As I closed the front of the cage so she was safe, a roar went up from the crowd and startled me. I had forgotten about my audience. There were whoops and cheers, more than there'd been for the wicker dragon. I was obviously winning over a few naysayers and that filled me with determination. I wasn't going to let Emory lose his primeship because of me. I was going to convert the whole lot of them into Jinx fans, one way or another.

Chapter 32

'We come to the third and final task of the challenge, the task to end all tasks that will test Jessica Sharp and her companions to the limit. Let us see who returns to us alive!' Elizabeth was working the crowd – as she said 'alive', she let out a huge wave of flame. She should have joined Farrier's circus; she excelled at theatrics.

'For the last task, Jessica must retrieve something of great value to her from Llanddwyn Island.'

The crowd gasped and then was silent. I looked at Emory and saw that his hands were grasping the arms of his throne and his jaw was tight. He wasn't happy.

'Jessica Sharp has twelve hours to return to us, or she will be lost forever to Emory Elite.' The crowd roared again.

Emory leaned back on his throne as if he were unconcerned or bored, but I knew he was neither. Fear skated down our bond. It took an effort, but I shut it down and focused instead on Nate. He was close by, hidden somewhere in the shadows. I couldn't think about Emory's fear right now, so I used Nate like a comfort blanket and drew his presence around me. He was filled with steely determination.

Once again I was in the dark. What was on Llanddwyn Island that was causing Emory such consternation?

I had no idea where to go, but heading to the waterfront seemed a safe bet. I started marching that way, with my friends at my back. As we passed through the turnstiles at the entrance to the castle, the brethren there knelt in front of me.

Once we were out of sight of the crowd, I relaxed. 'What gives?' I asked Shirdal. 'What's so bad about the island?'

'It's home to a bunch of nasties. If anything bites, it gets sent there.'

'Like what?'

'Kelpies, a sphinx, even the phoenix ... you have to give credit to Elizabeth, she knows how to make a good challenge.' Shirdal sounded impressed.

Nate melted out of the shadows. 'Hey,' he greeted us.

'Fuck!' Jack exclaimed. 'Make a bit more noise next time.'

'Sorry,' Nate grinned. *Lie.*

'Did you hear where we're going?' I asked.

'The island of certain doom?' Nate quipped. 'Yeah, I heard.'

'Catchy name,' I muttered. 'Listen, you guys didn't sign up for this. I don't blame you if you suddenly remember you've got hairdressers' appointments somewhere.'

Jack grinned and tousled his long dark-green locks. 'Can't you tell? I've already been.'

'And me,' Shirdal quipped. His hair, as usual, was unbrushed and possibly unwashed. That made me snort with laughter.

Amber sighed. 'Well, you're going to need me. There'll be a ward somewhere. If we fail, the Prime Elite will be grumpy and he makes life difficult when he's grumpy. I guess I'd best help you for my own sake.'

I bumped a shoulder into her. 'You know, you can just admit that you like me.'

'Whatever. I'll bill you for overtime.'

I grinned.

Gato said nothing but shifted from Great Dane form to battle cat mode. He was ready to rock and roll. My heart felt full. Even if I did die later on tonight, I was going to do it in the best company. 'Thanks guys, I appreciate it more than I can say.' My eyes filled with tears and I tried to blink them away.

'Don't get all snivelly,' Amber said brusquely. 'We have a task to complete. Do you have any idea of the item Elizabeth might have taken?'

I thought about it. 'Glimmer, maybe? I left it in my room. That's the only thing of value to me that I brought here.' I thought of Emory's missing Eye thing; it could be that, but that was an object of worth to him rather than me. 'How do we get to the island?' I inquired.

'It's protected by a tonne of runes, not just to keep stuff out but to keep the worst of the creatures in. You can't get in by plane or helicopter,' Amber explained.

'I could fly a couple of us in, but I can't carry more than two people,' Shirdal offered.

'Let's not split up if we don't need to,' I said. 'If we can't all fly in together, we need a boat.'

'Boat,' Amber agreed. We were already walking towards the waterfront but we picked up the pace. If we needed a boat, then we would need to go to the marina.

'Great. So, has anyone got a boat handy?' I asked hopefully.

'It's not something I carry in my pocket,' Shirdal joked unhelpfully.

I gave him a flat look. 'Jack?' He was one of the mer; they must have boats, right?

He shook his head. 'We have tails, we don't need boats.' A fair point.

I sighed. 'It looks like we're resorting to some good old skulduggery.'

'Skul-what?' Amber queried.

'Theft,' I explained. 'But we'll bring the boat back good as new. Come on. Anyone shout if they see a likely-looking vessel. We'll need a six-person one at least.'

We reached the river. The moon was high and the night was clear. I was relieved at the good weather. I didn't fancy a boat ride in a storm with a bunch of amateur sailors. Hopefully the sea would still be nice and calm further out.

'How about that one?' Amber pointed to a boat moored up a few feet ahead.

I shook my head. 'It's only a rowing boat. Ideally we need one with an engine.'

'How are we going to get the engine going without a key?' she asked.

'Magic,' I said, wiggling the fingers of one hand while pulling out my lock-pick set from my back pocket with the other.

'Ah. You have a varied skill set.' There was almost admiration in Amber's voice.

'A mis-spent youth.' When my parents died, I'd had a couple of years that I wasn't particularly proud of. I'd met and mingled with all sorts of nefarious characters. Those years were behind me now, and they'd helped form me so I couldn't completely regret them.

'There,' Shirdal called from up ahead. 'This one looks good – *The Scholes*. She looks seaworthy.' His tone was approving.

The boat was moored a little further out, and we'd have to get wet to reach her. Shirdal correctly interpreted my look of resignation and shifted into griffin form. 'Hop aboard,' he said cheerfully. 'I'll ferry us over.'

I was getting used to flying on Shirdal Airlines so I climbed onto his back with relative ease.

'No, thank you,' said Jack firmly. 'I have no issues with getting wet and you're not getting me on a griffin.' He hopped over the harbour wall, splashed into the water and started wading out to *The Scholes*. Gato had obviously formed the same opinion and jumped happily into the bay. He always liked an excuse to get wet.

Amber looked at the water, then at the griffin as she tried to decide which was worse. With a grimace she climbed behind me onto Shirdal's back. Her long skirt was hiked up around her waist revealing black leggings underneath. Handy. She looked calm, but once she was on Shirdal she clutched my waist tightly.

Nate, meanwhile, was squinting into the darkness. He was there one minute, and gone the next – he had phased onto the boat. He could have taken me or Amber with him, I thought mutinously, but never mind; we were on the Shirdal Express now.

Shirdal spread his white wings, and effortlessly lifted us up into the air. I heard Amber bite back a squeal. The night was cool and the forward motion created a little breeze on my skin, making me shiver. I hoped it wasn't in anticipation of what was coming.

We landed on the boat after a handful of beats of Shirdal's mighty wings. Amber and I slid off his back and he shifted back to two legs. Nate was lounging in the back seat of the boat, smirking at our dramatic arrival. Gato jumped up into the boat, edged close to Nate and gave a huge shake. 'Oh, for fuck's sake, Gato!' Nate groused. He was soaked. It was hard work to contain my snigger but, man, his face had been so *smug*.

Jack pulled himself aboard, ignoring the wet trousers which now clung to him. He obviously hadn't shifted into mer form because he would have lost his clothes. He looked about, then strolled into the cabin. 'This way, little thief,' he called to me.

I followed him and climbed up to the helm. The lock wasn't complicated and it only took a few moments to get the engine started. 'Weigh anchor,' I called.

'Why would we want to do that?' Shirdal asked. 'I expect it's pretty heavy – we don't need to quantify it.'

'Not weigh it like that,' I huffed. 'Just pull up the damned anchor!' The pressure was getting to me. We needed to get to the island and rescue something precious to me, and the island was small and deadly. Shirdal was goofing off and, although I knew it was his thing, I really wished I had Manners and Emory with me. They would be taking this shit seriously.

I was missing Emory so much. For a moment I was tempted to reach out to our bond but I resisted the temptation. He would feel how nervous I was and that just wasn't fair. I needed to knuckle down and keep going. I'd be back with him soon and before long we'd be laughing about that one time when I had stupidly accepted an ancient dragon's pissy challenge.

'Don't get your knickers in a twist,' Shirdal muttered. 'I'm weighing.' He paused. 'Shite, this *is* heavy.'

'Are you hauling it up by hand?'

'Yes?'

I grinned. 'There's a machine that— Never mind. You enjoy yourself.'

He grunted as he hauled up the final part of the anchor. 'Ridiculous weight,' he muttered. We were all grinning now. Suddenly the tension burst and we started to laugh – full-on guffaws at the absurdity of the deadly griffin struggling with an anchor. Shirdal winked at me and I grinned back. Goofball.

Good humour restored, we moved off. I had already put the island in as our destination on my phone's satnav, and I followed the course as best I could. Luckily the River Seiont was calm and it was far too late for many people to be out on the water. The moon was full, giving us light to see by as we left the river mouth and headed out to sea.

Jack had raided the ship's cupboards and found some food. As he handed out snacks, I made a mental note to replace them after we had returned the boat. I took the biscuits he offered; I needed some energy to see me through.

Behind me, Amber was painting runes on each of my companions. 'What are you doing?' I asked.

'Protection runes,' she said. 'They're not the most effective, but if they help deflect something even a little, it might help.'

'Good thinking,' I praised.

'It happens now and again,' she said drily. The woman couldn't accept a compliment without sass.

Jack stood next to me. 'You'll want to slow the engine. We're nearly there.'

I sent Jack a glare. 'Did you know where the island was this whole time?' I huffed. 'I was using satnav to navigate.' It was a bit unnerving, heading out into the sea. Usually with sat nav you followed the exact road it told you to, but in the sea there was nothing to follow, no yellow brick road to guide me to the wizard at the end. Or whatever awaited us.

'Yeah, but you were doing such a good job so I left you to it.' Jack grinned charmingly.

'Next time, you can bloody well steer if you know where we're going.' The sea was out of my comfort zone, and the waves were higher than I liked. I'd sailed a bit, and even rowed, but it wasn't the same on a river versus the high sea. The sea had a lot more oomph.

The island loomed ahead of us, craggy and dark. There was a lighthouse but it looked old and no guiding light was shining out from it.

'Kill the engine,' Jack murmured. 'Let's not forewarn them.'

I turned off the engine. 'Now what?'

'Now I scout ahead. You stay here while I try and find somewhere for us to berth.'

He headed to the back of the boat and stripped off his clothes without a hint of modesty before diving into the sea. I watched him with interest, wondering whether his back legs would fuse into a tail as he went, but his legs stayed human until they touched the water. All I saw was a flicker of a tail as he descended into the depths.

Sound carries over the water so we stayed quiet. We didn't really have any idea what awaited us on the island, besides Shirdal's deadly list of kelpies, sphinxes and phoenixes. I hoped he was wrong. I'd encountered kelpies once before and they had definitely wanted to kill me. I knew this was called a Challenge, and frankly Elizabeth didn't seem the type to pull her punches. She wanted to test me, so whatever we were facing was going to be dangerous at best and deadly at worst.

I've always been a bit of an adrenaline junkie, but I get nervous before the main event. I'm fine in the moment when I'm facing salamanders or dragons, but beforehand my stomach roils and it was doing somersaults now.

Gato stood next to me and leaned against my leg in silent support. I bent down and stroked him, but I stayed quiet. We all did as we bobbed up and down in the water.

We felt very vulnerable. Who knew what was coming?

Chapter 33

Jack leapt out of the water like a salmon flinging itself upwards during a run. His tail shimmered before becoming two legs again and he landed effortlessly on deck. He'd obviously practised that move. 'Do you want the good news, or the bad news?' he whispered as he dressed.

I kept my voice low too. 'Good news, please.'

'I've found a place for us to get onto the island,' he confirmed.

'Okay. What's the bad news?' I asked cautiously.

'There's a bit of swimming involved,' Jack confirmed. That didn't seem so bad.

'Can't we just land on the beach?' Nate asked.

'Not unless you want to start fighting the whole host of ogres that are waiting there,' Jack said, voice grim. Fuck. Ogres. They were hired mercenaries, and they were notorious for taking insult at the tiniest thing and brawling constantly. Not a group we wanted to tangle with if we could avoid it.

'I thought I saw a jetty,' I said. 'What about that?'

'There are two kelpies lying on it.'

I thought of the watery horses that had chased Emory and I one Christmas Eve. It had been terrifying and they had clearly intended us harm. Emory had said that they were some of the deadliest creatures in the Other realm. 'We do *not* want to tangle with the kelpies,' I said firmly. 'How many ogres are on the beach?'

'I saw about fifteen.'

Oof. 'That's way too many, even with Shirdal with us. I don't want to be responsible for anyone's deaths just for a stupid challenge. It looks like we're going for a swim, ladies and gentlemen,' I instructed our ragtag crew.

Nate was looking even paler than usual. 'I'm not a great swimmer.' His fists were clenched with determination but I could read fear in every line of his body; when I reached out to our bond, his terror almost overwhelmed me. 'Not a great swimmer' was a huge understatement.

'I'll help you,' Jack promised.

Lips pressed together, Nate nodded. He'd be fine with Jack's help. I hoped.

Jack turned on the engine and let it tick over quietly as we moved forward slowly. He directed us to a break in the cliffs; it wasn't deep or high enough to call it a cave, but it was a small rocky harbour with a bit of an overhang. There he killed the engines. 'Here we are. Everyone get ready for a swim.'

Amber stripped off her heavy skirt to reveal the leggings I'd seen earlier. 'Good thinking,' I commented.

She shrugged. 'The skirts aren't always practical. It's best to be prepared.'

I turned to Nate. 'Couldn't you phase instead of swim?'

He shook his head. 'I need to know where I'm going, or at least be able to see it, in order to phase. It looks like I'm getting wet.' He licked his dry lips. Nate shrugged off his jacket but kept on the rest of his clothes.

As I removed my leather jacket, Nate frowned. He had caught sight of my hand. 'Shit, Jinx, that must hurt like hell.'

The skin was raw and blistered. I had been trying to ignore the constant throbbing and the vicious shot of pain every time I moved my hand too quickly. 'A bit,' I admitted. *Lie.* Okay, a lot. I felt him reach out to me and feel my pain, then I felt his annoyance that I hadn't said anything sooner.

Nate gently took my hand and started to lick it. In any other circumstance, it would have been weird but vampyrs' spit has healing properties so I let him lick at me like I was a dripping lolly on a hot day. In less than a minute the skin had healed and the pain had completely disappeared. I gave a relieved sigh. 'Thank you. That's so much better.'

'You should have said something,' Amber groused. 'I could have painted some healing runes while I was doing the protection ones.'

'I didn't want you wasting your energy,' I admitted.

'It's *my* energy to waste,' she growled.

'Sure, but let's save it for when someone is bleeding,' I proposed.

'Enough.' Jack's pointed whisper cut across us. 'Let's move.'

He was right; we were dawdling. Amber and I exchanged reluctant glances before we both went to the edge of the boat to climb down into the water. Nate was pacing restlessly behind us.

Shirdal lowered the anchor by the expedient route of chucking it in, and we all winced at the resulting splash. 'I'll be the eyes in the sky. I'll find you when you're out of the water.' With that promise, he shimmered into griffin form, leapt into the air and rapidly disappeared into the clouds above us. I hoped he'd keep out of sight.

Jack shoved his clothes into a watertight bag he'd found in the cabin and slung it over his shoulder before diving elegantly into the water. Ten points from me.

I couldn't delay any longer; it was go time. I climbed down the ladder and stifled a curse as the icy water gripped my legs. Damn, it was cold. When I was fully immersed, I pushed away from boat to make way for Amber. I trod water, waiting to support her if she needed help. She climbed in quickly and efficiently.

Nate followed her. He joined us promptly, but moments later he was flailing in the water, panic flaring in his eyes. I reached an arm around his waist to help keep him afloat. He didn't say anything but he shot me a grateful look and his thrashing eased off.

'Cycle your legs like you're riding a bicycle,' I whispered. He nodded and his movements gained purpose.

'This way,' Jack called. 'We have to go underwater, but it's only a twenty-second swim before we come out in a cavern. Nate, I'll go first with you and Gato, then I'll come back to guide Jinx and Amber.'

That was the moment Gato was waiting for. He dived into the water without making so much as a ripple. Who knew he was such a water dog? He was a master doggy-paddler and he swam strong strokes until he was next to Jack.

'Ready, Nate?' Jack asked.

'Ready.' He sounded calm but our bond said he was anything but.

I could have pointed out that the undead didn't really need to worry about holding their breath under water, but it seemed like poor form. Fear has no rhyme or reason. I guessed Nate never had swimming lessons as a kid.

Moments later, all three of them had gone. Amber and I swam a little closer to where they'd disappeared and trod water again. I could see she was tiring. The cold was getting to both of us, but it wasn't long before Jack resurfaced next to me.

'I'll pull you through the water, Amber. Take a deep breath.' Looking a little relieved, she blew out a long breath before filling her lungs and diving under the surface. I hastily did the same.

Once beneath the surface, I opened my eyes – into pitch blackness. I felt a flash of panic until I saw a flash of Jack's tail ahead of me. I plunged after him, doing my best breaststroke and kicking my legs forcefully to keep up. I was struggling not to freak out. Jack had said twenty seconds but surely it was more than that by now?

I did a few more strokes. Suddenly the water ahead of me cleared and I swam up towards the light. My head broke the surface and I took in great gulps of air. Nate and Gato were standing on the rocks around the pool I was now in. Jack was courteously helping Amber out of the water like she was the Queen. Where was my helping hand? I dragged myself out of the water, clambering onto the rock with all of the grace of a flopping fish. I stood, water sluicing off of me.

I looked around. We were in a cave. Nate used his phone torch to light up the space around us. The cold had taken away my ability to think straight... Hold up – I had fire. I gave a mental head thump and I summoned it in my hands, as hot as I could manage. It danced on my palms and I expanded it; almost immediately I felt warmth rolling off it.

'Nice,' Nate commented. He stripped off his shirt and squeezed it out, then held it close to my flames to dry. That wasn't a bad idea. I grew the fire some more and we all huddled around it.

Finally Jack rolled his eyes. 'Enough. You'd think you'd never been in the water before.' Easy for him to say; his clothes had come over in the waterproof bag, though to be fair they were probably still damp from his earlier splash.

'It was cold,' I complained. 'Best to get warm and dry before we move out.' It suddenly occurred to me that I could have just used the IR to dry us all instantly rather than huddling around a small fire for ten minutes. Even after several months in the Other realm I still hadn't gotten used to having magic at my fingertips. I decided to brush past my moment of stupidity. 'We're going to need our wits about us, and thinking all the time about how damned cold we are wouldn't help. We'll think clearer now. You know the way out of this cave, right?' I asked Jack.

'Yeah, I checked when I did my recce. It's not far – it's not a very big cave system. This way.'

Jack took the lead confidently, drawing us away from our point of ingress. The tunnels were dark, tight and twisting. He hadn't let on that that getting out involved a crawl through a long narrow space. I'm not claustrophobic generally but even I was relieved when we emerged into the night air.

The night was lit not just by the moon but also by fireflies that definitely shouldn't have been hanging out in Wales. They were beautiful and I reached out in wonder – until Amber smacked my hand away. 'Are you mad? Don't touch the fireflies!'

I blinked. 'What?'

'*Fire*flies. The clue is in the name. If you touch one, it'll burst into flames. You might as well send up a flare announcing our arrival.'

I stared at her. 'Are you serious?'

'Have you ever known me to joke?'

'Actually ... no.'

'Well then. Come on, we're falling behind. Just ... don't touch the shiny things,' she said in a patronising tone.

'What if the shiny things touch me?' I whined.

'They won't. They have sonar like bats,' she explained.

The mention of bats suddenly reminded me of Audrey and her words of advice. Maybe I could use my empathy to suss out what was around us. I concentrated for a moment and let the ocean in my mind recede. Ignoring the minds of my companions, I reached out to feel the emotions of whatever else was around me.

The island was small and it wasn't hard to find the bunch of ogres. Their main emotion seemed to be a mixture of boredom and anticipation; I guessed they were looking forward to the fight. Hopefully, they could keep on looking forward to it while we sneaked around behind them. I could also feel something equine that had a fiercely protective feel to it and I guessed that was the kelpies.

I swept towards the massive lighthouse and I felt three things: one was bored, one felt ... ready, and the third was absolutely petrified.

It wasn't hard to recognise the being that was terrified – after all, I'd sat across from her in my office every day for weeks.

My 'something special' was Hes.

Chapter 34

'It's Hes,' I blurted out.

Ahead of me, Nate stumbled then whipped around to face me. 'What?'

'Hes. She's my something special that the dragons have told me to retrieve. I can feel her. She's scared.'

'How can you be sure it's her?' he demanded.

'I've worked beside her for weeks. She has a certain – aura. It's definitely her.'

'She's scared?' A muscle was working in his jaw.

I nodded, feeling awful. 'Petrified. I hate this. I hate that I'm responsible for her feeling like this.'

'The only ones responsible are the motherfucking dragons!' Nate snarled.

I felt his burst of hatred zing through me. Dragon–vampyr relations were notoriously bad, but I had hoped that Emory had alleviated a lot of that hatred. It seemed not; one lukewarm friendship didn't wash away centuries of distrust and antipathy. That was another reason why Nate had kept himself hidden in the castle. 'Nate—,' I started.

'No. Emory's not so bad, but his circle are something else. Who kidnaps a young woman and subjects her to god knows what just for some stupid challenge?'

I closed my mouth. The Other realm was full of things like the bullshit challenge, and the dragons didn't have the corner on stupid traditions, but now wasn't the time to argue. Tempers were fraying, and I decided to be the better person; I'd let the pot-shot at my mate's species go – for now.

There was a shriek from somewhere above us and moments later Shirdal arrived. His landing made the ground tremble. 'No sign of the phoenix.' His voice was foreboding.

'There really is a phoenix?' I asked apprehensively.

'Yes. It lives here. I expected some sort of aerial combat as soon as she sensed me in her skies but there was nothing.'

'So maybe she's on holiday,' I offered optimistically.

'More likely, she's already occupied.' His tone was grim. I hated to think what would keep a phoenix occupied.

I thought of Hes's fear and the *thing* I could sense with her. 'Crap, she's with Hes.' Poor Hes. Why was it always Hes that got kidnapped? First Mrs H, and now Elizabeth. The girl was going to get a complex.

Shirdal cocked his eagle head at me. 'Hes?'

'My assistant. She's my "something" that the dragons have taken,' I admitted. 'I can sense her.'

'Ah. Well then, we'd best press ahead. The phoenix gets nasty when the sun rises.' I'd hate to see what Shirdal's definition of nasty looked like.

'Shall we head to the lighthouse tower?' I suggested. 'It's the only building I can see and it's the right direction for the feeling I'm getting from Hes. Will you be able to take her down? The phoenix?'

'Oh no!' Shirdal said happily. 'She'll tear me to shreds and I'll go down in a blaze of glory. You'll tell Bastion the tale, won't you, so they can sing about me for centuries to come?' I wished he'd sound less happy about the prospect of his imminent demise.

'Let's just kick the phoenix's ass, take Hes and go,' I suggested.

'There'll be no ass-kicking. The phoenix is vicious – even the dragons fear her.'

'So how did they get her on side for this stupid challenge?' I asked.

'They probably didn't,' Shirdal replied scornfully. 'They'll have shoved Hes into the phoenix's territory while it was dark. As I said, it's sunrise that we need to worry about – that's when she feasts.'

My stomach lurched. 'Hes is really in danger?'

'Of the worst kind,' he said softly, his eyes glittering with sympathy.

Fuck. I was going to kick Elizabeth Manners' ass from here to Land's End when I got back to the castle. But first it was time for a daring rescue.

'Gato, shift to battle cat mode again. Amber and I will ride on you. Shirdal, you take Nate and Jack. We need to move. Now!' I barked out the orders and everyone started to move.

Gato shifted, growing in size, eyes flashing red and black spikes protruding from his spine. 'Don't worry about the spikes,' I said to Amber reassuringly. 'He won't hurt you.'

As I hopped on his back, the spikes where I landed slid inwards like blades in a stage prop. Once Amber had clambered on, Gato set off. Shirdal ran next to us, leonine and majestic. This time he didn't take to the skies but preferred to keep abreast of us on the ground. Presumably he didn't want to catch the phoenix's eye until we were ready.

The lighthouse reared out of the ground. Its white walls had seen better days; chunks of plaster had flaked off, the cheery red edging was faded and lacklustre. We ran around the base of it, which took longer than I'd expected because it was larger than your average lighthouse. There was no entrance.

'Where the fuck is the door?' I was starting to panic. We had an hour or two tops before daybreak and I was exhausted and cranky. I'd had my fill; I wanted to be at home, with Emory, not skulking around some random Welsh island at the arse-end of the night.

'Hidden.' Amber clucked her tongue. 'Stop! Let me get down, Gato. I need to paint some runes.'

'The phoenix will feel them,' Shirdal warned.

'Do we have a choice?' Amber asked forcefully.

'I can use the IR against her,' I said confidently. 'We'll be fine.'

'She's immune to the IR,' he cautioned. 'You can use the elements against her and maybe Glimmer, but—'

'I don't have Glimmer with me. I was only allowed to take one tool with me and I chose you lot.' I groused, gesturing to my companions.

'And your lock picks.' Shirdal pointed out.

I coloured. 'Well ... yeah.' I always carry them so I hadn't even thought that they might be breaking the rules. Anyway, screw the dragons and their stupid rules – they'd dumped my friend with a *phoenix*.

'And you have Glimmer,' Shirdal repeated.

'No,' I sighed. 'I don't.' His insistence was getting annoying.

'Then why is it on your hip?'

I blinked, looked down at my right hip – and, sure enough, there it was. I had never been happier to see my sentient dagger in my life. Glimmer had an uncanny ability to know when it was needed, and somehow – don't ask me how – it could travel to me no matter where I was. The weight of it on my hip was reassuring.

I drew it out of its sheath. 'Thank goodness for you,' I murmured. 'I'm so happy you're here.' Glimmer is an awesome weapon, and at that moment I needed every advantage I could get over a bloody IR-immune phoenix.

The dagger burst into song in my mind; it was happy to see me too. 'Don't distract me now,' I said aloud. 'I need to focus.'

'*I* need to focus,' Amber muttered, as she drew runes. 'You're chattering away like a bunch of babbling baboons.'

'Say that ten times,' Jack joked.

'A bunch of babbling baboons,' Shirdal started. 'A bunch of babbling baboons, a bunch of-'

'*Shut up*,' Amber growled. 'I am *trying* to concentrate.'

Shirdal mimed zipping his lips and throwing away the key.

'We can dream,' Amber bitched. She made her way around the lighthouse base, painting new runes every foot or so. Her gunk supplies were looking low, which couldn't be a good thing. I shelved that worry; we had bigger problems to solve – like rescuing Hes.

'I've got it!' Amber cried triumphantly. 'Here!' We dashed around the side of the lighthouse to where she was standing in front of a very visible door.

Relief rushed through me. I reached out to touch it but Amber swatted away my hand. 'Ouch!' I complained.

'What is it with you and touching everything? Let me just check it first for curses!'

Oh. That seemed sensible. 'Okay. You go right ahead,' I said graciously.

She painted on two quick runes that glowed once and faded. 'We're good,' she confirmed, relieved.

I tried to turn the round knob but nothing happened. I tried again and gave the door a shove for good measure. Nothing.

Underneath the handle was a large keyhole. I didn't have lockpicks big enough to deal with that. 'Shirdal, can you kick it down or something?'

'With pleasure.' The huge griffin backed up a few steps then ran towards the door. It didn't move as he bounced off it. Gato took a turn, bounding forward and flinging his spike-ridden body at the door. Nothing.

The two of them took turns thumping into the door but to no avail. They were making a lot of noise but no headway. The phoenix would certainly be expecting us now.

Glimmer was hot against my thigh. In desperation, I unsheathed the dagger again and shoved it into the lock. I wrenched it to the right – and the door clicked open. For fuck's sake; I could have done that before the pounding had announced our presence to all and sundry.

I pushed the heavy door inwards, stepped into a hallway – and stopped dead.

I had never seen a creature like the one that was standing in front of me but I knew without a doubt what it was: a sphinx. She was incredibly beautiful, with a human head and long tumbling golden hair, a pale lion's body and white wings like a griffin.

When her eyes met mine, they were oddly friendly. 'Hello,' she greeted me. 'Are you the challenger?' I nodded, mouth dry. 'Wonderful. The dragons told me to expect you.' She looked at my companions who had crowded in beside me. 'You're all welcome to listen, but no one may speak except the challenger. Am I clear?'

They nodded mutely.

'Hello, cousin,' she greeted Shirdal. 'A pleasure to see you. It's been too long since I've graced the mountains with my song. Perhaps I am due a visit.'

Shirdal said nothing but he bowed on his forepaws and sank low before her.

'Aren't you a sweetie?' she cooed. 'Maybe I won't eat all of you if the challenger fails.'

Jesus.

She turned back to me. 'Challenger, your courage has been tested but now it is time to test your wits. Answer me these five riddles and then you shall pass. Answer wrongly and you'll be devoured.'

'Five? Isn't it usually one or two riddles? Three at most?'

Her friendly smile dropped off her face like rain off a window. 'I set the rules here. There are five of you, so you must answer five riddles. Unless you really want fewer riddles and I eat a couple of your companions?'

'No,' I blurted out. 'That's fine. Let's do five.' I sucked at riddles but Lucy and I used to go to pub quizzes when we were younger and they had often come up in one of the rounds. Maybe I'd remember some of them.

The sphinx drew herself up. 'What can run but never walks, has a mouth but never talks, has a head but never weeps, has a bed but never sleeps?'

I didn't have to worry over that one; I knew it well. That one had come up time and time again. 'A river,' I answered calmly.

She smiled. 'Very good. Let us continue in the same vein.' She cleared her throat. 'A truth seeker calls her hellhound from the opposite side of the river. The hellhound crosses the river without getting wet and without using a bridge or boat. How?'

That one required a little more thought, but finally the answer came to me. 'The river was frozen.'

The sphinx clapped her paws together. 'Very good. Let's try this new one – I just learned it and I think you'll love it. Three doctors say that Bill was their brother. Bill says he has no brothers. How many brothers does Bill actually have?'

I found myself smiling back. A modern riddle, indeed. 'None. He has three sisters.'

'I knew you'd get that one! Lovely. Number four, then. What is so fragile that saying its name breaks it?'

I stared at the floor as I wracked my brains, but all I could think of was glass. I started to sweat. The seconds ticked on and the silence grew heavy as I desperately tried to come up with something that made sense. When I looked at the Sphinx, her smile had turned distinctly victorious.

I turned to my companions behind me. Shirdal gestured pointedly to his throat.

'I'll allow that, since I said you couldn't speak,' the Sphinx said. 'But now the rules have changed. You mustn't mime or communicate in any way. Break my rules again, griffin, and you'll be breakfast.' Even as she threatened us, she was still smiling. She was a psychopath.

Relief swept through me as I finally understood Shirdal's clue. 'Silence,' I answered.

She laughed. 'Wonderful. That took you a while – I was starting to worry. Last one, challenger, and this one has a time limit of sixty seconds for the answer. What can bring back the dead, make you cry, make you laugh, make you young, is born in an instant yet lasts a lifetime?'

I didn't need sixty seconds; I knew the answer in a heartbeat. It was all I had left of my mother. 'A memory.' My voice cracked. God, what would Mum think of me now, sneaking onto some hidden island to rescue a friend and face a phoenix? But I knew how she'd feel – she'd be damned proud. She'd raised me to be kind and help others, and I'd honour her by doing it until my dying day.

Which might well be today.

Chapter 35

Riddles completed, the sphinx stepped back to reveal a narrow staircase. 'Up you go,' she said cheerfully. 'The phoenix gets grumpy when you keep her waiting. Chop-chop.'

'She's expecting us, huh?' I said with dread.

'Darling, with the racket you made, the entire island was expecting you,' she said drily. 'Next time you try to do covert, can I suggest keeping the noise down?'

I felt slightly cheered by the fact that she thought there would be a next time. That was encouraging.

I sidled past the sphinx, giving her as wide berth as possible. She laughed a little at that, revealing big-cat teeth in her humanoid mouth. Maybe she really did eat the people who failed the riddles. I wondered how often that happened, or if she just rolled into the jungle and started chucking riddles out before going nuts on the animal population.

We climbed up the stairs and paused at the door at the top. 'Do we have a game plan?' Jack asked.

'Survive?' I was only half-joking.

'I'll distract the phoenix, while you lot rescue Hes,' Shirdal offered.

'I don't want you dying in a blaze of glory,' I protested.

'Aw, I knew you'd grow to love my charms.' He was all jovial humour, but I nodded seriously. Despite his obviously murderous nature he was constantly striving for good. I had never seen anything more impressive in my whole life; it was like watching a shark voluntarily become a vegetarian.

'I'll get Hes loose of any restraints, and phase her out of here,' Nate volunteered.

'After this, you should teach her how to phase herself. She's a vampyr in all but blood. If you'd taught her how to phase months ago, she could have rescued herself,' I pointed out. 'I know you two aren't talking these days so maybe someone else could teach her.'

'No, she's my responsibility.' The resolution in Nate's voice was clear. 'She's a vampyr because of me. You're right – I've been shirking. I'll rectify that when we're all out of here in one piece.'

'So get in, snatch Hes and get out,' I told him.

'That's a terrible plan,' Amber sighed.

Jack smirked. 'I think it's brilliant, simple but brilliant. Even a bunch of idiots couldn't screw it up.'

Yup, we were the idiots: here we were in the early hours of the morning, trying to sneak up on a deadly phoenix who definitely knew we were coming. Definitely idiots.

'Great. If we're all agreed? Let's go.' I drew Glimmer and clenched it in my right fist. Shirdal and Gato had already shifted and were battle-ready. They would go in first and draw the phoenix's ire and fire; hopefully they'd be quick enough to move out of the way before they got scorched.

As we burst in and fanned out, my eyes darted about searching for the phoenix. The large circular room was double height at least. It had been converted some time ago and all traces of the lighthouse equipment were long gone, but it could have done with some homey touches.

'Where's the phoenix?' I scanned the empty room. Could it be invisible? Nothing was beyond the realms of possibility. There again, I had no idea what I was looking for. Was it huge like the salamander, or was it parrot sized? Maybe I should have checked a few facts before charging in. Hindsight – don't you love it?

'There!' Shirdal pointed with one paw to the rafters where a small bird was sitting.

'*That's* the phoenix? Are you kidding me? Why have we been quivering behind the door?'

'I wasn't quivering, I was gathering resilience,' Shirdal exclaimed defensively.

'I was quivering,' Amber admitted. 'And I still am. Stop blathering and watch yourselves. Let's rescue Hes and get the heck out of here.'

'You'd be more likeable if you'd swear,' Jack said evenly.

'You'd be more likeable if you didn't,' Amber retorted. 'Swearing is a sign of a small mind.'

'Studies have found that to be untrue,' Nate joined in the debate. 'Swearing is a sign of intelligence.'

I turned my attention to Hes. She was tied to a chair in the centre of the room. Next to her was a large globe, but that was the sum total of the furniture except for an empty bookshelf fixed to the curved wall.

Hes was bound and gagged, and her eyes were red from crying. She was trying desperately to talk to us through the gag but her words were unintelligible.

'We're coming,' I reassured her.

She shook her head desperately and looked up at the phoenix in the rafters. Quick as a blink, Nate was next to her trying to undo her bindings but his fingers fumbled in his panic. I ran over and used Glimmer to saw through the thick rope. Once her hands were free, she pulled down the gag. 'It's a trap! You've got to go – she's going to eat you all!'

I looked dubiously at the tiny bird. Perspective had something to do with it, and she probably wasn't canary size – but she didn't look like she could eat a whole roast chicken, let alone me. It was hard to work up any fear.

'Grab Hes and phase out of here,' I ordered Nate. Our master-slave bond kicked into life and Nate was moving before I could apologise for being so abrupt.

He lifted Hes into his arms and dashed towards the shadows at the edge of the room – but then nothing happened. 'It's warded!' he shouted. 'The room is warded. We can't phase out!'

I felt his panic. The order I'd given him was still driving him but it was impossible to follow. Shit! 'Take her down the stairs!' I called, giving him a different order to follow.

He used his lightning speed to dash to the other side of the room but the door we had entered through was no longer there. 'It's gone!' he cried.

'Amber!' I yelled.

'I'm on it!' Amber drew out her gunk and looked at it dubiously. She was scraping the figurative barrel as well as the actual Kilner jar. 'I'm not going to make it with this. I'm going to need some blood.'

'You can have mine,' Nate offered.

'Yours won't work. I need someone who's still alive.'

'Try mine,' Hes offered.

I was about to chuck Glimmer to her to make a cut in her flesh but then thought better of it. The last thing we needed was to give Hes even more hybrid powers to worry about.

'I'll give you a bite if that's okay,' Nate offered.

'Just do it.' She held out her wrist.

'Get me a bowl.'

The phoenix started to laugh. 'So many plans, my little darlings. You're like ants trying to survive a flood. Scurry, scurry – but I'll still be eating you all soon. The sun is rising, my loves. You took so long with my dear friend the sphinx that now the sun is kissing the earth.'

She laughed and laughed and the sound that echoed round the stone walls of the lighthouse made me shiver. The madness in it was terrifying.

We needed to distract her so I summoned my courage. 'You're all talk, phoenix. I doubt you could manage to swallow a hellhound and a griffin, even if you were sitting down at an all-you-can-eat buffet. Come here, little tweety-pie. Let's play together.' I knew deliberately baiting a small bird sounded crazy, but what choice did I have? I needed to distract her and, in my experience, insults cloud people's thought processes.

'Insolent bitch! I'll save you for the last,' she spat. 'You'll watch and scream as I crunch your companions' bones – but first I'd like them cooked.' As she spoke her rage rocketed through me, making it difficult to think.

She was trying to take possession of my mind! Suddenly I needed to kill something *now;* all I could feel was the murderous need to snuff out life – all life. I summoned fire, growing it in my hands, ready to throw it at my nearest target: Jack.

Glimmer sang distantly but I ignored it as I gathered the flames. It sang louder and louder, almost screeching at me. My companions were shouting at me, too, but I ignored them. I could set this room on fire and burn everything to so much ash and soot ... it would be easy ... The room would be so hot – Emory would like it ...

And just like that, my brain rebooted. *Emory.* As always when I thought about him, love swamped my heart. It rose up and overwhelmed me, quashing the anger that was trying to consume me.

I blinked at the huge fireball before me. Holy fuck, what had I been about to do? The fire in my hands was huge now, nearly consuming the width of the room, and my friends were cowering near the walls. Amber was still painting runes with Hes's blood. Shirdal was shouting something at me but I couldn't make it out over the roar of the flames.

The fire was unstable and I was too inexperienced as a fire elemental to pull the flames back into myself. They had to go somewhere so I threw them upwards – towards the blasted phoenix. As the flames travelled up, my ears seemed to pop and suddenly I could hear again.

'Not at her! Don't send the flames to her!' Shirdal was shouting.

Fuck.

Chapter 36

We watched, rigid with tension, to see what would happen when the flames hit the phoenix. She didn't even try to avoid them; if anything, she flew into them. She laughed as they hit her – and then she started to grow. And grow. Her brilliant multi-coloured plumage flashed. That was all the warning we got before she plunged towards us with her claws outstretched.

Shirdal was there to meet her but he looked tiny next to her. That shouldn't have been possible because he was one of the fiercest predators I had ever met, but he was like a cub next to an enormous lion. He tried to attack her neck and chest but she fought him off easily with her lethally sharp claws. In seconds, he was cut and blood was glistening on his golden fur, but still he went back for more. He was trying to give us time, to give Amber time.

After what felt like aeons but was probably only a minute or two, Amber shouted triumphantly, 'I've got it!' The door appeared in a flash of light and we wrenched it open. Shirdal didn't let up from harrying the phoenix; he just went in again for more punishment to distract her from our getaway.

'Go! Quickly!' I held the door open. When the others were through, I shut it again and it disappeared. I had made the phoenix into this beast and I couldn't leave Shirdal to face her alone.

I waited until she did a low pass, and then I fired a jet at her, not of fire this time but water. She screamed as it struck her but in moments she was back in the rafters, too far away for the water to reach her.

Shirdal flew down to me. 'Get on my back!' he shouted. I didn't hesitate. I threw myself onto his back and he lifted us upwards. As we drew closer to the phoenix, I sprayed her with water again.

I couldn't be sure, but it looked like she was shrinking. It was working! 'Keep on her!' I yelled into Shirdal's ear.

He didn't answer but he kept following her, sticking to her like glue as she tried to duck and dive and roll away from us. If the moment hadn't been so tense, it would have felt like an arcade game. I was trying to hit a target with a water jet; if I won, the prize was to walk away with my life.

Shirdal was tiring and he was cut in dozens of places, but he soldiered on regardless. The tide had turned against the phoenix and I started to feel optimistic. *She* was running away from *us* now.

Then she started to laugh triumphantly and grow in size again; the water from my successful attacks must have dried off her feathers. She was so fast that my next two attempts to hit her failed.

I desperately debated what to do. If I couldn't hit her with water, then maybe I could fill the room with it and drown her. I aimed the water downwards this time and pulled a constant stream of it from within myself.

'What's your plan?' Shirdal asked.

'If I can't hit her, I'll submerge her instead.'

'And how are we going to get out?' His tone was derisive,

'I haven't got that far. One problem at a time.' I instructed.

'That is a pretty significant problem. I'm fine with being cut to shreds but being drowned isn't the way I want to go,' he complained plaintively.

'It'll be fine.' *Lie.*

We both swore as the phoenix spat golden fire at us. Shirdal dived to one side and narrowly missed the scorching flames. Her fire was *hot*, hotter than anything I'd ever felt before. She wasn't interested in eating us now; in her fury, she wanted to burn us to ash.

In an effort to distract her, I aimed the water at her again. Even if I missed, it would help to fill up the room ... and then the water stopped pouring from my hands. I had reached my elemental limit. I hadn't even known that there was one.

The phoenix was immune to the IR so I couldn't use it on her, but I could use it on the things around her. I summoned the heavy-looking globe, held it in the air for a moment, then shot it upwards with all my might, not at the phoenix but at the circular skylight in the middle of the lighthouse roof.

We were on an island; I might have been out of water, but the island certainly wasn't. Using the IR, I summoned the water from the sea until it came like a watery hurricane – a typhoon – and crashed through the skylight into the lighthouse. Shit. Too much water, way too much water. I tried to cut it off but when I couldn't, I directed it to the outside of the lighthouse instead.

Shirdal was soaked and flapping his wings with great effort to get us above the rising water. We shot through the hole in the roof and landed next to it. The phoenix was still in her tower. There was no time to celebrate that we weren't stuck in the tower because we didn't want her following us through our escape route while we did a happy dance.

I summoned more water from the sea and poured it into the lighthouse; it shot in as if it were pressurised from a fireman's hose. It had hit the phoenix a few times now and she was back to the size of a large – angry – parrot.

I felt a twinge of conscience. She was one of a kind; if I killed her with this flood of water, I would be responsible for making an endangered species an extinct one. Sure, she was murderous and bitchy, but I'd probably be a bit cranky in her position.

The water level had risen nearly to the top of the room and Shirdal and I were guarding the only exit. I had Glimmer drawn, and the griffin had his claws ready. 'How do you feel about letting her live?' I blurted.

'The deadly, dangerous phoenix?' he said incredulously.

'She's the last of her kind,' I mentioned.

'So let's make her extinct,' he huffed. 'She's ripped me to pieces.'

'You'll be fine. Don't be a wimp. Go on, let's let her live,' I wheedled.

He blew out a breath and I saw him visibly battle his murderous urges. After a tense moment, a flicker of a smile stole across his face. 'The assassin that let her live. That would be a tale, wouldn't it?'

'A mighty one,' I agreed wholeheartedly.

He retracted his claws. 'Fine.'

Taking advantage of us chatting together, the phoenix shot out of the hole beside us, but she was waterlogged and spluttering and she wasn't faster than Shirdal anymore. He had the upper hand now, quite literally, and easily he pinned her against the roof with one forepaw. 'We could kill you right now. You understand that, right?' he growled at her, eyes flashing with the urge to do just that.

She gave a feeble chirp. She was playing the weak victim card with all her might. 'I'm not buying it,' I said firmly even though I absolutely was. 'But we'll let you live if you promise not to hurt me or any of my companions ever again.'

'So mote it be,' Shirdal added, making the promise become a vow.

'So mote it be,' the phoenix agreed begrudgingly.

With reluctance in every line of his body, Shirdal lifted his paw off her throat. She looked like a colourful, bedraggled chicken and it was hard to take her seriously as a threat. The sun was rising from the horizon though, and I waited with bated breath to see what she would do next.

She breathed a small ball of fire and let it float in front of her to warm her and her soaked feathers. Then, like the sun, she started to grow. And she continued to grow – until she was taller than a dragon.

'You're pretty big,' I commented.

She screeched, 'I can be big, or little.' In a flash she was back to parrot size. 'I can spit fireballs that will burn through anything, even dragon hide if I so choose. I can soar higher and faster than a dragon and kill surer than any griffin.' She sniffed disdainfully.

'So how come there is only one phoenix left?' I questioned.

'There was always one phoenix, no more, no less. Perhaps God made perfection and knew it couldn't be improved upon,' she preened.

She hopped onto my shoulder and I struggled not to tense. That beak, so close to my neck ... 'Relax,' she purred. 'I gave my oath that I will never harm you or your companions. I am a bird of my word. Besides, I've seen what happens to oath breakers – the Other realm would destroy me if I broke it. My existence is solitary and miserable, but it's the only one I have.'

'Why did you get banished to Llanddwyn?'

She spluttered and cawed her outrage. 'Banished? I did not get banished; I choose to stay here. The Other realm grew boring. Every time I ventured out, people started cowering.' She sneered. 'They are so predictable.'

'But you like the sphinx?'

'I'm good with riddles. We keep each other entertained.'

'And the kelpies?'

'I keep my distance from those watery demons. We respect each other and that's enough.'

'What do you eat?'

'Mostly sea creatures. I ate a whale a little while ago and that was good. I do miss troll flesh, though, and the taste of a good dryad.' Her beak clacked happily as if she were remembering ripping into the flesh. Eww.

'Well, it's been … interesting … meeting you, but I'd best be going,' I said politely. 'I need to check if Hes is all right. You freaked her out.'

'She was fun to play with. She would have been tasty to eat, but I'll let it slide this one time.'

'And every future time,' I glowered.

'Yes, I know,' she said impatiently. 'Human flesh tastes so good when it's been barbecued. Never mind, other humans will wander onto my island.' Her beak clacked again in anticipation. 'Of course, you're not quite human are you?' She eyed me. 'I thought I had you with my influence but you got out. Such a shame. It would have been fun to watch you massacre your friends.'

A chill ran down my spine. We might have been conversing quite civilly, but she was fucking feral. 'Anyhow, we'd best be going,' I said lamely.

'No problem.' She launched off my shoulder into the air. I hoped she'd stay in Llanddwyn; the world had enough problems without a homicidal phoenix making an appearance.

Her voice called back to me on the breeze. 'Watch out for the ogres gathered at the base of the lighthouse. I'd be mad if they got to kill you when I couldn't.'

At the base of the lighthouse? Fuck. Could this infernal Challenge get any worse?

Chapter 37

The griffin and I could fly away from the ogres, but the same couldn't be said for the rest of the team.

'Well,' Shirdal said merrily, 'it looks like we might die today anyway.'

'Will you stop sounding so chipper about it?' I protested. 'I want to make it home.'

'To Emory?' Shirdal tried to waggle his eyebrows suggestively, but it looked ridiculous on an eagle's face.

'And a hot bath! And dinner,' I listed on my fingers.

'It's breakfast time now, sweetheart,' Shirdal confirmed.

'I don't give a shit what time it is. I want food,' I moaned. 'Preferably cake. It's been a long fucking night.'

'Don't say that,' Shirdal objected. 'No fucking has been had. Emory would have my head if he thought there had been.'

I ignored his weak attempt at humour. 'Come on. Let's go and save the others.'

'Or die with them,' he suggested cavalierly.

I ignored that piece of overwhelming optimism and climbed on his back again. 'I feel like a horse,' he muttered. 'I've only had a couple of people on my back in the last few centuries, and now you're on and off it like a yo-yo.'

'Sorry. Do you mind?' I asked.

He sniffed but didn't answer; no, he didn't mind. He leapt off the lighthouse roof and his wings struggled for a moment. As we dived too fast, panic clawed at my throat and I gripped his body tightly with my legs. Then his wings started beating strongly again and we slowed.

We landed hard. Shirdal was exhausted. I felt horribly guilty; he was bleeding because of me, yet he had kept on going. 'Thank you, my friend.' I leaned forward and gave him a quick hug before I dismounted.

We had come down next to Amber, Gato and Jack. Hes was still cuddled into Nate.

And the five of them were facing an ogre army.

Maybe I'm being over-dramatic, but there were a dozen ogres, maybe more. And our most powerful weapon – Shirdal – was already bleeding and tired. Maybe this challenge really would be the death of me.

I was all out of water, but I hoped I had some flames left. I summoned fire and was relieved when they leapt into my hands. But before I could grow the fireball into a bigger threat, one of the ogres stepped forward.

He had a crow on either shoulder, like some kind of ogre pirate. He raised his hands in the universal sign for surrender. 'Whoa, lady. Drop the flames. We're here to help you. Emory Elite hired us.'

The fire in my hands sizzled and died as my mouth dropped open. 'What?' All of that time we'd wasted slinking in on a silent boat, getting drenched in an underwater cave … and all that time the ogres were on our side?

When I saw Emory I was going to— I didn't know what I was going to do, but it would hurt. Couldn't he have mouthed 'I've hired some ogres to help you' before I was sent on the challenge? How was I supposed to know they were allies?

'You're here to help us?' I repeated dumbly.

The ogre grinned. 'Yeah, though you seem to have things pretty well covered. The phoenix looked pissed when she flew away.'

'You saw that?' I asked.

'Yeah. We were waiting for you at the beach until we heard someone pounding something.'

That would be Gato and Shirdal trying to hammer down the door.

'We headed this way,' he continued, 'and here we are. We can escort you back to Caernarfon, if you like.'

I shook my head. 'No. We're okay.' After all we'd been through, I didn't want the dragons to think we'd got through the challenge because of a bunch of ogres. 'But you can help us get our boat,' I suggested.

'Sure.' The ogre whistled and two of his men peeled off to retrieve our boat.

'Do you have any healing supplies with you?' I asked. 'Or food?'

'Food yes, potions no. Injured ogres heal or die.' He gave another whistle and someone started handing out food.

'Who are you?' I asked curiously, wondering why the other ogres were jumping to obey his instructions.

'I'm High King Robert Krieg.'

I blinked. 'Oh. Should I have bowed or something?'

'There's lots of things that you should have done, but I'll let it go for now since Emory is paying me a small fortune for what turned out to be a very easy job.' He looked disappointed.

'Were you hoping for death?'

'Death? No, but maybe a little dismemberment.' He sighed. 'It's been boring.'

'Sorry to disappoint,' I said drily. I blocked out the bloodthirsty ogres and focused on my friends. Amber was pale and swaying; she was all but out. 'Gato, can you send Amber to the Common for a recharge?' I suggested.

'Thanks,' Amber muttered.

Gato barked twice and tapped his tail. He stood on his hind legs, touched his snout to her forehead and sent her back to the Common realm where, for her, the sky would suddenly be blue and everyone around her would look human.

'Are you okay, Hes?' I asked my young assistant.

She managed a wan smile. 'The phoenix was horrible, but I'm fine.' She was still in Nate's arms and I could feel his wave of protectiveness. Things had been broken between them since Hes had made a poor decision, but everyone deserved a second chance. Now it looked like Nate might forgive her, and I was pleased for both their

337

sakes. They'd both been pining and frankly it had been getting annoying. I'd contemplated an intervention but this was better; there was nothing like a crucible of fire to make an old argument look small and petty.

'Nate, can you help Shirdal?' I said. 'He's bleeding.' Although the griffin looked terrible, it was nothing that a bit of vampyr spit couldn't sort out.

'I'll be all right,' Shirdal protested. 'Most of the wounds are already healing.' He was right; the smallest cuts were already closing up, though he still had a nasty deep slash across his chest.

Nate licked his lips involuntarily.

'Stop it, boy. You can't drink griffin blood,' Shirdal said gruffly. 'It makes you vampyrs go spacey. Best stick to Common blood – Other blood isn't good for you.'

'A little bit is fine,' Nate disagreed. 'Griffin blood doesn't do the same thing to us as wizard blood. It just makes us a little – high. I can spit in the wound, but it won't heal properly if I don't lick it. I'm happy to help.'

'Of course you are. I'm tasty,' Shirdal grumbled. 'Go on, then. Give it a lick,' he grumped.

I knew he must be feeling worse than he was admitting if he was willing to let a vampyr help to heal him.

Shirdal lay down and closed his eyes as Nate knelt by his side, bent forward and started to lap at the wound. The rest of us tried to ignore the wet, sucking noises.

I was relieved when he was finished and the big wound was closed. Shirdal stood up and tested his forepaw delicately, then with more weight. 'Excellent. Thank you Nate,' he said. For once there was no sarcasm in his tone.

'No problem.' Nate rose to his feet, swaying.

'You've got a little ... ' I tapped the side of my mouth.

'Oh!' He dabbed away the smear of blood and giggled. I started to smile. He was high all right; I could feel it down our bond.

He slung an arm around Hes. 'No taking advantage of him,' I admonished Hes. 'He's high as a kite.'

'I wouldn't!' she protested.

Hmm. The jury was out on that one; she didn't have a track record for reliability. But I was working on forgiveness, and I was nearly there. Forgetting was another thing entirely.

Nate had fed but the rest of us were still hungry, so we tucked into the ogres' supplies, grateful for the biscuits and chocolate. Now that I wasn't starving or in danger of impending death, my thoughts turned back to the challenge. Surely I had proved myself? I just wanted to get home, back to normal life.

I tried to quash the thought that, if I became Prima, life would never be normal again.

Chapter 38

The ogres helped launch the boat. I gave them a jaunty wave goodbye, which they blithely ignored. Rude.

I started the engine with the help of my trusty lockpicks but I gave the helm to Jack. 'Do you mind steering?' I asked, tiredness lacing through my voice.

'Aye, aye, captain.' He gave me a mock salute.

I slumped down next to Gato. 'Are you okay, pup?'

He barked and closed the distance between us to lean on me. He touched his nose to my forehead for a quick blast in the Common realm. 'Thanks,' I muttered. 'That's a good idea. I was starting to feel itchy.' Having a hellhound was incredibly helpful, no wonder they were in such demand.

Plus, they were incredibly cute. I gave him a kiss on his huge head, and rested with my arms around him.

I had used a huge amount of magical energy, so it was no wonder I could barely stand. Plus I'd had no sleep in twenty-four hours and I'm a girl that needs her eight hours. I can cope on six but I'm not happy about it.

My head was muzzy and I felt grumpy. Hunger still clawed at my tummy. Those biscuits hadn't hacked it.

'You look a mess,' Nate giggled.

'Thanks,' I replied flatly.

'You have dried blood on you,' Nate confirmed, his eyes too wide.

'She wears my blood well,' Shirdal announced. 'Like a warrior. She and I were a fierce team, like avenging Valkyries. We could have killed the phoenix but we let it live because of the compassion in our hearts.'

I snorted. 'My heart had compassion. Yours wanted to stomp on her.'

'To be fair, she did do a number on me,' he said. He shifted and sat down next to me as a man. As always, he was dressed in rumpled clothes with unwashed, unbrushed hair. I knew his appearance was an affectation because he didn't have the slightest odour about him. Shirdal enjoyed his games, and pretending to be unimportant was his favourite. He liked people to underestimate him; they only did it once.

I rested my head on his shoulder. 'Thanks for coming with me.'

'You're welcome, Prima.' He said it respectfully, with none of his usual jokiness present.

For once, I didn't argue about the title. This time, I felt I'd earned it.

The boat ride had felt lightning fast on the way out, but on the way back it seemed horrendously long. I just wanted to be *warm*. Was that too much to ask? The slow rocking of the vessel was making me sleepy and I closed my eyes to rest them for a moment.

'Wake up, Prima,' Shirdal murmured. 'Time to face the dragon music again.'

'The dragons keep playing the same tune over and over,' I complained, sitting up and rubbing my gritty eyes.

'Then you'll have to help them change it,' he suggested softly.

The nap had rejuvenated me, and I was feeling more optimistic. Was I happy that Elizabeth Manners had stolen my assistant and put her on an obscure island, guarded by a sphinx and a phoenix? No, but I had overcome it and that victory had energised me. Elizabeth thought she had put insurmountable tasks in my path, such as raging fire and vicious salamanders, but I'd become a pyro-animal whisperer. I had *achieved.*

I wasn't going to let her crap in my hat anymore. I was done proving myself. If she didn't accept the challenge as proof that I was good for Emory then she wouldn't accept anything I could do. I loved Emory; that alone made me worthy of him. I *was* good enough, and I knew it from the tips of my slightly singed hair to the bottom of my squelchy toes.

I re-tied my hair then grabbed the leather jacket that I'd stowed in the boat while we went swimming, though I didn't put it on. I had grime and Shirdal's blood on me and I looked gross, but that made me look hard-core. I don't put great stock on appearances but I know that there are some out there who do. My appearance said I could kick ass and take names. Hopefully it would give some of the dragons pause, and they would cut Emory some slack as we moved forward. He had been trying to protect me from his court but maybe now they would understand that, nice as his protection was, I didn't need it.

I searched around the cabin for a pen and paper then scrawled a hasty note to the boat owner, apologising for borrowing it without permission. I explained that it had been a matter of life and death and I added a postscript that we had eaten some of his cookies. I emptied all of the cash out of my pockets and left it there as thanks. Luckily we hadn't caused any damage, and the money would more than cover the cost of the fuel and biscuits.

Gato portalled Amber and I back into the Other realm. The hour recharge would hopefully stop us being booted to the Common Realm when we weren't prepared for it. The itchiness had faded, and my nap had given me a little more energy to face the coming bullshit.

We climbed out of the boat into the water and waded to the harbour. Shirdal was next to me, too tired to offer to fly us to land. I owed him a massive gift. What did griffins like – besides murder and a heroic death?

I was grateful to be back on dry land once more, land that didn't have kelpies or a phoenix. The sky was a rich lilac; it looked like it was going to be a beautiful day. I hoped that sky wasn't deceptive.

I looped my arm through Amber's and although she shot me a horrified look, she didn't untangle our limbs. Nate was coming off his giggle-fest and walking hand in hand with Hes. They still had shit to talk about, but they seemed to be on the path to relationship redemption. Gato was in Great Dane form, relaxed and happy. Shirdal jogged to catch up with him and switched into his griffin form so that the beasts could walk next to each other. It was cute.

Jack cleared his throat awkwardly. 'I'll say my goodbyes here. I'm not into pomp and ceremony. Besides, I didn't quite mention to Father where I was going. I didn't expect it to take this long and he's gonna be a bit pissed off.'

I winced. 'I'm sorry for getting you into trouble.'

'I'm not five years old!' He laughed, waving it away. 'I won't be sent to my room – but I might need to do a bit of grovelling. I was supposed to be at a ceremony last night. He'll get over it.'

'Thanks for sticking around, Jack, I really appreciate it. We wouldn't have found the way onto the island without you,' I said solemnly.

'Apart from the fact that the ogres we were fastidiously trying to avoid turned out to be friendly,' he pointed out with a grin.

'Well, how could we have known that?' I grumped.

'When I was scouting, I noticed that they were flying the Welsh flag but I thought they just had national pride,' Jack admitted.

'And now you think they were trying to convey they were on Emory's side by flying the dragon?'

'Maybe. Maybe they're just Welsh. The Welsh take their nationality very seriously. *Hwyl Fawr.*' Jack waved goodbye to us all.

'What?'

'Goodbye in Welsh. Goodbye, Jinx. Don't forget to use your wise words.' He winked and dived back into the river. I watched the ripples until all evidence of him disappeared.

'Shall we?' Amber said impatiently, forced to pause with me due to our interlocked arms.

'Yes, let's go,' I agreed. We turned and trudged back to the castle. My legs were tired. Everything was tired. My aches had aches and it was hard to keep moving forward.

We finally got back to the castle; Amber unlinked her arm from mine. I could almost see her straighten her metaphorical witchy hat, and gather her bitchiness around her like a cloak. It was only just past 7am and the castle didn't officially open until 10am so I expected it to be deserted, but to my surprise the courtyard was heaving.

Cheers erupted as we walked in and someone started playing music. It was way too early for music.

The crowd drew back and created a corridor so that we could walk to the centre of the courtyard where Emory was sitting on his throne.

The giant wicker dragon had burnt away or been removed; all that remained was some ash on the ground. The salamander was still in her cage. I reached out a hand to her; her skin was cool so I sent her a ball of fire to warm the cage again. She chittered happily and snuggled down into her bed of flowers. The cage was full of flowers – someone had put more of them into her cage while we were out risking life and limb to rescue Hes. At least Sally was happy.

I continued towards Emory. He was looking relaxed and, as I reached for the bond between us, I was overwhelmed for a moment by his joy, relief and triumph at seeing me safe in front of him. I grinned. 'Hi.'

'Hi, Jessica.'

'I got Hes back.'

'So I see.' He leaned back into the throne, the epitome of a bored ruler, then stared at Elizabeth. 'Are we done here?'

I tensed. Surely we had to be done? If she announced a new challenge for me, I was going to spray water at her until she changed her mind.

Elizabeth was back in human form, dressed in a ridiculous ballgown. Oddly, she looked triumphant. 'The challenge is concluded. Jessica Sharp is worthy to become our Prima, the first challenge-tested Prima in five centuries!' The crowd whooped and cheered. Considering a lot of them had wanted me dead only hours before, they were inordinately happy that I was now alive. I'd take it; I wanted all the allies I could get.

'Spread the word near and far, Emory Elite is betrothed to Jessica Sharp. Their wedding will be within three moons!' Elizabeth shouted.

Wait – what?

Chapter 39

A riotous celebration of our safe return continued until half an hour before the castle was due to open its gates, then everyone was shoved forcefully in the direction of the door. There were a lot of beer bottles littering the courtyard and the brethren had to do a quick turnaround to clear the place up before the visitors arrived. It looked to me like the party had been going on the whole time we were away at the island; no wonder there had been so much whooping and cheering – the crowd was already tipsy when we got back.

'One day,' I said to Elizabeth, 'you and I are going to have a chat about what is acceptable behaviour. Kidnapping is not ok. I'm going to discuss it with you at length. There'll be shouting, rude words and hand gestures. But not now. Now I'm exhausted.'

'I'll make a note in my diary for a future rollicking,' Elizabeth said, still looking happy.

'You can't kidnap people,' I reiterated. 'It is officially against the rules. It's not ok.'

'Ultimately, there isn't anything I wouldn't do to ensure that the Revival Prophecy comes to pass.' Elizabeth shrugged.

'We'll talk prophecies another day. On the same day as the shouting day,' I suggested. I really was exhausted.

'As you please, Prima.' Elizabeth bobbed me a curtsy and left. Fabian and Leonard came over. Fabian offered his congratulations that I had survived the gauntlet. Leonard grunted something inarticulate which I took to mean, 'Well done, Jinx.' Leonard was on his usual glaring form. He stalked off without looking back.

'I'm glad you made it back okay,' Veronica said warmly. 'I was worried. I did what I could to help with the wicker dragon but there was nothing I could do about the island.'

'That was you, with the wicker dragon?' I smiled at her. 'Thank you for the assist.'

'Not that you needed it.' She smiled. She touched my arm. 'Well done, Prima.' She ducked away before I could respond but the whole thing had made me feel just a tiny bit more accepted. I *did* have allies here.

The other surprise was Evan. After making "you're going to die" faces at me earlier, I wasn't expecting him to be chipper that I'd survived, but he came over with a bunch of other younglings and coolly congratulated me on my success. The other kids were all giggling, looking at him like he was a rock star, he *knew* Jinx the Prima-to-be.

Emory then compounded it by greeting Evan familiarly, and telling him that he'd like a chat with "his ward" properly tomorrow. They had stuff to discuss. Evan did his best to act coolly disinterested but he failed miserably. You could see the excitement vibrating off him as he shot me a grateful look.

Finally the celebrations wound down, and Emory and I were alone. He took my hand and led me down the corridors running through the castle. I was so happy to be warm. Now I just needed to peel myself out of my ridiculous outfit.

Emory nodded to the brethren member standing guard outside the door. As soon as the door slammed shut behind us, he took me in his arms. 'Goddamn it, Jess.' His lips closed on mine and he pushed me against the wall. The kiss was hot and hungry; things could have got really interesting really fast if my tummy hadn't given an embarrassingly loud growl.

Emory pulled away and laughed. 'Let's feed the beast.'

I looked with longing towards the bathroom. Despite the warmth of the room, I was still cold. Being soaked to the bone really had chilled me. I felt like only a soak in the tub would get rid of it. It was a toss-up: hunger or cold?

'Are you injured anywhere, my love?' Emory asked anxiously.

I took stock of my body. 'No, I don't think so.'

'Your burn ... '

'Nate sorted that ages ago.'

'Good. I'll stand down the healer.' He went to the door and murmured some instructions to his brethren guard. When he came back, he tapped my forehead. 'What are you thinking in there?'

'I'm trying to decide if I care more about food, or getting warm and clean in the bath.'

'Why choose? Hop in the shower to wash off the blood, then I'll feed you while you're soaking in the tub.'

I brightened. 'That's a great idea.' I paused. 'I wouldn't have thought of showering off the blood first.'

'You don't want to soak in the blood of your enemies,' he pointed out.

'It's Shirdal's blood,' I said cheerfully. 'But I don't particularly want to soak in the blood of my friends, either.'

'Shirdal's?' Emory raised an eyebrow.

'I was riding on his back a lot.'

'I'm getting jealous.'

'Of Shirdal?' I asked incredulously.

'The only man you should ride is me,' he growled possessively.

I smirked. 'We can definitely get to that later.' My tummy made a noise again. 'After food,' I added.

I stripped off and hopped in the shower while Emory bustled about. I heard the room door open and close and assumed it was someone delivering food. Emory has many talents, but cooking isn't among them.

By the time I was clean, the bath had filled. It seemed excessively luxurious to shower *and* bathe, but today I was going to allow myself that. 'Is everyone else being looked after?' I called out.

Emory came into the bathroom. 'I've put them all in the guest suites down the hall. The healer is in there now, checking over Shirdal.'

'Thank you. And Amber? She was close to exhaustion.'

'I have a healing wizard with her too,' Emory reassured me.

'A wizard? Not a witch?'

'My healer in Wales is a wizard. He's a good man.'

'I'm not sure Amber will be good about giving up the reins.'

'She'll be clutching the reins when she dies,' he joked. 'But I think she's actually tired enough to let someone else take care of her for once.'

'And Gato?'

'He's fine. I just checked on him. He's eaten a huge dinner and is lying by the fire.'

Something in me relaxed. 'Great. Thanks.'

'Come on, let's get you in the bath.'

'Where are my leather clothes?'

'I've sent them away for cleaning. Don't worry. They'll be back. You looked entirely too sexy in them. In fact, I might order a dozen more outfits just like that.'

'I still prefer jeans and a T-shirt, but for you I'll wear leather occasionally.'

I stepped into the hot bath. Emory had been generous with the bubble bath and I couldn't see my toes for bubbles. He'd even put in rose petals and the delicate aroma scented in the air. I gave a sigh as I finally started to feel warm. My eyes slid shut and for a moment I had to battle not to fall asleep. Only gnawing hunger prevented me from drifting off.

'Ready for some food?' Emory asked. 'Grapes? Chicken skewers? Blueberries? Cake?'

I opened my eyes. 'Yes – all of it.'

He laughed and started passing me food. Eventually I realised I was thirsty. 'Can I have something to drink?'

'Water? Champagne? Tea?'

'Tea, please. Can you send the champagne to Amber? I owe her a bottle. Or six.'

He returned a moment later with a tray, complete with a teapot adorned with a tea cosy and a huge mug. He knew I wasn't one for dainty china teacups.

I pulled my eyes open again with an effort. 'So, when Elizabeth said we'd marry in three moons … '

'It's tradition. Don't worry, I'm sure we can move it.'

I chewed my lip. 'What if I don't want to move it?'

He stilled before flashing me a huge smile. 'Then we have a wedding to plan.'

I stood up and let the water and bubbles sluice off me. 'If there's to be a wedding, I think we should start practising.'

'For what?'

I pressed my still-wet form against him and slid my arms around his neck. 'For the wedding night.'

His eyes smouldered. 'Practice *does* make perfect.'

Chapter 40

After a rejuvenating sleep, I was happy to be reunited with my friends – especially Gato. None of us had slept for long because otherwise we wouldn't have slept that night, but boy had we needed those few hours.

'I'd better go,' Amber said abruptly. 'I have things to do down south before I'm ready for the coven leadership contest.'

'Leadership contest?' I asked.

'To determine who rules over all of the British covens and becomes the next witch symposium member,' Amber explained.

'You're young for that, aren't you?'

'I'm forty-two. I'm old enough,' she confirmed. She didn't look a day over thirty. I wondered if it was good genes, good facial care or a sneaky potion regime that kept her looking youthful. One day, after some drinks, I'd ask her.

'No doubt.' I thought about it. 'If you're going down south, I think that Lucy could really use some help.'

'Did it ever occur to you that there is more to my job than running around after you two?' she asked with exasperation.

I grinned at her. 'That's what having friends is like.'

'Lucy and I aren't friends,' she groused.

'Maybe not yet, but you will be,' I said confidently. 'A friend of my friend is a friend of yours, even if you don't know it yet. Besides, I think you could do with another friend as much as Lucy could.'

'Why are you trying to shove us together so much?' she asked with suspicion.

'I don't know,' I admitted. 'I just have this gut feeling that she's going to need you. Will you go?' Once, what felt a long time ago but was really only a matter of months, I had accidentally absorbed a bunch of Mrs H's seer magic. The last couple of months I'd occasionally had a gut feeling so strong that it was almost overwhelming. My intuition often told me more about a situation then I knew consciously, but this was even stronger. It felt prophetic: Lucy was going to need Amber.

Amber huffed, 'I'll go, but someone had better offer me more champagne at the end of all this.'

I laughed. 'I sent bubbles before! Listen, don't tell Lucy about all this challenge business. She'll only worry, and she needs to focus on herself and her pack. Oh – and Amber?'

'What?'

'Take your healing supplies,' I advised.

She sighed and rubbed tired eyes. 'I'll get my driver to take me down south now, but I'll stop at Rosie's first. I need some time to re-charge. That quick hour wasn't enough.'

'Gato could send you back to the Common realm now, if you like.'

'No, it's okay. If I'm absent from a portal for too long, people gossip. Besides, the halls are a good place to get a feel for the issues that we're all facing.'

'Good thinking. Um, one more thing.'

'What?' she asked again, arms folded. Her patience was wearing thin.

'Just a heads-up. I've sent Bastion to help Lucy too.'

Her glare increased in intensity and she marched off without another word. 'Love you!' I called after her. *True.* I was really getting the hang of this friendship thing. It was nice.

Amber sent me a rude hand signal as she stalked away without a backwards glance.

'She loves you too,' Shirdal commented. 'I've never seen her so warm and friendly with anyone else.'

'*That* was warm and friendly?'

'For Amber.' He grinned.

Hes and Nate were sitting together on a loveseat, looking relaxed. They had clearly … reconnected.

'There's one thing I don't get,' Hes said to me.

'What?'

'The break-in at the office. If it wasn't the dragons and it wasn't Bentley or the centaurs, who was it?'

'I don't know.' I said grimly. 'But I intend to find out.' Now that I had the challenge behind me, I still had a to-do list as long as my arm. I had so many irons in the fire that I was in danger of burning down the castle. I had a business to run, the Eye of Ebrel to find for Emory, a burglar to find for me, and a wedding to plan for us.

Piece of cake.

I sat on Emory's lap and enjoyed a moment of happiness before turning my mind to business. 'The Eye of Ebrel,' I started. 'You were kidding when you said there would be doom if it was lost, right?'

'No.' Emory sighed. 'Sadly not. The Revival Prophecy is quite clear; without the Eye, the fate of dragon-kind is sealed.'

'Sealed in a good way?' I asked optimistically.

'No, not in a good way. Sealed in a total-doom-and-destruction way.'

'Total annihilation seems like high stakes.' I swallowed.

He gave me a kiss. 'I have total faith that you'll find it before the gates of hell open on us all.'

Yikes. It's a good thing I work well under pressure.

What's Next?

Betrayal of the Court

Well, what did you think of *Challenge of the Court?* I hope you enjoyed it. I was incredibly nervous about dusting Jinx off for another outing. If you're desperate for more, then never fear! I never leave you waiting for long. The next book in this series is *Betrayal of the Court* coming out on 18th May 2023. Before we plunge into *Betrayal* I need to let you know that some of the events in Lucy's trilogy get referred to in it. For *maximal* reader enjoyment I thoroughly recommend reading Lucy's trilogy first, which starts with *Protection of the Pack.*

Reviews

As always, I appreciate reviews SO much. I really do read them all. One of them recently said they hate the use of the word "whilst" in my writing as it seems old fashioned. I have used "while" this time, just for you dear reviewer. So please do review, I promise I listen to them. The really nice ones make me beam for hours. Reviews and positive buzz from readers makes a huge amount of difference to us little Indie Authors and I really can't thank you enough for taking the time to review for me, wherever you can.

Patreon

If you'd like to support me *even more* then you can join me on Patreon! I have a wide array of memberships, rangeing from £1pm – £300pm. No one has taken me up on the biggest tier yet but a girl can dream! I give my patrons advance access to a bunch of stuff including advance chapters, cover reveals, art and behind the scenes glimpses into what goes on into making my books a reality.

Thanks so much for reading my work. I'll be seeing you in the back of the next book, or on my socials if you can't wait that long.

Take care,

Heather x

Glossary - The Jinx Files

Jinx's Other Log – An aide memoire

Amber - A feisty red-headed witch. Business-like, money minded, she lost her partner Jake who was coaxed to death by Bastion (see below). She's one of the contenders to become the next Coven leader.

Bastion – paramount griffin assassin. Laconic and deadly. He can coax (make someone take a course of action that they're already considering). He thinks of me like an niece, and although he kills people, I still think he's a good man under his kill count. Has a daughter, Charlize.

Chris – Emory's brethren pilot. Always on standby with a helicopter.

Emory – yum yum dragon shifter king. King of a bunch of creatures. So far I've ascertained that he's the Elite of the following creatures: centaurs, dryads, gnomes, mer, gargoyles, griffins, satyr.

Elvira – Inspector Elvira Garcia. She used to be kind of betrothed to Stone, and she loved him. She's prickly but I think she's warming to me. I think she's an honest person, underneath the prickles.

Elizabeth Manners – Greg Manners' mum, member of Emory's dragon circle.

Fabian – member of Emory's dragon circle. Saw him once at Ronan's ball raising money for making more Boost. Query his motives for being there.

Gato – my Great Dane turned out to be a fricking hell hound. He can grow huge with massive spikes and he can play with time like it's his favourite ball. He can send me between the realms for a magical re-charge. He also houses my father's soul. He used to have Mum too but she died closing the daemon portal.

Glimmer – A sentient magical blade, created by Leo Harfen, the elf. It can take magic from someone Other, and be used to make someone Common become magical. Or, make someone magical have an even bigger skillset. The transference of power always changes the magical gift somehow, in unknown ways.

Greg Manners - brethren soldier. I used to turn his hair pink to get a rise out of him but lately the only one getting a rise out of him is Lucy. He's her second in command and all round enforcer of all things Lucy, so nowadays I don't pink his hair.

Hes – my once-Common assistant. I rescued her from Mrs H's clutches, but Glimmer made her magical, she's a vampyr that doesn't need blood.

Lucy – my bestie! I turned her into a werewolf using Glimmer. Now she's accidentally a werewolf alpha, with her kick-ass wolf Esme.

Nate – Nathaniel Volderiss is the son and heir of Lord Volderiss. He also has a master/slave bond with me. We can sense each other and he has to obey me. I need to be so careful in how I phrase things so I don't accidentally force him into an action he doesn't want. He used to date Hes but when she betrayed his trust he dumped her to the kerb.

Reynard – He was once a squat, grey-skinned little gargoyle but the Other Realm waved a wand and now he's something else. Something new. The Other realm doesn't like new. Watch this space.

Roscoe – Head fire elemental, used to run Rosie's Hall where I got introduced to the Other Realm. Partner to **Maxwell Alessandro** (see Lucy's files).

Shirdal – head honcho of the griffins. He appears to have a drinking problem but everything is deceptive when it comes to this man. Always dressed in rumpled, mismatched clothing I once saw him kill thirty men without breaking a sweat, yet I trust him ...

Stone – Inspector Zachary Stone, he died in a hellish fiery portal, closing the daemon portal to the daemon realm. He was raised Anti-Crea but despite his father's best efforts, he ended up being a good man.

Tom Smith – Emory's right hand man (brethren). He's loyal, taciturn and loves to hide in bushes.

Printed in Great Britain
by Amazon

38082476R00211